DEAD STAR ISLAND

DEAD STAR ISLAND

ANDREW SHANTOS

Alliance Publishing Press

Alliance Publishing Press

www.alliancepublishingpress.com

Published by Alliance Publishing Press Ltd
This paperback edition published 2015
Copyright © Andrew Shantos 2015
Andrew Shantos asserts his moral right to be
identified as the author of this book.

ISBN: 978-09928116-2-4
Typeset in Sabon
Book & Cover Design by Mark James James

Biography

Andrew Shantos always knew he wanted to write, but he didn't have an idea for a book.

After scraping through his Maths degree by the skin of a Rizla, he helped his father launch *Highway Electrical News*, a magazine about street lighting which nearly featured as the guest publication on *Have I Got News For You*.

In his twenties, Andrew left a number of bands due to artistic differences.

Finally, three years ago, on a beach in Cyprus, Andy was thrilled to finally come up with an idea that combined his love of music, dead rock stars and ferrets, though his wife claims the idea was actually hers.

They live in Brighton with their two small children and have almost settled the argument.

For Gaynor

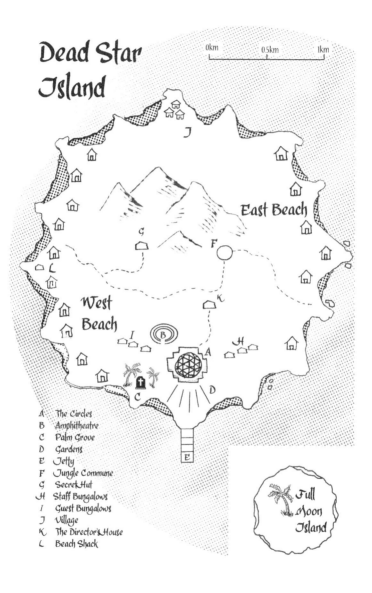

Dead Star Island

East Beach

West Beach

A The Circles
B Amphitheatre
C Palm Grove
D Gardens
E Jetty
F Jungle Commune
G Secret Hut
H Staff Bungalows
I Guest Bungalows
J Village
K The Director's House
L Beach Shack

Full Moon Island

0km   0.5km   1km

The killer rose at dawn.

Padding through the jungle, by paths almost invisible in the false light, the Déjà Vu Killer arrived at the appointed place. There, the killer waited, shadowed among the trees, looking across an expanse of white sand. The rifle was heavy, its barrel cold, as if it might melt in the heat. Where was John? He was late. Late for his death. Had it been like this, more than thirty years ago? The first time John died.

Movement. Barely discernible, an itch on the optic nerve: a black flicker, out where the sand tapered to a dagger-point and pierced the sea. The movement separated into two figures, expanding until their faces showed: exhausted, blotched with red, sweating from their morning run. They were standing now at the water's edge.

Elvis was with him, as expected. He was framed against the sea in his lycra running shorts, telling John, 'Come on man, we're nearly there.' Elvis took out a comb, ran it through his hair: black teeth through silver.

'You're such a bloody tart,' John told him, then grinned and said, 'Give us it here, will you.'

The masked assassin watched from between the trees. It was good to see John so happy: the contentment of someone who has made a decision. Like they all had. The killer waited for him to stand. But John was taking his time: rubbing sweat from his beard; pointing to the water, suggesting a swim.

'Not yet, man,' Elvis said, 'we got an eight mile run to finish.' John stood up. 'Alright mate, let's do it.'

He gazed across the beach, past the trees, towards where the assassin waited; then up, at the low, white sky. He put on his spectacles and his eyes became shadows: dead, behind round, tinted lenses.

Now. The Déjà Vu Killer lifted the rifle and took aim. Yes. It would be exactly like last time.

1

When he woke they were still watching him.

He lay there, looking up at the cabin walls, feeling the boat move gently under him. Didi was scampering around somewhere behind his head.

The faces looked down at him from each wall. He looked back. He knew them all, of course. Who wouldn't? Each photograph in colour, hanging in its frame, signed in black marker pen: actors, rock stars, singers. Captured in time, watching him from inside each frame. But there was something else, a feeling he'd had all day, like an itch. Something about them wasn't right. He couldn't decide what it was.

Fur against his ear, warm and soft: Didi. She was about to speak.

One of the faces moved.

Didi yelped and burrowed into his shoulder. He lifted his head, muscles tensed, waiting for something to happen. The face moved again. The eyes closed, suddenly flicked open, watery and blue. Then he realised; it was the window. Gunzabo relaxed back onto the floor, nodded wryly at the face looking through: gaunt, almost skeletal, skin pulled across sharp bone. 'Hello, Tommy. You got a cigarette?'

No answer. Of course not. The ferryman just stared back. It had been like this since he'd been picked up at the airport. They had driven in silence, just the two of them, fifty kilometres to the coast. Then twenty-four hours of muteness across unchanging ocean.

'What time is it, Tommy?'

Didi giggled. 'He's not going to tell you, Gunzabo. I'm not even sure he can speak.'

He gave her a quick glance. He took off his baseball cap and loosened the hair from his scalp. He dried his hand on the nylon of his tracksuit, lingering at the point where it sagged over his missing arm. It was the same day, he decided; the damp patch where he had wet himself was warm. And he still felt drunk. He was quite pleased with this deduction. Some skills you never lose.

He looked back at the window, now an empty rectangle of daylight. He stood up, knees creaking, felt an explosion of pain as he bumped his head on the low ceiling. Muttering obscenities, he wandered over to the table at the end of the cabin. Remnants of the party lay scattered and broken on its surface: waxy packets crumpled under wedges of cheese and preserved meat; shreds of smoked fish; half-empty dips and pâtés; an open wicker basket; inside, a chequered blanket covered in shards of French bread. Not much of a party though, really. Only him and Didi. Unless you counted the faces on the wall.

He picked up a magnum of Bollinger and poured the last dribble into a flute. He drained the champagne, glass vertical against his lips. The photographs. Suddenly he realised what was wrong. They were too old. Every one of them. Those legendary faces he knew so well: smiling, singing, smoking, laughing. Dead before their time. But the eyes seemed wiser, the faces more worn than they should have been, as if they had aged beyond death while hanging in their frames.

'Gunzabo, look at this.'

Didi was sniffing inside a cabinet. He knelt down to look. Two more photographs, piled at the back: framed, signed, instantly recognisable. Both men. One wearing a pair of round spectacles, tinted red.

He studied the bare patches of wall where the photographs must have hung. Two more dead superstars. That made sixteen.

'Why have they been taken down?' asked Didi.

He did not know. No one had told him anything yet. Not Tommy. Not even Christian, when he'd got that phone call back in England two days ago.

'Mario,' the voice had said. 'Hi, how are you?'

He did not answer, just clamped the phone to his ear in shock. Mrs Pottinger was standing next to him, on court, her topspin backhand as feeble as ever.

'How long has it been, Mario?' They both knew how long: not long enough. 'You know who this is, right?' Of course: nobody had called him Mario in fifty years. 'There's a plane leaving London Gatwick in five hours. Can you make it?'

'Where to?'

There was a pause, then, in a lowered voice, 'East Java. Thomas will meet you there. You can trust him.'

Tommy. It was a good name for a mute. But he definitely didn't trust him; the man looked like he had been exhumed.

'So what are we doing, stupid-head?'

Didi was nibbling a stray piece of French bread on the floor.

'Finding out where in hell we are.'

'Hallelujah.' She jumped up and wriggled into his empty right sleeve.

Stooping, he mounted the steps and went outside.

He had arrived at an island. Trees formed a sharply rising canopy which became lost in cloud. The beach, deep and wide, angled away as if the boat rested on the point of an enormous star. Tommy was standing on the sand, a lone emaciated figure, eyes deep in shadowed sockets. There was no sun. Mist swirled in the air, hot, like steam.

He stepped onto the jetty. Wooden boards flexed; his stomach heaved. Overcome with dizziness, he stumbled blindly onto the beach and fell to the ground. The sand was wet between his fingers, cold and clammy, like a corpse.

He looked up, seeing only fizzing darkness, until gradually a picture formed: Tommy lurching along the stretch of beach, sea to the left, and to the right a wall of trees, leaking mist from their upper branches. He hurried across the sand, following Tommy round a sharp curve. As he turned the corner, almost back on himself, the jungle fell away to reveal buildings in the middle-distance; white edges sliced the mist. He stepped onto a decked path flanked by sun loungers. A man in white cotton uniform smiled in greeting.

He nodded back. 'What's this place called?'

The man smiled but did not reply.

'You speak English?' More smiles and confusion. 'Greek? *Πώς το λένε αυτό το νησί;*'

Gunzabo frowned and moved on; he'd run out of languages.

Sand gave way to grass, decking to a paved footpath. They passed through a series of enclosed gardens, rockeries and immaculate open lawns. Further paths left their route on either side, leading to still more, mist-shrouded gardens. At intervals the path rose over a small cobbled bridge and he crossed five streams in this way. Staff dressed in white cotton worked soundlessly, tending the grass, flowers and miniature fruit trees; others walked swiftly on errands, silent and polite wraiths who smiled and bowed their heads as he passed.

He entered a herb and spice garden; its walls were dense bushes of basil, thyme, coriander. Through the mist and mingling scents of a hundred plants, a figure came floating towards him: a woman, slim and tall. She was dressed in a red sari, a faint smile on her face, black hair pulled forward over her shoulder in one long plait.

'Welcome to our island,' she said. 'My name is Lastri. It's a great honour to have you here, Mr Gunzabo.'

He stared at her, full of grief.

'Call me Gunzabo,' he mumbled.

She looked just like his wife.

She was not classically beautiful, but her skin was perfect, hair and clothes immaculate, her eyes as black and clear as a starry night. Perhaps she was forty, but he could not be sure; her face had an ageless, eternal quality, though it lacked the bright vivacity of youth.

'I hope you had a pleasant journey.'

'It was alright once we found the champagne.' He pushed down the emotion, composed himself enough to look steadily back at her. 'Where's Christian?'

The woman smiled regally. 'The Director is waiting for you, Gunzabo. I'll take you to his office.'

They passed through a portico into a beautiful rock garden filled with butterflies; at its centre was a hexagonal pond with a statue of Orpheus looking over his shoulder.

'Where are we?' he asked.

Lastri stopped. 'You do not know?'

He indicated Tommy: mute, staring into space.

'Dead Star Island,' she told him.

She moved on. Gunzabo strode beside her. 'Why am I here?'

This time she did not stop. 'The Director will tell you, I am sure.'

They were walking through an enclosed meadow of knee-high grass. He gazed at her, marvelling at the smoothness of her neck; down to her shoulder; coiled hair obscuring collar bone. He wanted her to look at him. He scratched an intolerable itch on his phantom arm.

'Why are *you* here?' he asked.

They emerged onto a terrace. On the other side, across an expanse of marble tiles, an imposing, dome-like structure rose into the mist. Lastri stopped. She hesitated, looked searchingly into his eyes. Suddenly he saw his wife again. He clenched his eyes shut, determined not to remember.

'This is The Circles.'

He came to. She was gesturing to the building: a colossal hemisphere of black glass. He shivered despite the heat, blinked away the memory of his wife.

'A hotel?'

She shook her head. 'Leisure complex. The residents have their own villas.'

He followed Lastri's eyes to the beach, tracing northwards.

'Who are the residents?'

'Those who seek privacy. Those who wish to escape the outside world.'

A ridiculous idea popped into his head. He looked closely at her. 'How many residents are there?'

'Sixteen,' she said quickly, then murmured, 'Fourteen.'

The faces in the cabin. Was he right? Surely not.

Something moved at the edge of his vision. He turned to the building. At the base of its curving glass wall, black as obsidian, a door was sliding open. A woman rushed out, short and wide, wearing a floral dress. She put her head down and came galloping towards them like a rhinoceros.

'Thomas!' the woman shouted.

Gunzabo glanced at the ferryman. No reaction.

'Thomas!' she yelled again. 'We've got to go. Now!'

She was nearly upon them. Her gigantic breasts bounced like melons in a truck.

'It's happened again,' she cried out. 'I think it's happened again!'

She stopped, drenched in sweat, cheeks scarlet from the short run, and burst into tears.

Lastri moved next to her, put a hand on her arm. 'What has happened?'

'Oh, whatsits! Oh balls!'

The woman's fleshy chin trembled with each anguished sob. 'What is it, Mrs Bradley? Tell me. Please.'

The woman closed her eyes. She let out short controlled breaths in an attempt to calm down. 'Christian's already gone there. He said Thomas should go too, break down the door.'

Lastri lowered her voice, speaking reassuringly to Mrs Bradley. Gunzabo edged closer, straining to listen to the conversation.

'It's Marilyn, that's what it is!' she burst out. 'No one's seen her in twenty-four hours. The cleaners couldn't get into her villa. Oh it's just awful, what's happening to my life! It'll be me next, I just know it. I can't sleep, I can't concentrate on the television I'm so nervous. Oh, blinking whatsits!'

Lastri moved her hand away. She was staring at Mrs Bradley, as if she did not believe her. 'You think Marilyn may be dead?'

'Of course she's dead. She must be. It's the Déjà Vu Killer, I know it. It'll look like an overdose. We've got to go.'

Lastri glanced at Gunzabo. 'And our guest?' she asked.

Mrs Bradley looked uncertain. The two women moved away, conferring quietly before Mrs Bradley rushed over to Tommy and engulfed him in her bosom. He stood, zombie-like, as she sobbed into his face. 'Oh, love, it's been so hard without you. Come and sort it out, will you?'

Gunzabo stepped forward. 'I'll come.'

'I'm afraid that won't be possible,' Lastri told him.

He gazed back at her in surprise. 'You know my profession? I was famous throughout the Mediterranean for—'

'Christian has given specific instructions. You are to be taken to your room,' Lastri said coolly. 'You have had a long journey, you will want to freshen up, I'm sure.'

'I must insist—' he began. But she wasn't looking at him anymore. She was looking past his shoulder. He felt a circle of darkness in his back. He turned round to see Tommy staring back, standing squarely in his way; beyond, Mrs Bradley was already charging across the meadow, flattening the grass in a line towards the sea.

He met Tommy's gaze for a moment: watery, blue; no other colour in the man. He watched him lope off after Mrs Bradley. Then he glanced at Lastri, ready to be taken to his room.

They stopped at the last of a line of three bungalows, at the end of a narrow path a hundred metres west of The Circles. Across the gardens, the sea was grey and flat; the mist had retreated into a low white sky. Lastri, calm and assured, slid open patio doors, then turned to him.

'Can I get you anything, Gunzabo?' she asked.

He reached around in his tracksuit pocket and pulled out a crumpled wad of banknotes.

'That will not be necessary. We do not have money here on our island.'

'What about beer?'

'We have fifty-two varieties. Would you prefer Asian, American, Latin American, Australian? Or perhaps European?'

'It all tastes the same,' he said, peering inside the bungalow: spacious, tiled floor, large white bed. 'Bring two, will you? Better make it four.'

'Four?'

He shrugged indifferently. 'I'm an alcoholic, not a mathematician.' He glanced at her. 'Sit and have one with me.'

She was gazing out to sea. 'I'm afraid I do not drink beer.'

Neither spoke for a moment. 'I must go,' she said eventually. 'The residents expect dinner whatever the circumstances.'

'Bring four anyway. I'll drink on my own.'

'I'm sure you won't,' she said, smiling. 'Not for long, anyway.'

* * *

'So what do you think?'

Gunzabo poured the next bottle of beer into his glass. 'It's quite nice, isn't it?'

'I mean the incident. Mrs Bradley.'

'Someone's dead, I suppose. Sounds like a serial killer, maybe.'

Sweat dripped from his nose. He gulped his beer. The jungle hummed and throbbed behind the bungalow. He pretended not to notice Didi, looking tetchily up at him from the patio floor.

'So are they bringing you out of retirement?' she asked.

'Either that or someone's desperate for tennis lessons.'

She smiled, nose wrinkling cutely. 'There's a fair bit of money flying around. They could probably afford a two-armed tennis coach.' Then shaking her head, she added, 'They must be mad.'

He gave her an irritable look. 'Let's go.'

'Where?' she asked, scrambling up his leg.

'Wherever Marilyn lives.' He drained his glass. 'Used to live.'

'Well they went off in that direction.'

He glanced west across the gardens, where the beach tapered to a star-like point and turned sharply north.

'It might be a bit dangerous,' Didi murmured.

'Maybe.'

He shoved a beer in the pocket of his tracksuit bottoms. Holding the other bottle in his hand, he headed for the beach.

2

Paving stones curved down towards the sea. To his left were the gardens; to his right the jungle had been cleared some twenty metres, leaving a sparse pebble-strewn hinterland guarded by sculptures of men and mythological beasts. He glanced at a hydra; its nine heads writhed motionlessly in granite. He continued, away from the jetty, onto sand, past a cluster of trees: towering palms which formed a perfect circle, gloomy and magnificent, oddly silent. He lingered for a moment, considered entering the ring of trees. No, he decided. He wanted to find Marilyn.

He walked north on a corridor of fine white sand, sea lapping at his feet, dissonant noise of a million creatures pulsing through the jungle. As he walked, he rubbed the stubble on his chin, trying to dispel a vague sense of unease. Didi poked her head out of his sleeve.

'I'm sure there's someone following us,' she whispered.

He glanced over his shoulder. Jungle, sand, sea. Still as a postcard. He studied the treeline. Nothing. He moved on. Still there was the feeling, the same as on the boat, of being watched.

He came to a break in the trees, where the jungle perimeter was now marked by a cast iron fence, and a gate which was locked. A metal plate read:

BRIAN

He peered through the railings: an expanse of lawn; circular swimming pool, edges streaked with black, as if something had recently been dragged out; beyond, a house on wooden stilts. In the centre of the pool, on a raised island, a giant sculpture towered skywards: a Buddha, painted black.

'I could break us in?' said Didi. 'Have a little look around?'

Gunzabo looked at the wooden house: empty, silent, windows boarded.

'Not yet,' he told her, dropping his empty beer bottle on the sand. 'Let's find Marilyn.'

He continued north. The beach widened; squinting into the distance, he saw thin triangles of sand-fringed jungle: layered star points, one above the other. He angled towards another gate: locked once again, railings choked with vegetation. Pushing aside tresses of vine, he made out a near-replica of the previous residence: garden, pool, wooden house in what he assumed was the local style, but with a manufactured, almost too-perfect feel. He stepped back to read the metal plate:

RIVER

He frowned. 'River what?'

Gunzabo carried on, reached another star-point, ducked under trees, turning back on himself, onto another stretch of beach. Again the sand opened out, pushing the treeline backwards, until the jungle gave way to more railings, another garden, and a white, single storey villa. He surged towards the gate. 'Marilyn,' he murmured, reading the sign, pushing against the bars; the gate creaked open. He nodded approvingly; he was too old for scrambling over fences. He tossed his final, empty bottle into the undergrowth and went in.

The villa was white and still; the garden was silent. Nothing moved. There was no Tommy, no Mrs Bradley. No Christian. Where were they? What had happened? Moving under cover, he made for the villa. The front door was ajar. He put an ear to the opening: no sound. He peered through the windows, but they were either shuttered, or rendered opaque by the paleness of the sky. Cautiously, he let himself in.

The interior was dark, silent, cold. Didi jumped down, ran through faint strips of light unfolding across marble tiles. He waited for his eyes to adjust to the gloom, fully alert. The air smelt of musty decline. He saw something round, white as bone. Tommy? No: a china plate, hanging on the wall. And now, chaise longues and antique sofas formed around a Persian rug; mahogany cases lined the walls. There was no one here. He relaxed, felt heat against his back from the garden outside. He closed the front door; the click reverberated through the house.

'Jack?' It was a woman's voice. 'Is that you?'

He stood, listening. Didi came scampering back and ran up his leg. Again, the voice spoke, feeble and shrill. 'Jack? Goddam you, stop playing your stupid games!'

He moved towards the voice, across the tiles, groped blindly down a dark corridor. He paused in the black, open doorway of a room. He could hear the rhythmic sucking of a pump. Tiny multi-coloured lights punctured the darkness, winking on and off in response to a medical beep; others double-pulsed like a heartbeat; others were permanently on.

The woman's voice came again from somewhere inside. 'Will you come in and stop this nonsense!'

He marched briskly into the centre of the room. 'Gunzabo. Pleased to meet you. I heard you were in trouble, so I—' He tripped over a cable on the floor, crashed into something large and metallic. It started beeping urgently. He fell again, flailed about, grabbing wires and knocking into metal objects with sharp corners.

'What on earth are you doing?'

He looked wildly around the room. Everything now was beeping. 'Where's the light switch?'

'By the door. Keep it low though, will you. I don't like too much light.'

He groped for the switch, twisted it to its lowest setting, whirled round.

A decrepit old woman was propped up in bed. She was covered in transparent tubes. A clear plastic mask covered her face, secured by elastic bands, which ran over her ears and disappeared under a platinum-blonde wig.

'You'd better see if you've unplugged anything,' she croaked. 'The iron will stop working.'

'The iron?'

'Here.'

He moved his gaze from her trembling index finger to a large grey box next to the bed. Tubes ran from the box into her wrists; others curled up from another machine into her nostrils. There were no lights on either machine.

'Is it still on? Is it hot?' She tried to take a breath, but it was more of an inward squeak, as if she was in a vacuum. Her face was blue.

Gunzabo scrambled about on the floor, grabbing cables, tracing with his fingers to where each wire terminated. Both machines were plugged into a junction box; three cables lay loose on the other side. He heard a choking sound, looked quickly over to the woman. She was trying, but failing, to say something. He plugged the cables into the junction box. Nothing happened.

'Try a different combination,' hissed Didi.

He tried again; still nothing. The woman was now purple and making rattling noises.

'Over there,' said Didi. 'Something else came out.'

He hurried over to the far wall, found a plug dislodged from its socket. He pushed it back in. A fan started whirring; tiny lights came on. The pump resumed its steady rhythmic sucking; clear liquid in the plastic tubes began moving. He sighed with relief.

The woman's involuntary noises quietened; he watched her face slowly return to a wrinkled, deathly-white.

'Yes, that's better. Let me know when it's ready, will you? Jack and I are going out tonight. I said I'd iron a shirt for him.'

'None of these boxes is an iron, madam. They appear to be keeping you alive.'

'Alive? Nonsense.'

He moved beside the bed and sat on a high-backed chair. 'You caused quite a scare earlier today.'

'A scare? Oh no. Bobby came round, we played gin, we had a stroll on the beach. Down near Malibu.'

He glanced at her legs, impossibly thin under the sheets. 'Mrs Bradley said you shut yourself in. People were worrying you may have been...'

Her face sharpened. 'May have been what?'

He paused, deep in thought. 'How long have you lived here?'

'You seem to imply, young man, I have been here an awful long while.' Her mouth, under the mask, was puckered in annoyance. 'What is it to you?'

He looked at her in sympathy, as she lay there, tiny, confused. 'I apologise,' he told her.

'Stop beating around the bush. Tell me why you're not Jack.'

He shifted in the chair to face her squarely. 'I have just arrived on this island. I am a detective. I believe there may have been a recent murder. Perhaps more than one. I want you to tell me anything you know about this. Anything at all. No point, no detail is too minor.'

Her face was aghast; if it could have turned whiter, it would have. 'A murder? What? Where? Oh my God! Call Jack, you must. Oh my. A murderer!'

He took her hand. Marilyn was beside herself. Her eyes blazed wide; she tried to push him away, but there was no strength in her arms. 'Lock the doors,' she whispered.

'Of course.'

Disengaging her knobbly fingers from his hand, he stepped carefully across the room, shut the door, switched off the light, then returned to the chair. He sat next to her in the dark without talking, as the pump sucked in and out and the lights of the machines pulsed gently in primary colours. Didi was gnawing a cable on the floor. He scowled at her, pushed her away with his foot.

'Are you feeling better?' he asked Marilyn.

She gave him a baffled look. 'Jack?'

'It's Gunzabo.'

'Gunzabo? Never heard of him. Where's Jack? Can you get him for me?'

'I don't think so.'

'Oh you must. We're going out tonight. Why are you sitting here in the dark? Switch the light on, will you?'

He turned on the light.

'I don't know you,' Marilyn said, glaring at him suspiciously. 'Why are you here? Have you come to rob me?'

'Do you not remember? I am the detective. Investigating the murders.'

'Murders? What? Oh my God!'

It began again. This time Gunzabo lied and he consoled her, saying, 'Silly me, of course not, I was joking. I came to take your temperature, that's all. You are absolutely fine.'

She gazed back at him, lips quivering.

'Oh, I see,' she murmured. 'Well that wasn't a very nice joke.'

Gradually, she settled down and closed her eyes. He watched her eyelids flutter while she slept. Despite her extreme age, there was something remarkable about her: a compelling beauty, greatly faded, crumpled even, but still there; and a certain dignity, like that of the dead, ready to be buried.

For a moment, he worried that she had stopped breathing,

one of those moments where time pauses.

But the pump sucked; her chest rose; the medical equipment flickered and beeped contentedly. What was the time? There was no clock, but he saw, on the bedside table, a sheet of paper: a handwritten note, folded in half.

So sorry you didn't see me today. You looked so beautiful asleep in your bed. I couldn't bring myself to wake you.
Michael

'What are you doing?' Marilyn snapped in her feeble voice.

He looked up guiltily.

'Are you trying to steal my jewellery? You are, aren't you? Get out now.'

'No, no. Someone left you a note.'

'Nonsense. You're a thief and you've taken my jewellery. Give it back now and go.'

Gunzabo put the note back on the bedside table.

'I don't want to see you again,' Marilyn told him. 'Tell them to find Jack.'

'Of course.'

She began coughing. She clawed at her mask, trying to take it off, coughing now in a weak, prolonged fit. She recovered briefly, yelling, 'Get out,' her face white, wrinkles deep with outrage, trying to get out of bed. The beeps increased in frequency until they became a flat sustained note. Shouts came from outside the room. Someone rushed past: a flash of blue polyester uniform. Gunzabo stood up, stepped back as two more nurses arrived. He left the room and stood in the corridor, watching Marilyn's flailing arms while they administered an injection. Finally the single note divided into beeps. The room settled. It was time to leave.

'You nearly finished her off in there,' said Didi, 'charging around like a bull in a care unit.'

Gunzabo was striding along the beach, back towards his bungalow. What the hell was going on? It was starting to aggravate him. 'I wasn't the one chewing through the cable of her life support machine.'

'I couldn't help it, it's in my nature.'

He glanced at her and his mood softened. She was looking up at him from his empty sleeve, nose wrinkled quizzically.

'What the hell is going on, Gunzabo?'

He looked out to sea: empty, grey, leading to a flat horizon, devoid of ships or boats. He thought of the faces again. 'Not a very common name, is it?'

'What, River?'

They were passing one of the houses on stilts.

'That too.'

'So what?' Didi asked.

His gaze lingered in the distance. Dark clouds were forming. He sensed something, in the far reaches of his peripheral vision: a flash of white. He snapped his head round. He looked back up the coast. Someone was definitely stalking him. But the forest was motionless, its noisy, abundant life hidden behind a wall of vegetation.

He carried on, eyes narrowed. 'Let's find someone who can tell us.'

'Your best mate?'

He grunted. Much as he hated to admit it, he really wanted to see Christian.

3

The day was waning, but the air was like cigarette smoke, hot and thick in his lungs. He arrived at the terrace and stood for a moment, observing The Circles. Its glass walls seemed to compel the light, to hurry the onset of dusk. He marched across the tiles. A door hissed open; black glass gave way to a restaurant interior. He went inside.

There were no diners. Half a dozen staff moved swiftly, laying tables with cloths as white and starched as their uniforms; glasses and cutlery gleamed under tastefully dimmed spotlights.

'Have you come for dinner, Gunzabo?'

Lastri was standing at the bar. She looked so beautiful he could not breathe.

'We usually have the tables outside, but we're in rather a heatwave at the moment.' She dismissed the woman beside her.

'What time will the residents arrive?' he asked, weaving through the dining tables.

She inclined her head to one side. 'Perhaps later. We cannot know. The residents often prefer to take their meals at home. Ah, look.' She bowed graciously; an elderly man had entered the restaurant. 'Good evening, sir.'

Despite his advanced age, he was striding vigorously, dressed in tennis whites.

'How're you doing, honey?'

Gunzabo caught a brief glimpse of the old man's face as he swept past: tanned and lean, a light sheen of perspiration, thick white hair, white sideburns.

'Who is that?' he asked.

The man had gone outside.

'Elvis,' said Lastri. 'He may come later to eat.'

'Who was he playing tennis with?'

'I expect with Diana.' She gave him a faintly mischievous look. 'They are very good friends.'

He was about to ask another question when the elevator rang. A man stepped into the lift: tall – almost Gunzabo's height – and smartly casual in a cream linen suit. As the doors closed, Gunzabo saw the man's eyes in the elevator mirror, looking back at him. Probably in his sixties. Christian? He could not be sure; the lighting was too dim. Besides, they had been children when he last saw him. Where was he going? He glanced at a sign, next to the spiral staircase leading upstairs:

LLG: Spa & Roman Baths
LG: Gymnasium, squash & tennis courts
G: Restaurants
1: Lounges & Bar
2: Offices & Reception

The screen above the elevator changed to *1*. He waited a few seconds, until he was certain the lift had stopped, then hurried up the stairs, taking them two at a time.

'I'll reserve a table by the window for you,' Lastri called after him.

He emerged into a room on the next floor: a lounge, dimly lit, spacious, furniture arranged in sections to form intimate pods. A member of staff – female, dressed in white – stood behind a bar at the far end.

'Did someone just come through?' he asked.

The woman indicated a curved wall of glass doors leading outside. He nodded, moved past sofas and coffee tables, seeing a ghostly version of himself in the tinted glass, superimposed over a patio overlooking the gardens. Two doors slid open; he stepped into the heat.

He stopped at a balcony, stood gazing across the gardens. It was evening now; lamps glowed in the falling dusk. The beach was a hundred metres away. Waves whispered into the sand. All around him insects sounded. For an instant, Gunzabo was a child again, when they used to head north to Kyrenia to spend the summer months by the sea. His mother would let him stay up late and they would stand quietly on the veranda, the air pulsing with heat and cicadas, while Christian and his own mother slept inside.

'Are you following me?'

He turned, quickly, saw the man in the linen suit. Gunzabo nodded a greeting. 'Are you creeping up on me?'

'Haha, maybe.' The man held out his hand. 'Ken Winter.'

'Gunzabo.'

'Ah yes, that's right, the detective,' Ken said, releasing his vicelike grip. 'I hope you're good.'

'Did you not follow my most famous case?' Gunzabo asked him. 'Stavros the Bull? It was a sensation throughout the Balkans.'

'Must have passed me by, that one,' Ken said. 'I left Europe years ago. Swapped London for the States. Then I came here.'

'What do you do here?'

Ken gave a non-committal look, running his fingers through ruffled grey hair streaked with highlights. 'This and that.' He grinned and Gunzabo saw perfect teeth, their white purity obvious despite the evening gloom.

'I'd say you're the dentist.'

'Ha, I wish. Cost me a fortune, these gnashers did. Like the rest of me. I'm utterly fake you know.' Ken grinned again. 'No, I'm not a dentist. Much less important. I'm the doctor. Haha.'

'The doctor?' Gunzabo looked at him closely. 'Did you attend Marilyn earlier? I understand there was a scare.'

'Had one of her funny turns,' Ken said. 'She's a bit forgetful at times, poor cow. Bit paranoid too. Wanted a tea towel. Freaked out, chucked out the nurses, sat there going loopy.'

'How old is she?'

'Forty. In her head.' He smirked. 'Anyway, I came up here for a smoke. Cigar?'

'Why not.'

Ken lit their cigars with a silver lighter. 'What happened to your arm? If you don't mind me asking. Professional curiosity you know.'

'Accident.'

'Hope you got plenty of compensation.'

Gunzabo didn't answer. He looked up into the empty sky. Suddenly in his mind he heard the skidding wheels of the car, heard her voice, too late now, screaming for him to stop.

'Thomas Bradley bring you here, did he?'

He blinked and he was back on the island. 'Yes,' he said.

'Met his wife yet?'

'Mrs Bradley?'

'Funny old couple, aren't they?' Ken smirked again. 'Little and large.'

'What's that?' Gunzabo pointed to his right, at the ring of trees from earlier. It was set apart from the gardens, on the beach itself, the trees darkening to silhouettes against the water.

'Where the residents get buried,' said Ken. 'When they finally peg it, for real. Palm Grove.'

'Mrs Bradley was concerned Marilyn might have been dead. She mentioned a killer.'

'She did, did she?'

'Has there been a murder on the island? I presume that is why I have been brought here.'

Ken took a deep drag on his cigar. 'Déjà Vu Killer, they're calling him.'

'Why?'

'Because of the way he's killing them. Same as how we faked their deaths in the first place.'

Gunzabo thought again of the photographs in the cabin. 'Who?'

'John. Shot three days ago. Brian, last month.'

'How did Brian die?'

'Drowned in his pool.'

Gunzabo looked up into the night. The sky was a lightless void now, so black and close it seemed to Gunzabo he must be underground. 'You attended each murder scene, I take it?'

There was a flash of lightning out to sea. Ken sucked on his cigar, frowning as much as his static forehead would allow. 'Looks like another storm tonight, worse luck.'

'Another one?'

'There was one last night too. Right pain in the arse. Messing with my plans.'

Gunzabo glanced at Ken. He was about to ask what plans, but he dismissed the question, and instead leaned against the balcony, fending off memories of the accident, trying to make his mind as empty as the night sky.

'The recent shooting,' he said after a while. 'What can you tell me about it?'

Ken tapped his cigar. He looked at Gunzabo, but didn't answer.

'You're the doctor,' Gunzabo persisted. 'You must have seen the body, at least.'

Ken held his gaze, eyes apologetic. 'My lips are sealed. Strict orders of the management.'

A gust of wind blew across the balcony. Gunzabo glanced sourly away. The management. 'Where can I find him?' he asked.

'He'll be up in his house, I expect.'

'I want to see him.'

'Good luck getting there in the dark. He lives up in the hills.'

Gunzabo ground his teeth in frustration, staring at the clusters of light which stretched into the distance up the coast, where he had walked earlier.

'That's West Beach,' Ken said.

'You're allowed to tell me that, are you?'

Gunzabo moved his eyes out to sea, then across and up the other side of the island, where more lights stretched north-east. 'More residents?' he asked.

'The cheaper end. But don't tell them I said that.'

Gunzabo studied Ken thoughtfully. 'The residents. I think I know who they might be.'

Ken raised an eyebrow. 'Do you now?'

'Yes.'

'Think you're clever, do you?'

'Yes.'

'Good. Because we're all as frightened as kids.' Ken stopped smiling. 'Everyone thinks they're going to be next. Especially the residents. It's not good for business.'

'So why don't you tell me?'

'I told you. The management.'

Gunzabo stared back, exasperated. Suddenly he felt tired and old. No more questions, he decided. He would wait until he saw Christian. He stood next to Ken, breathing out smoke into the night, listening to the sound of waves and insects and the rising wind.

'Some of the boys are playing cards later on,' Ken said. 'Fancy joining us? No high stakes or anything, just enough to keep it interesting.'

'I heard there was no money on the island.'

'Who told you that? The staff? Haha.'

'I have a few pounds sterling. Not much.'

'I'm sure we can work something out.' Ken tossed his cigar

over the balcony into the invisible gardens below. 'How about you don't accuse us of being murderers?'

'I can promise that.' Gunzabo paused. 'On one condition, of course.'

'What's that?'

He looked unblinkingly at Ken. 'That you're not the murderer.'

Ken looked straight back at him. He laughed. 'You're something, you really are. In that case, we have an understanding. See you at Heath's. Eleven thirty.'

'I'll set my alarm.'

'Bit late, I know. Got a few things to attend to. Don't forget your wallet.'

They shook hands. Gunzabo lingered for a few minutes, his thoughts dark and in the past. His eyes tracked the coast, fixing on the lights of each villa, watching them glow in the darkness and cast their ghostly rays into the jungle. Who would be next? No one, if he could stop the killer. But that would involve someone telling him what was going on.

4

'Come on then,' said Didi, 'where are we going?'

She was scampering up and down the ornate ironwork dividing their veranda from the unoccupied bungalow next door.

'To bed,' Gunzabo told her.

'What? It's just got interesting.'

'A detective needs his sleep.'

'I noticed how you've suddenly stopped being retired.' She wrinkled her nose petulantly. 'What about cards?'

'It's not for a few hours. Wake me up, will you?'

It started raining: a sudden, fierce downpour that hammered the tiles. Gunzabo went inside.

'You can go home now,' he called out, as he slid the door shut.

A figure moved away in the darkness.

It was cool inside; the air conditioning was on. He felt his weariness leave him. He stood at the closed doors, moodily pressing at the empty space under his shoulder, looking past his reflection and into the blackness. Rain was hitting the glass like shingle. Howling gusts of wind threw furniture across the patio. He tried to think about what had happened that day, think through each event, each conversation. But always his mind returned to the past. And the only way he could stop thinking about his wife was to think further back, to his mother, and to Christian. That last time he saw him. They were only children, they had just come home from school. He remembered the look of fear on his mother's face. And she was saying, 'What did you tell them, Christian? What have you said?' Christian was staring moodily at the floor. His mother started screaming. Rhea came outside and she began screaming back, until she took Christian away. They left Cyprus. So did he, once he was old enough to join the police in Athens. Twenty years, married to the job. He had given up meeting anyone. God, how Lastri looked like his wife! He shook his head violently. He would not think of either of them. He needed a drink.

He moved away from the patio doors. He noticed a map on the wall. *Dead Star Island.*

He frowned; he should have seen this earlier; he'd lost his touch.

He studied the map: a sixteen-pointed star, houses marked as small squares around its edges. A circle indicated the main complex, with a cluster of squares for the surrounding bungalows. And there, on the southernmost point, an oversized ring of trees, gravestones in the middle. *Palm Grove.* Drawn in a separate box in the corner, was a smaller, circular island. *Full Moon Island.*

The phone rang. Gunzabo picked it up immediately.

'Hello sir, how are you?' asked a female voice on the other end of the line.

'Alright.'

'I'm glad, sir. We are just calling to let you know that dinner at The Circles restaurant has been cancelled.'

'I see.'

'Sometimes it is getting like this. We shall send some food to your room, sir. Mr Winter asked us to say cards has been cancelled. Best to stay in please, it is a little dangerous outside.'

'OK.'

'What would you like for dinner, sir? I can ask chef to prepare whatever you desire.'

'Send me anything.' Gunzabo paused, looking around the room. 'Is there a minibar?' he asked.

'Yes, sir.'

'Good.'

He put the phone down and looked for the minibar.

'You're normally so good at hunting down the booze,' said Didi. She was curled up in a chair, watching him. 'Do you want to know where the minibar is?'

He looked back at her. 'Yes.'

'I don't know if I should tell you. You'll only get half cut again.'

'It's better than being in tiny pieces.'

'Stop feeling so sorry for yourself.'

Didi jumped off the bed and scampered over to the wardrobe. She disappeared inside. He heard her scratching about, until a door opened, revealing a discreet cabinet: shelves of crisps and nuts and miniature spirits; a refrigerator packed with wine and mixers. It was like the hostess trolley in first class on a transatlantic jet.

'Your reputation precedes you, Gunzabo,' said Didi. 'They gave you the room with the secret drinks cabinet.'

Gunzabo grunted and said, 'What do guests without pet ferrets do for a drink, then?'

He emptied some nuts onto a plate.

'I don't know,' said Didi, munching happily. 'I wonder what ferrets without pet humans do for food?'

He smiled and settled back in his chair with a whisky and soda.

He woke with a start. It was still raining, but the storm had lost much of its intensity. Didi was nuzzling his face.

'I heard something,' she whispered.

A gust of wind rattled the shutters.

'Probably just one of the staff, turning down the room.' He rolled over onto the other side.

'The maid did that hours ago. She brought dinner too.'

He rolled back again; a food trolley, next to the bed, was

laden with condiments, bread rolls, a silver domed platter and a smoked salmon starter. He lifted the platter and inspected his main course: fillet of beef cooked medium-rare; potatoes dauphinoise; wild mushrooms in a red wine jus. He hadn't realised how hungry he was. He ate a forkful of potato: cold, but delicious.

Something flitted past the window outside. He jumped up. 'What was that?'

'What I was talking about.'

The rain lessened to a distant hiss. He heard a scrape of metal against stone outside. He switched off the bedside light, quietly slid open the veranda doors and peered into the darkness. Didi scuttled out between his feet and disappeared.

'Didi,' he said softly. There was no sign of her. He stepped out onto the veranda. The marble tiles were cold and wet, but Didi had not left any paw prints, of course. He edged forward, moving more confidently as his eyes adjusted to the dark. A surge of excitement coursed down his back.

Didi reappeared. She ran up his pyjamas and onto his shoulder.

'There's someone out there,' she whispered.

'Who?'

'I couldn't see, but whoever it was, they were carrying something over their shoulder. Something long.'

'A body?'

'No, thinner. Lighter. This way – down towards the beach.'

He was on the same path as earlier, feet gently slapping wet paving stones, gradually descending towards the shore.

'Careful, old man,' said Didi. 'Watch the step.'

He put his foot into a deep puddle.

'Sugar,' he whispered.

Didi ignored him. She was on Gunzabo's head, squatting on her back feet like a meerkat, claws sharp against his scalp.

'Down there.'

'Where?' he said, casting his eyes about, trying to discern the black shapes swirling in the darkness. 'I'm not a nocturnal burrowing mammal, you know.'

'Neither am I, dickwad. Towards the trees. The graveyard, where everyone's buried.'

He shuffled forwards with his arm out in front.

The rain stopped. The wind died. He stood motionless on the path.

Silence reigned for a few heartbeats.

A wave splashed nearby, fizzing through sand.

He held his breath, listening intently. He heard a scraping sound; someone quietly muttering. He edged forward. Lightning flickered in regular pulses. He glanced up, grateful for the light.

'Watch the step,' said Didi.

Too late. His foot met empty space. He lurched forward, spinning in the air as the ground seemed to rise towards him and thud into his shoulder. He grunted with pain, winded.

'Oh, sugar, sugar, sugar,' he moaned.

'He's getting away!'

'Who?' Gunzabo said. He rolled over to look.

'I told you, I don't know,' said Didi. 'Him.'

A figure appeared from the other side of the trees, sprinting across the sand to the waterline, gone within seconds. Gunzabo lay in a puddle, clasping his shoulder.

'That didn't work out, did it?' he said.

'It's what's called a catastrophic blunder,' said Didi. 'We could have caught him in the act.'

'Which act? Necrophilia?'

Gunzabo struggled to his feet. He carefully tested his body. 'Just a few bruises, Didi. No need to worry yourself.'

A burst of thunder roared overhead. He looked up and a torrent of rain slapped him in the face, fierce as a water cannon, as the storm suddenly returned to life. Lightning flashed. A nearby tree erupted in sparks, instantly extinguished by the downpour.

'We've got to go back, Gunzabo,' Didi shouted. 'It's getting dangerous.'

'Not yet,' he shouted back. 'Use your ferret night vision to guide me.'

'There's no such thing. Besides, I'm like a drowned rat.'

He shuffled along, Didi wrapped round his head, hand stretched out into the gale. Somehow in the darkness he sensed an even darker mass ahead; he moved into it, put his hand against tree trunks, lurched blindly between them. Everything stopped. He was in the eye of the storm. He stepped on something hard; he knelt down, fingers pushing through sand until he felt metal: the edge of a wide, dull blade.

'What is it, Gunzabo?'

'I'm just checking.'

A gust of wind rushed between the trees. Something fell onto the ground nearby. He crawled a few metres, groping blindly: a coconut, half buried in the sand.

'Lucky that wasn't my head,' he said.

'It might have knocked some sense into you.'

He glanced up at her, clinging to his head. 'It might have turned you into a set of ear muffs.'

'Did you bring a light?' said Didi.

Gunzabo stood up and edged forward in the dark. 'If you'd let me smoke I'd have one.'

'If I let you smoke you'd be as dead as me.'

He shook his head and muttered in the darkness. Didi was now lecturing him on his levels of alcohol consumption. He tripped over something rectangular poking out of the ground.

'For Peter's sake,' he muttered.

There was another burst of wind; his sodden pyjamas flapped against him; another coconut thudded into the sand, followed closely by two more.

'We've got to go, Gunzabo. You'll get killed.'

The storm now raged through the grove. A flurry of coconuts landed around him in dull rhythmic thuds.

'Come on then, let's go.'

He reached around on the ground until he found the metallic blade – a shovel, he realised. He picked it up and hurried through the trees, back onto the open beach.

The wind hit Gunzabo immediately. He fell into wet, fluffy sand. He pushed himself up, carried on, found the path. Somewhere ahead a tree fell with a crash.

'This is more like it,' he yelled into the wind. Rain sprayed into his mouth. 'Beats tennis lessons with bored housewives, doesn't it, Didi?'

He battled his way up the path, anaesthetised by the wind, blinded by the rain, using the shovel to feel the way ahead, scraping its blade against the paving stones, jarring it against the steps he'd fallen down earlier. The exterior lights of the bungalow appeared. He hurried now, more confident of his footing. He reached the veranda, staggered inside, pulled the doors shut and collapsed in a saturated heap into bed.

Gunzabo was fast asleep. Outside, the tropical night was buzzing with life; the air was perfectly still, the sky inert. The leaves and branches of the gardens' flora finished dropping their tiny packets of rain onto the ground. Only the shimmering pools of water hinted at the storm that had now passed.

A scream pierced the stillness: an anguished howl which reverberated through the trees. Then another, of pure rage. Then there was nothing again.

5

Gunzabo woke with the sound of tyres and panicked shouts still in his mind's ear. He never saw the crash in his dreams but he heard everything, compressed into an instant: engine at its limit; tyres shrieking; a vehicle horn; wind whistling through an open window; a scream in his right ear; the final thud that always led to oblivion.

Then silence. A heavy softness; warmth; and now cool, conditioned air in his lungs as he lifted his head from the mass of pillows. He blinked, trying to process the light streaming into the bungalow. The island. It was real. He sank back into bed and stared at the ceiling. Gradually, in between the sadness and loss, was a new feeling: he wasn't alone. Someone was next to him, in his bed. He felt a touch of fear; the tiniest fraction of hope. He turned, then he saw: it was a shovel. Disgusted, he tossed it on the floor; the metal blade clattered across the tiles towards the patio doors.

A woman was standing outside. She took a step back, looked at the shovel on the other side of the glass. He got out of bed, and as he approached the doors he saw with relief that it was not Lastri, but an older, plumper version. She was clasping a tray of food. Dragging his eyes from her chest, he nodded, slid the doors open. Hot air rushed in.

'Good morning, sir,' she said.

'What time is it?' he asked, looking past her. Down on the beach, a circle of palm trees wobbled in the sweltering, hazy heat.

'It is ten thirty, sir. I am sorry to wake you. It is just... The Director would like to see you, sir. At eleven.'

'I'll need at least an hour.'

'An hour, sir?' she said nervously.

'At least.'

He took the tray. She gave an uncertain smile, showing white, uneven teeth. 'What should I tell The Director, sir.'

'Tell him to stop getting his pants in a mess. I'll be along later.'

Gunzabo ate breakfast on the veranda. It was superb. Still hungry, he ate his dinner from the night before.

'Didi,' he called into the room, 'there's a sausage here for you.'

Didi scampered over. 'Stick it in your trousers,' she said. 'It might impress all these women waiting on you day and night.'

He stuffed the sausage in his tracksuit pocket.

'That was supposed to be a joke.'

He shrugged; it was worth a try and he didn't have any spare socks.

'Well?' Didi said. 'Are we going?'

He stood, hesitating on the patio.

'You were desperate to see him yesterday.'

He gazed up at the sky's white purity. He could still hear echoes of the dream. Too many reminders of the past. He pushed at his empty sleeve.

'What's the matter?' Didi said.

'My phantom arm. The heat makes it ache. It's why I came to England, remember?'

'That's not why you came to England, Gunzabo.'

'I don't talk about that.'

'Maybe you should.'

'I'm too old. It's just the way it is.'

Didi was looking up at him, a concerned look on her face. He gestured for her to climb up his leg. 'Come on, then.'

She scurried into his empty sleeve. For a brief moment, he almost felt whole again.

* * *

35

Inside The Circles the tables were being laid for lunch. He stepped into the elevator. His hand hovered over the button.

'He can wait a little longer,' Gunzabo muttered, pressing the button for the lower ground floor.

He wandered through rows of empty treadmills, rowing machines and cross trainers; then into a dance studio, where staff mopped the floor and polished wall-to-wall mirrors. He roamed squash courts, tennis courts, an Olympic-size swimming pool. He was tempted to jump in, just to destroy its shimmering perfection. He went down a floor to the spa. A middle-aged woman smiled at him from behind a desk.

He made his way down a corridor. Force of habit made him try the doors as he went. They were all locked.

'Maintenance,' he explained to the woman; she was leaning over, watching him.

He tried another door; it opened unexpectedly and he fell inside.

He was in a storeroom. He got up, dusted himself off, rummaged through shelves full of work tools: ordered collections of screwdrivers, spanners, wrenches, saws; all marked *T Bradley*.

'Is this Tommy's little man-cave?' said Didi.

Gunzabo grunted. He was reading the rosters and notes tacked to the walls: all signed by Tommy.

'Gunzabo, look at this.'

Didi was on the floor, sniffing a plastic container. He knelt down. The container was full of salt-like crystals; ten litres worth. On one side, *NaF* was printed above a skull and crossbones. The container next to it was half full; five more were empty.

'Sodium fluoride,' he murmured. 'What do you need that for, Tommy?'

Footsteps sounded from the corridor. He flashed a look at the doorway: empty. But the footsteps were coming closer: slow, zombie-like. Tommy. He needed to hide. The sodium fluoride.

Hurriedly pushing aside a container, he crawled in and lay flat against the wall as someone entered the storeroom. He saw, in the gaps, a pair of boots moving. They stopped in front of him. Blue jeans collapsed into folds; knees descended; a hand thrust towards Gunzabo, pulled out the container he was hiding behind. Blue eyes flicked up.

'Ah, Tommy. I was hoping to see you.'

No response. Just an unblinking stare.

Gunzabo crawled out, stood up, smiled. 'Sodium fluoride. What do you need that for?'

Keeping his eyes on Gunzabo, Tommy picked up the container, stared at him for one last second, then stalked out of the room.

Didi poked her head from one of the toolboxes.

'Shall we follow him, Gunzabo?'

She jumped onto his arm as he stepped into the corridor and hurried after the footsteps.

'What do you think?' he asked her.

He was next to the elevator.

'Why bother with the caretaker when you can see the boss?' she said.

She shook her whiskers towards the open elevator door. He was trying not to think of the past, but it was catching up. Reluctantly he went in. Leaning out of his sleeve, Didi pressed the button for the second floor.

'Let's go and see Christian,' she said.

The elevator door opened onto a bright, spacious reception area. He stepped out, towards the centre of the room, where a metallic tree trunk rose through the floor from the levels below. On this topmost floor the tree divided into a shining network of finely sculpted silver branches; sitting in the upper reaches, two dozen brass birds motionlessly preened their sharp feathers among the leaves.

He wandered over to the reception desk: empty, save for a screen, keyboard and mouse. The curving glass wall offered spectacular views towards the interior of the island: in the near distance, a semi-circular amphitheatre protruded from the jungle; beyond, the terrain rose unevenly, like a rain-forested Hollywood Hills; here he saw a house, a white cube with dark windows, like a die, dropped from the mist above. Gunzabo squinted at the house; he made out a balcony, which he supposed must overlook the entire southern part of the island; tiny figures in white scurried about, sweeping the veranda, taking rubbish outside.

'Do they ever stop cleaning this damned place?' he muttered.

He stepped across to the windows on the other side; these overlooked the beach. He saw the jetty to his left: a wooden skeleton tacked onto the southernmost point of the island. On either side of the jetty, a beach stretched away, one to the east and the other west, zigzagging up either side of the island.

'Yoo-hoo,' called a voice.

Mrs Bradley was standing at the desk. 'Bonjour.' She pronounced this to rhyme with sewer. 'Sleep ok did you, love?' She carried on, without waiting for a response. 'Dreadful, wasn't it?'

'Hmm?'

'The storm. I woke up with such an awful cold this morning. Who'd have thought it? A hundred and ten degrees, and old Muggins here gets a cold. Here to see Christian, are you?'

He feigned indifference, but kept his eyes fixed on her.

'Ooh, you are late. He won't like that. He's a real stickler, you know.'

'He always was.'

He watched her pick up the phone.

'Bonj,' she said. 'Yes he's here, love. Yes. Thomas? He's feeling a bit better now, thank you, love. Yes. He was just tired. I know, poor lamb-boy.'

Mrs Bradley put the phone down. 'He'll just be a minute, love.' She lowered her body into the seat behind the desk. 'You're just like my Kevin. He was always late.'

Gunzabo stood at the window looking out to sea. Grey, triangular wave-tips moved across the water like the ghosts of dead seabirds.

The phone buzzed. Mrs Bradley picked it up. 'Hello, love,' she said. 'Yes, of course.' She turned to him. 'The Director will see you now.' She gestured towards the door on her left.

He rubbed his arm and went through.

6

'Come in, sit down.'

The Director was sitting behind a desk in his office. There were no windows; the ceiling spotlights were dimmed to an orange glow. Gunzabo's eyes slowly grew accustomed to the twilit room.

'Hello, Christian,' he said.

'Hi!' Christian grinned at him, a brief flashing of teeth.

Gunzabo sat down and looked around the room. 'I see we're not alone,' he said, not bothering to hide his distaste.

'Ha! *Ja.* I have my friends with me.'

They were surrounded by a menagerie of stuffed animals: lizards and birds stood in frames and on shelves; on the floor a tiger lay in a state of permanent rest; a Komodo dragon pointed its tongue at Gunzabo's knee. Placed between the larger animals were penguins, puppies, kittens, monkeys, baby seals; a gigantic python lay coiled around the entire room.

He sat in the gloom while the air conditioning blew chilled air onto his face. He resisted the urge to shiver. Christian grinned at him again, wrinkling his eyes behind frameless spectacles and showing small even teeth. 'How's your mom?'

'Dead.'

'Mine too.'

Christian spoke in a soft voice with a Californian accent. No trace remained of his Cypriot roots. He seemed more Swiss or German than anything. He was wearing a headset connected to the phone on his desk; Gunzabo watched him stroke the metal arm of the headset, running his finger and thumb along its length to a small microphone in front of his chin. Christian smiled again, with his mouth only; his grey eyes remained humourless.

'You've been busy.' Gunzabo glanced around the room again at the host of motionless animals frozen in their prime.

'Do you like them? It's a small hobby of mine.'

'Not so small.'

Christian adjusted his spectacles. Gunzabo wondered if this was a nervous mannerism.

'So how long did you stay after mommy and I left?' Christian said.

'I was there during the invasion. I finished school. After my mother died I went to Athens. There aren't enough murders in Cyprus to be a detective.'

'But you're in the UK now?'

'I was thrown out.'

'Of the police force?'

'Yes,' Gunzabo said.

'I thought they were jobs for life.'

'Even the unions were glad to see the back of me.'

'Oh I'm sorry,' laughed Christian. 'That's so sad.'

Gunzabo didn't respond. He hadn't seen Christian since they were children, and now, sitting in the gloom, seeing him here with his frameless spectacles and his headset and dyed, mousy brown hair, he still couldn't stand him. Christian was laughing silently at him, shaking his right leg under the desk, foot arched, only the toes touching the floor.

'Sounds like I could have made a movie about it,' Christian said.

'A bad one,' shrugged Gunzabo. 'A cheap afternoon movie with a sad ending.'

Christian's smile disappeared. 'I don't make bad movies, Mario.'

'I didn't know you made good ones.'

'For a while. In Los Angeles. But it's hard to make money, it's such a treadmill. So I kinda branched out, saw an opportunity.' The look of mock reproach was gone and he grinned. 'And here we are.'

'Hmm.'

'It's a long way from Limassol, isn't it?'

'Thank God,' Gunzabo muttered.

They were silent for a while.

'Still prefer them dead, then?' Gunzabo indicated the animals around them.

'It happens to us all. Eventually. You should meet Cerberus.'

Christian smiled at the line of Jack Russells in front of his desk, each dog captured forever in its own particular pose: one alert, sniffing the air; others resting with their legs tucked under them; some kneeling obediently, gazing up at their master. Gunzabo leant forward to study their perfectly preserved, lifeless forms. The specimen on the far left was remarkable. He reached out his hand. Just as he touched the dog's nose, it nipped his finger. He jolted back; Didi gave a muffled shriek. The dog wagged its tail energetically.

'There he is: Cerberus the Thirteenth.' Christian's smile was almost subliminal, a quick baring of his small teeth. 'He's getting a little old now. He'll be joining the others sometime soon.'

'He's lovely. Hello boy.' Gunzabo tickled Cerberus under his chin.

'He really likes you. He isn't that friendly usually.' Christian paused briefly. 'It was so good of you to come. I can't tell you how grateful we are.'

'There aren't many places I wouldn't go for a million dollars.'

'Ha, *ja*, that always helps. But I was adamant. It must be a friend, someone I know and trust, to help us with this... situation.'

Gunzabo stopped stroking the dog. 'Tell me about the situation.'

Christian became serious. He adjusted his spectacles. 'We are all in shock. The residents refuse to leave their homes. The staff are terrified. People are talking about leaving. Of course, that could never happen...'

He pursed his lips in an expression of sadness that Gunzabo couldn't help but mistrust. 'We have a serial killer on the island, Mario. People are calling him the Déjà Vu Killer. He's killed two residents in a month. Our island paradise is threatened. So I called you, my old friend, the only person in the world I can rely on. I followed your career closely for years. I know what happened to you.' He paused, wrinkled his eyes in sympathy. 'But I know all the fine things you achieved, and what you are still capable of. *Ja*, you have fallen – I know you won't mind me saying that. But when you walked in this room, your intellect, your instinct... it shines like a beacon. Your detective soul spoke to me across the ocean, Mario. I knew it had to be you that we called upon, to... cleanse our island, return it to paradise.'

Gunzabo sat listening in his grubby tracksuit, hungover, numb from the freezing air. He resisted the urge to lie down in that twilit zoo of dead animals and curl up beside the tiger. 'Tell me what happened to John.'

'He was shot dead whilst running on the beach, three days ago.' Christian shook his leg frantically as he spoke. 'The killer ran off into the jungle.'

'Where is the body?' asked Gunzabo.

'Buried, according to John's wishes.' Christian adjusted his spectacles. 'I can get you the form if you like. We ask all our residents about religious preferences and suchlike.'

'Buried in Palm Grove, I take it? The graveyard.'

Christian stared back at him. His fingers were clamped round the stem of his headset. '*Ja*.'

Gunzabo leaned forward. 'The shooting itself. What happened exactly? Who attended him?'

'Some staff, tending the gardens nearby. Ken Winter – our doctor – was there almost immediately. There was nothing he could do. I'm sure Ken will tell you the precise locations of the gunshots. I believe there was one to the neck, a chest wound that pierced the heart.'

'He died instantly.'

'*Ja.*'

'When did the burial take place?'

'Yesterday morning. We don't dally here, Mario. It's too upsetting for the residents when someone passes away. And these particular circumstances are especially disturbing for us all.'

He watched Christian shift in his chair. 'What about the other murder? Brian, I believe.

'Oh *ja*, I nearly forgot. Four weeks ago, two of our residents found Brian floating in his pool.'

'And were the circumstances suspicious?'

'At the time, no. Many of the residents indulge in narcotics. They get a little bored. But since John's murder, some have been questioning this version of events.'

'Who was it that found Brian?'

'Jimi and Bruce. They were very upset.'

'I'll need to question them.'

'Of course.'

Christian was watching him intently with his small grey eyes.

'What are these?' asked Gunzabo, glancing at a pile of brochures on Christian's desk.

'Oh, promotional material. I've been going through our archives. Some of these go back forty years or more.'

Gunzabo moved his hand towards one of the brochures. It looked glossy and new. 'Elysian Fields,' he said, catching a glimpse of the cover.

Christian moved it out of reach, slipping the brochure into a drawer.

'You weren't supposed to see that one,' he said.

Gunzabo looked at him quizzically. He picked another from the pile: also of high quality, he noted, though with a dated design. The cover read, *Death: Your Next Career Move?* He flicked through the brochure, scanning its contents, then looked at some of the others: *Monastic Bliss*, *Playboy Paradise*, *The Modern Ancient Greece*, *Life After Death.*

'They seem a little contradictory,' he said.

'Our residents have all kinds of reasons for coming here. We must appeal to them all.'

'Do they get what they expect when they arrive?'

'Oh *ja*,' Christian replied softly. 'They get it all.'

'You have a few spaces now.'

'*Ja*, we have. And *ja*, I am reviewing our recruitment programme. But I'd prefer it if you kept that information to yourself.'

'Of course,' said Gunzabo. 'Everything we discuss is in the strictest confidence. Between me and you.' He glanced around. 'And the animals.'

There was a pause. Christian watched him from behind the desk. Gunzabo looked back with undisguised contempt.

'Oh, I'm sorry,' Christian said, wrinkling his eyes. 'Would you like some refreshments?'

'Why not.'

'How about a Greek coffee for old times' sake?'

'I'll have an espresso.'

Christian span round in his chair and pressed a button on the phone. He gazed at Gunzabo as he ordered coffee. A few minutes later Mrs Bradley bustled in with a tray of pastries and coffee.

'Something to keep your peckers up, boys.'

'Thank you so much, Joan,' Christian said.

'I did my best not to sneeze on them, but I can't guarantee it.'

'Poor Joan.'

'Where do you want your lunch today, love? The others will be downstairs at one.'

'Oh, *ja*. I'll be there.' Christian looked at Gunzabo. 'It's good for morale.'

'And you, Gunzarby. We'll lay a place for you, shall we?'

'Why not,' Gunzabo said, ignoring the slight narrowing of Christian's eyes.

'Don't forget dinner tonight,' Christian said to her. 'I hope Thomas is coming too?'

'Oh, he wouldn't miss it for the world,' said Mrs Bradley. She froze, waiting to sneeze; it didn't arrive. 'Maybe Gunzarby could make up four for Scrabs?'

'Gunzabo isn't interested in Scrabble. He's a busy man, what with all these lunches and lie-ins.'

'Right you are,' said Mrs Bradley. She blew her nose loudly and left the room.

Christian served their coffee. 'It'll rot your teeth,' he said, stirring in three sugars for Gunzabo.

'It already has.' Gunzabo took a pain au chocolate and dipped the corner in his drink. He flipped through the brochures as he ate, skimming through bland editorials and postcard shots of the beach and jungle. He waited for a reaction, expecting another brochure to be taken away from him, but Christian just sat there, shaking his leg, letting his coffee go cold. What was he hiding? What was special about that first magazine? He finished his coffee and tossed the remaining brochures back on the desk.

'How long have you been here on the island?' he asked.

'Oh I'm sorry, you've finished reading, have you?'

Gunzabo smiled. He'd caused some irritation at least. Not enough, though. Christian grinned humourlessly, sharp teeth flashing. 'Let me think. We arrived in '72. Before that we were out in the desert in Nevada. You heard of Area 51, right?

We were kinda like that.'

'Hmm.'

'I guess you could call it a commune. I just had the idea one day. Somebody was talking about James Dean, and how sad it was, his dying ten years before. And then somebody else said, he's probably living on a ranch, hiding from all his fans. And I thought: maybe he *is*. Or, at least: maybe he *should have*. So we started the commune. Jimi and Janis came, and then Jim.'

Gunzabo smiled inwardly. So he was right. 'Why did they come?'

'I can be persuasive.' Christian wrinkled his eyes. 'Then Jack and Bobby and Marilyn got in touch. They said, "We want to be part of this too." They'd been alone for years, they wanted company.'

'They just phoned up one day,' Gunzabo asked him, 'called your secret commune?'

'Through an intermediary, *ja*. But they said, not here, not in the US, and I'd been thinking the same. We were too close to what we were trying to escape. And it was a little too austere. Everybody likes the simple life for a few months. But then it gets boring. You start thinking, "Where's the Bollinger? Where's room service?"'

'I think that most days.'

'So we came here. Of course, it wasn't that easy. It took time to find this place, negotiate with the authorities, complete the building work.'

'For your six star resort.'

'Sixteen. When we're at full capacity. And not just stars.' Christian's eyes widened with almost erotic pleasure as he whispered, 'Superstars.'

Gunzabo looked across the desk, saw how much Christian was enjoying himself. There was a look of glee on his face that made Gunzabo want to strangle him.

'The photographs on the boat, is that what you're talking about?'

Christian didn't answer; he gazed at Gunzabo, silently laughing, legs shaking under the desk.

'And the staff?'

'They love it here. We've got a wonderful team, looking after the residents makes us feel good. And we get to do it in a tropical paradise. How cool is that?'

'With a crazed killer on the loose.'

'That's the awkward part. It's where you come in, Mario.'

'I'll need a detailed map of the island. A list of all the residents, all the staff.'

'Of course. I'll ask Joan to provide you with everything you need.'

Gunzabo paused, rubbing his chin, staring at the animals. 'Where were you at the time of the two deaths?' he asked, fixing his eyes on Christian.

'I was at my house all night, Mario. I came here to my office in the morning, as usual. Then I was informed and I went to see the evidence for my own eyes. I'm talking about Brian.'

'And John?'

'I was off the island, on business.'

'Was anyone with you?'

'Thomas took me there. He came back for me after it happened.'

'He didn't stay while you were there?'

'No.'

'I see.' Gunzabo rubbed his chin again. 'Did you kill either of those two men, Christian?'

'Why would I do that?' Christian answered softly, gazing back at Gunzabo. He sat motionless in his chair. 'They are all my friends. We're one big family.' For once he did not smile. 'No Mario, I did not kill anyone. My aim by the way, is that everybody on this island should reach at least one hundred years old. Ideally more, much more.'

'Like Jack and Bobby?'

'Oh no, they died years ago. Don't worry about them. Everyone else though.'

'A hundred and twenty seven club?'

'Ha, *ja*. It's possible, you know. You too Mario. You could reach a hundred. Just think.'

'I'm too old already.'

'There's always euthanasia. It's been brought up by our longevity committee on several occasions.'

Gunzabo opened his mouth to put his next question to Christian, when the door opened and Mrs Bradley rushed in.

'Yes, Joan?' Christian said.

'Oh – I just – oh I can't believe it's happening!' She burst into tears.

'Is something wrong?'

'It's not working! I can't connect. I changed the batteries. I wiggled it about. Kevin's waiting for me online. For our weekly chat.'

Christian frowned. 'Can you be more precise, Joan. What isn't working?'

'Well, my mouse. I can't miss my chat with him, I just can't!'

'Did you try restarting your workstation?'

'Yeah, I did all that. Please Christian, have a look will you?' She started weeping. Her neck was flushed with crimson blotches.

'Oh Joan,' Christian said. He was looking at her with great tenderness. It was the only true feeling Gunzabo had seen in him. 'Let's see what the matter is. I won't be a minute, Mario.'

They left the room. Gunzabo waited thirty seconds, listening to the activity outside. This was his chance. Leaning over the desk he stretched his fingertips towards the drawer; it was open. He grabbed the magazine: *Elysian Fields*, the cover read, over a stock photograph of a young, tanned couple; then a strapline: *An interview with Bob*. Much like the others, just newer. But the insignia, that was odd. In the top right, an outline of an owl. He looked at the other, older versions: each one had a sixteen-pointed star, somewhere on the cover. No owl. Why had Christian changed the island insignia?

Mrs Bradley shrieked with excitement outside. 'Oh, you're a star! You're so clever, Christian!'

His time was up. Quickly, Gunzabo slipped the magazine back into the drawer. He sat down in his chair just as Christian returned.

'Joan's always so desperate to maintain contact with her son...' Christian remained in the doorway, eyeing him suspiciously. 'What have you been doing?'

Gunzabo looked back, keeping his face expressionless, enjoying Christian's uncertainty.

'Interview over, Mario. I have important business to attend.' He ushered Gunzabo out. 'We'll meet the same time tomorrow.'

The door closed, almost onto Gunzabo's nose. He stood there for a moment, trying to look through the peephole. No luck. He needed a drink. He went downstairs to the lounge.

'What a touching reunion,' said Didi.

'I'm doing it for the money,' Gunzabo told her. 'Nothing else.'

'I bet he was bullied.'

He grunted, feeling a certain satisfaction. He took a sip of gin and tonic. Didi was right, as usual. 'There was a ferret-sized space on the wall next to that gibbon, I noticed.'

'What, the one swinging on the branch? Or the one holding its dead baby?'

'The one with the dead baby,' he told her.

'I almost feel guilty to be alive. So what are we doing now?'

Gunzabo shifted in his chair. He looked through the windows

at the sea and the gardens below. It was rather pleasant watching the workers perform their duties from up here. But he was feeling restless. He eyed his glass, wondering whether to order another double, or a triple. A woman appeared, ready to take his order. He ordered a bottle of beer; something he could take with him. In the distance, against a backdrop of grey sea, the ring of palm trees was beckoning him.

7

Sand crunched underfoot; the sky contracted with his approach; trees soared ever higher into the white. Now he stood in the sultry afternoon heat, gazing up the full length of the palms: brown, darkening to black; a cascade of green foliage. He moved through the circle of trees, feeling the jagged coarseness of bark on his hand as he entered Palm Grove.

The air inside the grove was cool and still. It felt like evening. The waves sounded distant, muffled by the wall of trees.

He was standing in an enclosed circle of sand; in the centre, a jet-black obelisk rose towards the heavens, flawlessly polished, its surface smooth and unadorned with carvings or writing of any kind.

Around the obelisk was a semicircle of marked graves, like the spokes of an unfinished wheel.

'Maybe they could bury us here.'

Gunzabo glanced at Didi. She was poking her head out of his sleeve.

'I want to be home by next week,' he said. 'And not in a box.'

Didi dropped down onto the sand, scampered in and out of the wall of trees which marked the grove's perimeter until she had completed two full laps, then came running back towards Gunzabo.

'If the serial killer gets us though, can they put us here?'

Gunzabo smiled. 'Yes, Didi.'

He wandered around the interior, inspecting the graves: each had a wooden sign at its head. Most looked weathered and dull, but some were new, a silky chocolate colour, and engraved with charcoal letters. The first read:

> *DEAREST BRIAN*
> *LIFE NEVER ENDS*
> *YOU WILL ALWAYS REMAIN*
> *OUR SWEET FRIEND*

'Remind me to get cremated,' he muttered, and moved to the next grave.

> *OUR BELOVED STEVE*
> *FATHER, SON AND SPIRIT TO US ALL*

The next read simply:

> *JACK & BOBBY*

Then:

> *MAHAMRITYUNJAYA MATA*

Close beside it was another:

> *RAJIB, YOU LEAVE THIS LIFE FOR ANOTHER*
> *I AM HEARTBROKEN*
> *YOUR MOTHER*

He moved to the end of the semicircle, and an unmarked grave, its presence indicated by a mound of freshly dug sand and a single blue flower.

'Do you think that's —'

'Yes, it must be.' He knelt at the grave. The sand was raised and compacted in the approximate shape of a coffin. He shook his head grimly. 'The world mourned him and all this time he was alive.'

Didi said, 'Up until three days ago. Would have been nice to meet him, wouldn't it?'

Gunzabo studied the grave. He pressed on the raised mound of sand, then glanced at the other graves: they were flat, marked only by the wooden signs.

'When did they bury him?' he muttered, and looked up at the circle of open white sky framed by the tree tops.

'Yesterday morning, according to Christian.'

He looked back at the freshly compacted sand. 'You wouldn't know there'd been a storm, would you?' He picked up a flower placed at the head of the grave.

'What type of flower's that then?' said Didi.

'Iris. I wonder why this particular—'

He became alert. Something had changed in the grove. Trees swayed above him; the obelisk tapered sharply into open sky; the light played faintly across the sand where he knelt at the grave. He frowned; the tranquillity had gone, but he could not quite determine why. He stood up; the blood rushed to his head and he was overcome by dizziness.

'Gunzabo,' whispered Didi urgently. 'Behind you.'

He turned round, blinking his eyes, hand pressed against his forehead, and looked towards the grove entrance. As his sight slowly returned, an image of a woman assembled itself: dressed in sky-blue, she was holding something in her arms. A baby, he thought, staring in disbelief and hope; an apparition straddling worlds.

'Megara? Is that you?' he whispered. 'My darling. I'm so sorry.'

Deep in his abdomen a dark well of emotion, so carefully buried, expanded and rose. His chest flooded. He reached out with his one hand as the figure came to him.

'Gunzabo. What's the matter?'

He came to his senses and saw it was Lastri. She was dressed in a blue sari. She had recently been crying; her eyes were red, her strange beauty diminished. She came close, gazing at him with concern. He pressed against his shoulder and looked at the graves. 'I thought for a second I'd seen an angel,' he mumbled.

Lastri smiled compassionately. 'I brought these for John. My son picked them from his grandmother's garden.'

She placed a bouquet of flowers on the sand, next to the blue iris, and gave a cry. 'The headstone. Where is it?'

Gunzabo stood rubbing his shoulder, pale and distraught from the vision of Megara, watching numbly as Lastri cast around the centre of the grove. She disappeared among the trees. 'Thank God,' she exclaimed. She was at the outer fringes, nearest the water, and she came towards Gunzabo, holding a stake attached to a rectangular sign.

'How on earth did it get over there?' she murmured. 'Help me will you, Gunzabo.'

They pushed the stake into the ground at the top of the grave; there was still a deep hole and it went in without difficulty. They stood up together. Lastri gazed into his eyes; he looked back at her; she was beautiful again.

'I must go,' she said. 'I have to prepare for evening service.'

'Yes, of course.'

Lastri hurried out of the grove. He watched until she had gone, then turned to the newly marked grave. Didi peered out from his sleeve. The new headstone was different to the others. Carved by hand, it simply read:

Revolution

He stood at the grave a minute longer, looking at the compacted, raised sand, noticing again the other graves, flattened the previous night. He thought of the storm, of groping through this very same place, rain and wind lashing through the trees. There were still coconuts, half buried in the sand around him. How did this grave survive such violence? It looked so fresh.

He smiled. Yes, of course. He saw now exactly what had happened. But he did not know why. And he did not know who. Was it the killer? He pictured the figure last night, dropping the shovel – perhaps here, where he was standing – running away across the beach. Coming back later.

He wondered what the time was. He was feeling hungry. Then he remembered: lunch, with Christian, the Bradleys, others too. That might be interesting. Perhaps it was one of them who had been digging up John's grave.

8

Gunzabo was starving by the time he reached The Circles. The terrace was empty, the tables confined to the restaurant interior, and he was grateful for the cool, conditioned air inside.

'Gunzarby, over here.'

Mrs Bradley and Christian were seated at a table in the near corner, alongside a striking woman who looked to be in her early fifties.

'Gunzabo, isn't it?' the woman said, in a delicate voice.

He looked at her with amused surprise. So she wasn't dead either.

'Pleased to meet you,' he said.

She smiled faintly, allowing him to take her hand.

He looked into her eyes and for an instant saw a look of need, almost to the point of being scared, gone as she smiled again and tucked short blonde hair behind her left ear.

'I see your face every morning,' he said.

She smiled enquiringly.

He sat down. 'On my coffee mug.'

'There were lots of those, weren't there?'

Gunzabo studied her face: immaculate as a Roman statue, white foundation, a dusting of rouge, ruby lips. She was older now, of course; lines in her forehead rose from the inside of each brow.

'It was from your wedding.' He was thinking now of her portrait, so young and innocent, glowing with happiness.

She looked down briefly, lashes dark with mascara; and then her eyes showed again, blue and vulnerable.

'Your husband is on the back,' he said.

'Ex-husband,' she answered.

'Looking like a gay soldier.'

She smiled at this and raised herself up in her seat, legs crossed, in black tights. She looked at him with composure now, as he asked her why she'd chosen to come here and if her family knew.

'Those who I love understand and gave me their blessing,' she told him, 'but I prefer not to talk of the past. My work is all that matters.'

Ken joined them at the table. 'So, you've met the shrink?' He sat next to Gunzabo. 'Don't listen to a word she says. She's completely nuts. Haha.'

She made no acknowledgement of Ken's arrival, looking only at Gunzabo; he felt her eyes searching his, as if she was trying to find a way in. She looked sad now and somehow he knew the sadness was for him. He turned away. Christian was sitting with his leg shaking under the table, saying nothing. Mrs Bradley was eating her third bread roll. Ken called over a waiter and breezily ordered drinks for everyone.

'Solved the mystery yet?' he asked Gunzabo.

'Yes. It was you.'

Ken looked at him and roared with laughter. He drained his glass of wine. 'In the cellar, with the wine bottle?' He simulated hitting Mrs Bradley over the head with the Sancerre, then topped up her glass.

'You're going to get me sloshed, Kenny,' giggled Mrs Bradley. 'You know how frisky I get when I'm tipsy.'

'I certainly do, Joanie. Let's go up to Christian's office and shag among the animals.'

Ken winked at Gunzabo, gave Diana a sideways glance and reached for a cigar, putting it back as the starters arrived. 'Any theories, then?'

Gunzabo shrugged. 'I don't have much information at this

point, just a few isolated details about the murders.'

'What do you want to know?' said Ken.

He paused, collecting his thoughts. 'John. You attended the murder scene. What happened?'

'Shot by an armed assassin, dead as soon as I got there. Bullet to the heart.'

'Who else was there?'

'Lastri, a few other villagers. Elvis of course. They were out on their morning run.'

'Do you have a death certificate?'

'Of course.'

'I'll need to see it. And Brian?'

He didn't take his eyes off Ken, watched him frown, then shrug. 'Someone drugged him, pushed his quad bike into the swimming pool. With him in it.' Ken took a large forkful of prawn cocktail. 'So eighties, Christian, I love it.'

'You think someone did this? Not just a simple case of misadventure?'

Ken glanced quickly at Christian, as if seeking confirmation he should answer. Christian smiled and said nothing; he seemed to be enjoying Ken's discomfort.

'Well, it's the Déjà Vu Killer, isn't it? Killing them the same way they faked their deaths. Too much of a coincidence to be an accident. Who's next, that's what I want to know. Don't go out for a drive, Diana. Haha.'

Diana blinked, still refusing to look at Ken. She placed her cutlery carefully on her plate. 'One thing we do know: whoever killed them is one of us.' She spoke with timid confidence. 'One of the population that is.'

'You are certain about this?' Gunzabo said. 'An outsider couldn't be the killer?'

'No one knows where the island is, love,' said Mrs Bradley. 'It's top secret.'

'There are people who know *about* it,' Diana said. 'Not many, but a few have to know. How could this place function in such an... idyllic way, with such comforts? But nobody knows *where* it is.'

'Not even us,' said Ken. 'Except Christian, of course. You do, don't you? Or we're never getting off.'

Gunzabo listened thoughtfully. If no one could come here uninvited, neither could anyone leave. Not without Christian's consent. He watched Christian's eyes wrinkling with contentment, lips opening slightly as he sipped some water. For a moment, as brief as one of his grins, his eyes flicked towards Ken and narrowed with hatred.

'Your husband knows, of course,' Gunzabo said, addressing Mrs Bradley. 'He brought me here, after all.'

'Oh yes, my Thomas knows. He won't tell me though. Not even to let my Kevin come and visit.' She put a glum look on her face.

'How would that work?' Ken said. 'He thinks you're dead.'

'I know. I do feel bad.'

'He doesn't. I wouldn't worry yourself, he got that lovely insurance payout. Mind you, he'll have spent it on narcotics and prostitutes by now.'

'Oh you are a devil,' said Mrs Bradley. 'My Kevin? He wouldn't do that. I didn't bring him up to waste money on women and drugs.'

'Who said it was a waste?' said Ken.

Gunzabo drank his wine and watched Ken sit back and light a cigar. Diana frowned at the smoke drifting over the table; Mrs Bradley craned her head towards the kitchen, eager for the next course. Christian grinned contentedly; waitresses came and took away the plates.

The main course arrived. It was simple but delicious: barbecued lobster, French fries, a green salad, lime dressing, a selection of dips. As he was shaking salt over his food, Gunzabo noticed an insignia on the salt cellar: a sixteen-pointed star. The cutlery, plates and glasses were all embossed in the same way. Christian, his food untouched, was still grinning at him. Irritated, Gunzabo ate his meal in silence.

When everyone had finished eating, he took out a notebook and pen from his tracksuit top, placed the notebook by his empty plate and addressed them all.

'You all know why I'm here,' he said. 'To find the killer before he strikes again. You say he must live here, so firstly I must know the names of everyone, the entire population, starting with the residents. There are fourteen, I understand, some of whom live on West Beach and the remainder on East Beach.'

Diana and Ken looked towards Christian, who rocked back in his chair, looked back at them with his small grey eyes, then turned and flashed his grin at Gunzabo.

'Their names?' Gunzabo said.

'Joan will get you that list, I'm sure.'

Mrs Bradley was eating Christian's main course. 'What list?' she said, through a mouthful of lobster tail.

Gunzabo waited, pen in hand. 'You can tell me now.'

Mrs Bradley finished her mouthful. She made a face as she tried to remember. 'Alright, let's see,' she said. 'Well, East Beach, there's Janis and Karen. Keithy of course. Blimey, I'm such a scatterbrains.' She scratched her fleshy chin, then said, brightly, 'Oh, but it doesn't matter. They weren't on the island anyhow.' She lowered her voice, adding, 'When John was... you know.'

'You mean the East Beach residents?'

Gunzabo opened his notebook, drew a vertical line down the middle of the page and wrote two headings: *West Beach* in the left hand column, *East Beach* in the right. He carefully noted the three residents' names.

'Where were they?' he said.

'Full Moon Island,' Ken said. 'Partying.'

Gunzabo looked up, remembering the map in his room.

'I'm surprised you weren't there, Kenny-Wenny-Bongo,' said Mrs Bradley. 'We all know how much you like a party.'

Gunzabo made more notes as he questioned Ken about Full Moon Island: it was twenty miles away at least, Ken told him. Thomas Bradley had taken all six East Beach residents there, along with a few of the staff. Tommy stayed there with the boat and took them back to Dead Star Island the next morning, following news of John's death. He then left to get Christian from the mainland.

'Was anyone else on Full Moon Island?' Gunzabo said.

Mrs Bradley shook her head. 'A few staff, that's it.'

'Was there any way they could have left the island, come back here? Another boat, for example?'

'The other one's in about six different pieces, love. My Thomas has been meaning to fix it for weeks. It's sitting on the beach near the village.'

'Which village?'

'Where the staff live. Up past West Beach.'

Gunzabo looked at his list. In the right hand column he had the names of the three known East Beach residents: *Janis, Karen, Keith*. He added three question marks for the unknowns, then *Tommy*. In the left hand column, for West Beach, he wrote three more names: *Brian, River, Marilyn*. He put a cross through Brian's name.

'The other residents,' he said. 'I need their names.'

Mrs Bradley began to speak, but Christian interrupted her. 'Find out, go see them. Mingle.' He did not smile or blink; spotlights gleamed on his glasses. 'They'd love the company.'

Gunzabo stared at him, bemused and exasperated. The others shifted uncomfortably in their seats. He turned back to Mrs Bradley.

'The West Beach residents. Where were they when John was murdered?'

'In their villas, love. Well I expect they were, it was early. Apart from Elvis of course.'

Gunzabo wrote one more name in the left hand column: *Elvis*. Yes, out running with John. The last person to see him alive. 'And the staff?' he asked.

'That one's easy,' Mrs Bradley said. 'All the staff were at roll call. Us too.'

'Roll call?'

'Every day, at seven in the morning. There's a head count, and everyone was there.'

'Everyone?'

'Apart from the staff on Full Moon Island, yes. Us and the villagers.'

But not you, Gunzabo thought, glancing over at Christian. He turned back to Mrs Bradley.

'You're saying that at the time of the shooting, every staff member on Dead Star Island was at the same meeting? It's not possible that someone crept off?'

'Nope,' said Mrs Bradley firmly. 'I did the headcount myself, everyone was in line and accounted for. I'd only just finished, and then the shots were fired.' She blew her nose noisily, and added, 'Apart from Diana. You weren't there, were you love? I nearly forgot.'

'I slept in that morning,' Diana said. 'I don't always attend.'

Gunzabo drew a horizontal line across the middle of the left column in his notebook, writing in the bottom section: *Villagers, Mrs Bradley, Ken, Diana???*

He put his pen down, sat back and drank his wine. The others were looking at him, waiting for him to speak.

'I'll need a room in The Circles,' he said. 'Somewhere private. Perhaps Mrs Bradley can arrange the interview schedule.'

'Schedule?' said Mrs Bradley.

'I need to question everyone, in turn, and in private.'

'Oh, I see. In that case—'

'That won't be possible,' Christian said softly. He flashed his teeth at Gunzabo. 'I'm afraid our residents simply won't tolerate the interruption to their tranquillity.'

Gunzabo laughed ironically. 'You know, of course, this will delay the investigation, perhaps even prevent any chance of success?'

'Oh, I'm sorry. But we have very strict service level agreements. And we have very demanding people who have paid huge sums of money to be here.'

'The staff then. I'll start with them.'

Christian smiled sadly. 'That's just not possible I'm afraid, Mario. We have an island to run. The residents simply would not tolerate the disruption to their routine.'

Gunzabo looked around the table. Nobody said a word; Ken shrugged; Mrs Bradley blew her nose; Diana stared at the table expressionlessly.

'How do you suggest I conduct this investigation?' he said.

'Do what you do best, Mario,' said Christian. 'Investigate. Find out who is killing our residents. You have our full cooperation, naturally.' He grinned as he rocked on the back legs of his chair. Gunzabo had to restrain himself from shoving Christian backwards. Any more of this and he would be killing someone himself. Would that forfeit the million dollars? Probably. He poured himself another glass of wine and waited for dessert.

9

Dessert was mango *tarte tatin* with a passion fruit sorbet. It was delicious, easily the equal of the previous courses, and served with a dessert wine, which was sweet but with enough acidity to complement the food perfectly.

Gunzabo mulled over his notebook, frustrated at the blank spaces in each column, looking up as Diana stood, pushed her chair under the table and announced she had appointments all afternoon. She shook his hand and left. Gunzabo watched her walk across the terrace, rendered ghostlike by the tinted glass, until she disappeared from view.

'Appointments?' he asked.

'Diana's the therapist, love,' Mrs Bradley told him.

'She's not a resident?'

'She was, but she didn't like it. She got a bit bored, poor lamb. She likes helping others.'

'Who sees her?'

'Well, the residents, of course.'

'Which ones?'

'A fair few,' Ken said. 'She does the brains, I do the brawn. Fully holistic treatment here, Gunzabo.'

'Oh yes,' Mrs Bradley said, 'Diana's extremely holistic.'

Ken laughed.

'How did she come to the island?' Gunzabo said.

'Oh, it was a classic,' Ken said. 'Years of planning that one. Went like clockwork. All those paparazzi? They were ours. Car stops, she gets out, snogs the boyfriend. A few tears, then she's on the back of a motorbike, straight to the airport for resettlement.

We set up the crash, in come the body doubles. Loads of fake blood, photos, then about five million in bribes. Job done.'

'You speak as if you were there,' Gunzabo said.

'Nah, it was our European operation. I was in the States by then.'

Waitresses arrived with coffee and chocolate truffles. Christian was quivering both legs under the table, his face suffused with a mixture of pleasure and annoyance at Ken's description. As Gunzabo stirred sugar into his coffee, he thought about Diana's funeral, watching it on television in a bar in Athens. He'd been working on the Hydra murders at the time.

'I went down to Palm Grove,' he said. 'The graves, I presume these are all residents who died here?'

'Oh *ja*, none of us can live forever.' Christian wrinkled his eyes.

'It does get you, when they peg it,' said Mrs Bradley. 'They're like sons to me. All of them.'

'Even the women,' said Ken.

'But when Steve passed away, that got us all, that did. Didn't it?'

No one answered.

'He was our father figure.'

'I thought he was like a son to you,' said Ken, lighting another cigar.

'When did Steve die?' asked Gunzabo.

'Oh, twelve, thirteen years ago?' Mrs Bradley sighed. 'He was a good egg, was Steve. Always had time for you.'

The table was silent for a minute. A waitress brought more coffee. Gunzabo's thoughts came back to Ken's description of Diana's resettlement.

'How long have you been here on the island?'

'Seven years now,' Ken said. 'It's alright, I suppose. I keep myself busy, do the odd op. You're happy with your breast reduction, aren't you Joan?'

'Oh yes,' said Mrs Bradley. She popped a chocolate truffle into her mouth. 'Like a pair of cantaloupes they were. Chafing and weighing me down in the heat. Oh, it was awful. I still suffer with my back, mind.'

Gunzabo glanced at her still enormous breasts. Ken followed his gaze. 'You should have seen them before,' he said, blowing his cheeks out.

'Kenny was surgeon to the stars,' Mrs Bradley said.

Ken raised his cigar to his lips, took a puff and shook his head nostalgically. 'Loved me, they did. Waiting list as long as your arm. Best thing I ever did, moving to the States. Beats miserable old England.'

'We're so lucky to have him,' said Mrs Bradley. 'Aren't we Christian?'

Christian sipped his water, tightened his eyes slightly and gave a forced grin.

'You still can't do anything about my piles though,' she said.

'Modern medicine has its limits unfortunately, Joan,' said Ken. 'And your rectum is beyond those limits, by quite a distance.'

Gunzabo listened while Ken smoked his cigar and reminisced about all the stars he knew personally; which ones he'd operated on; others who constantly begged him to fit them in; who had the best parties; who used to live next door.

'Happy days, they were.' Ken poured himself another drink and shook his head wistfully. 'It was the fifth marriage that screwed it all up. Right shocker. Took me to the cleaners.'

'You mean she would have done, if you hadn't jumped off the Golden Gate Bridge,' said Mrs Bradley, smirking.

'Yeah, tragic it was, my suicide.'

'So you knew about Dead Star Island?' Gunzabo said.

'Oh yeah. Cigar?' Ken took out his silver lighter and held the flame out.

'Kenny was our Business Development Manager,' Mrs Bradley said.

'Head of recruitment,' said Ken. 'Five years, I did. Over in LA.'

Gunzabo considered this while he took a puff on his cigar and glanced at Christian. His legs had stopped shaking, but his left eye was twitching as he stared at Ken. Gunzabo wondered why the conversation was causing him such discomfort. He looked as if he was about to leap on Ken and tear off his limbs.

'While you were in Los Angeles,' Gunzabo continued, 'did you recruit anyone for the Island?'

'Oh yeah. Back in the nineties, I was on fire, I was. I'll tell what happened—'

'I don't think you will,' Christian said, interrupting with a snarl. He pushed his frameless spectacles back into place and leaned towards Ken, who bit his lip anxiously and muttered, 'Yeah, sorry.'

Christian leaned back again, teeth showing in a brief smile, small eyes deadly serious. 'It's all been very interesting, I'm sure,' he said. 'But the detective has work to do. And so do we.'

Gunzabo nodded at the others as they rose, said goodbye and left with their heads lowered like guilty children.

Gunzabo patted his stomach and stretched backwards in his chair. He fancied a little siesta. But he needed to finish off the list of residents. Mingle, Christian had said. Alright, he would. He checked his sleeve, saw that Didi was still asleep, drank the remainder of Mrs Bradley's dessert wine, then went outside and down to the beach.

He headed up the island under a low, claustrophobic sky. The sea was calm and inviting, the sand soft and white; the jungle throbbed with hidden life. He stopped at Brian's gate and looked into the garden: silent, frozen in time. He moved on, past River's place, then Marilyn's; both were equally quiet and lifeless.

He continued up the coast, came to another star point, then a new, curving section of beach. He angled across sand, to a railing and a gate. He rattled the bars: locked. Next to the gate, was an American style mailbox, a vertical line of Chinese characters on its side. He opened the flap, found a letter inside, embossed in gold with a sixteen-pointed star.

Dear Bruce
Finally it's that time of year again! We are thrilled to
invite you to the annual Dead Star Island dinner and
talent show. We cannot wait to see you there, so please
contact Mrs Bradley with the details of your act as soon
as you can.
Christian Adhis, Island Director

He put the invitation back and peered through the railings. The garden was simply arranged, its perimeter marked by delicate trees and shrubs. A stream ran along one side into a small rock garden. At the front of the house, across its full length, was a wooden balcony and a table with a tray of uneaten breakfast and jugs of milk and fruit juice.

'Where is everyone?' Didi said.

'Somewhere else,' he answered, taking his notebook out.

'Hiding from the Déjà Vu Killer, I expect.'

He wrote another name in the left hand column: *Bruce*. 'Let's go,' he said.

Further up the beach he came to another residence: beautiful, tranquil garden; the house, like the others, single storey, intricately carved and on stilts. He moved away.

'Gunzabo,' Didi whispered.

She was peering backwards, through the railings.

'What?'

'Someone's in,' said Didi.

He caught a brief glimpse of a figure moving across an open window. 'So there is.'

'This is John's place,' Didi said. 'Isn't he supposed to be dead?'

He advanced cautiously into the garden towards the house, keeping to one side under the cover of trees. He crept up to the front window and stole a look inside: someone was kneeling on the floorboards, picking through a bag of running gear. Tommy. He watched as Tommy moved to the bookcase, pulled each book off the shelf, examined each in turn before placing it back in its original position.

'Get down,' Didi hissed.

Tommy's head snapped up. He stared into space, as if he was using an entirely different array of senses. Gunzabo knelt low, listening intently. Didi quivered in the hollow of his shoulder. There was a creaking sound and Gunzabo heard steps across the wooden floor, into another room. He crept along the side of the house to the next window, cheeks tingling with pleasure. He looked down at Didi. 'Exciting, isn't it?'

'Don't talk so loud. He scares me stiff.'

He shot a look through the window. Tommy was sifting through piles of clothes and bedding.

'What's he doing?' Didi whispered.

'Amateur detective work.' He frowned, the excitement replaced with annoyance. 'This should have been me. Why did you let me sleep in this morning?'

'Because I'm not your mum, fish-face.'

He was still formulating a response when Tommy began walking towards the window. Gunzabo quickly ducked down. He pressed his back against the outside of the house. Looking around for cover, he inched along the wall towards a weeping fig the size of a tree. He heard a noise. Coming from above him. He stopped, held his breath. All was quiet. He raised his chin, slowly, until he was looking straight up the wall and found himself eye to eye with Tommy, only centimetres away.

'Tommy, we must stop meeting like this,' he said, staring up at Tommy's upside-down face. 'Doing some detective work for me?' He scrambled to his feet. 'You're empty-handed. A shame.'

Tommy pulled his head back from the window. Footsteps sounded through the house. Gunzabo stayed by the weeping fig, waiting for Tommy to come out, stand menacingly nearby, or perhaps stare from afar. But there was just the sound of footsteps and the creak of floorboards, starting and stopping in the same pattern as before. It was almost disappointing. Shaking his head in perplexity, Gunzabo walked round the front, up wooden steps, onto the porch and inside. He found a drinks cabinet, settled into a sofa, drinking his whisky while he watched Tommy work methodically through the remainder of the house. Finally, Tommy went outside empty-handed, without even a sideways glance.

'See you later,' Gunzabo said. 'Better luck next time.'

He turned to Didi. 'Our turn now.'

'Didn't we just watch Tommy do it for us?'

He looked at her, offended. 'Is Thomas Bradley the foremost detective of modern Greece? Has he solved unsolvable murders? Did he catch Stavros the Bull?'

Didi was rolling her eyes.

'No. He is a janitor. He knows how to mend things, steer boats, stalk around like a zombie. He does not know how to search a house for clues.'

'He seemed pretty thorough to me.'

'We'll see, Didi. We'll see.'

He examined the contents of the kitchen while Didi played on the work top. It gave him great pleasure: at last, proper investigative work.

'I wonder how the Bradleys have stayed together so long?'

Didi said. 'Love is blind, I suppose.'

'Hatred isn't.'

'Talking about Tommy, or your old mate Christian?'

He examined a pair of round spectacles. 'He's not my friend. This is business.'

'Hard work, this *business*, isn't it? Having all these *business* lunches and these *business* drinks.'

'It's what happens when one rises to the top.'

He moved into the living room, over to a pile of papers at an open writing bureau. 'Love letters,' he muttered, reading each in turn. 'All from someone called Iris.' He thought of the blue flower on John's grave. 'Interesting. Ah, now these...'

'What?'

'No, also from Iris. The handwriting is different. A little more interesting.'

'John had two lovers, both called Iris?'

'It seems so. But not at the same time. The chronology is clear. Only the later ones are different.' He put the letters back on the desk.

'What do they say?'

'What do all love letters say? Think of an eighties ballad. With two female singers.'

He moved to the bookshelf. Tommy had already flipped through each book, checking for loose pieces of paper; Gunzabo repeated this and found nothing. One book he pulled out again: *A Brief History of the Nazis*. It was the only work of non-fiction on the shelf.

'Do you know this trick?' he asked Didi, shaking the book, then flipping the spine back into the palm of his hand. The booked opened up. 'Usually you just get the sexy bits. But who gets turned on by Fascism? Apart from Christian.' He began reading:

Fluoridation and mind control:-
Fluoridation, primarily by means of sodium fluoride,
is rumoured to have been used by the Nazis, both
prior to, and during the war. There is certainly strong
evidence that it was used by the Russians in the 1920s,
ostensibly as a supplement for strengthening teeth
and bones. The credentials of this compound as a
medication for mass mind control have never been fully
established, as well as its reported effect of causing
sterility in both sexes; there is however, a catalogue of
anecdotal evidence...

Didi looked up at him. 'Is that a clue?' she said.
'It's a clue, Didi.'
'What for?'
'A detective must be patient. Just keep it in mind.'
'Let's carry on looking.'
'See, you're getting the hang of this now.'
He moved steadily through every room, inspecting every item, large and small. He fetched a chair and felt on top of the wardrobes and the kitchen units, then tried the bookcase, running his fingertips through dust until he discovered a scrap of paper.

'See?' he said, triumphantly. 'How does a scrap of paper get on top of a bookcase without being put there? And did the janitor find it?'

On one side was a name, printed on glossy paper, like something torn from a magazine: *IAN FIELDS*; on the other side was a handwritten code: *KB230574*.

'Is the plot thinning or thickening, Didi?'
'It's sort of stewing with the lid on.'
'Doesn't your ferret's intuition tell you anything?'
'Oh shut up, Gunzabo. Stop enjoying it all so much.'

He carried on the search, but an hour later Didi was bored and scratching the sofa so petulantly he conceded it was time to go. Besides, he needed a drink; whisky made him too dark and sombre. He made his way back through the garden, onto the beach and continued north.

It was by now the hottest part of the day; he took off his trainers, wading along the water's edge with Didi on his shoulder. The beach turned sharply right; he passed under low branches overhanging the sea. The sand opened up again, revealing a new beach, and a wooden shack near the water. As he approached, Gunzabo saw an old man sitting cross-legged in the doorway, fully naked but for a pair of mirrored aviator sunglasses. A small fire crackled invisibly on the sand as he mumbled a mantra, hands on his knees, palms facing upwards.

'Hello my friend,' said Gunzabo.

The man gave no response, other than increasing the volume and intensity of his chanting. Gunzabo looked over the man's shoulder into the shack: grubby bedding, soiled clothes, damp towels strewn amongst cooking equipment, food, video cassettes, magazines; candles flickered precariously atop piles of still more video cassettes, threatening to turn the entire shack into a funeral pyre.

He moved off, looking back as the old man called after him, 'Come back later, man. I've got a thousand more Shri Ganesh's, then I'm all yours.'

Further on, he came to another property. He looked into an unkempt garden, covered in litter, dominated by a swimming pool filled with murky, green water. At the far end, three men were lying on dilapidated sunbeds.

'Hello there,' he called out to them. 'Can I join you?'

One of the men looked up. 'Come on in, have a beer.'

Things were looking up: something to drink, and finally some residents to talk to.

10

Gunzabo walked towards the men, stepping over rubbish, eyeing the swimming pool next to him: a variety of aquatic life darted about under cans, bottles, magazines, cigarette butts.

Two of the men looked to be asleep; the other was playing *Heartbreak Hotel* with great skill on an acoustic guitar. He was dressed in a floppy military-style hat, vest and knee-length combat shorts.

'Say, are you the detective?'

He was an old man but Gunzabo recognised him immediately, remembered his gentle, dark, searching eyes from a thousand posters.

'Yes.'

'Right on.'

The old man didn't stop playing. Lean and powerful despite his years, he was still handsome with a clearly-defined jaw and muscular cheeks; frizzy hair showed under the rim of his hat: tight curls of grey mixed with white.

'Help yourself, Mr Detective,' he said, in a deep melodious voice, nodding towards a cool box.

Gunzabo picked out a beer.

'Hey, Bruce,' the man said. 'Where's the bottle opener, man?'

One of the other men grunted from his sunbed, nose buried in a cushion.

'What was that, man, I didn't quite hear you?' the guitarist said.

'I don't know. You had it, man.'

'I didn't have it, man. *You* had it, man.'

Bruce said something unintelligible into the cushion.

'I can't hear what you're saying. Are you gonna get your fat ass up and find our guest the bottle opener?'

Bruce dragged himself up into a sitting position, pulled his string vest back down over his belly and squinted in the afternoon brightness. 'I said I feel like death. Go get it yourself.'

The guitarist's eyes flashed, losing their softness for an instant. 'All I'm asking is a simple question. It doesn't require some kind of complex philosophical response.'

'Give it here.' Bruce rubbed his bald head and blinked a few times. He reached for the bottle, flipped it three hundred and sixty degrees into the other hand, raised it to his mouth, prised the cap off with his teeth, then threw it back: all in one rapid, fluid motion. The bottle flew with perfect precision towards Gunzabo's missing right hand, flashing over his shoulder and into the pool.

'You a bit slow, baby,' said Bruce. 'I'll give you some training if you want, speed up your reflex a little.' He opened another beer and handed it over.

'You should learn to throw better,' Gunzabo said. 'Like you used to in the movies.'

Bruce grinned, showing teeth which were straight but bad. 'You wait till later, the next one will take your head clean off.' He was looking at Gunzabo's missing arm. 'What happened, man? You're like a crime boss in one of my films.' He flicked his head back and grinned again. 'You wanna get yourself a nice long hook.'

Gunzabo was about to answer when a staff member appeared with a tray of cocktails: a young woman, dressed in white who smiled shyly as she placed a drink next to each of the residents.

'Thanks, baby.' The guitarist glanced over to the third man. 'Hey, River. Your snowball's here.'

River didn't move; he was fast asleep. The guitarist turned

back to Gunzabo. 'Hey, I'm sorry, man, would you like a cocktail? We're a little wiped out, making us a little ratty about certain things, that and lose our manners.'

'Why not,' Gunzabo said.

'How about a daiquiri? Will you drink a daiquiri? One more, baby.'

The waitress smiled and the men watched her as she glided away. Gunzabo stretched out his hand to the guitarist. 'Gunzabo.'

The guitarist smiled, almost shyly. 'Pleased to meet you. Jimi.'

Gunzabo turned to Bruce. 'Gunzabo,' he said.

Bruce's hand was clammy and veinless, like the hand of a fat child, and as he released his grip, Bruce took his eyes from Gunzabo and looked accusingly at Jimi. 'What's got into you, man?' he said. 'You never play guitar, not anymore.'

Jimi blinked twice, slowly, opening his eyes each time like he had just woken up. 'I decided to start over, man. Lose the static, you know. It's just so absolutely, completely on top of everyone right now.' His slim, muscled arms shone in the light; the tassels sown onto the brim of his military hat swung gently as he played guitar.

Bruce shook his head. 'Everyone gone crazy-mad.' He yawned, rubbed his swollen, creased eyes, slapped his head, then ran his fingers along white eyebrows.

'Had a few late nights?' Gunzabo said.

'We've been borrowing Heath's console,' answered Jimi.

'I don't know what that is.'

'You should try it sometime, it's beautiful.' Jimi gave Gunzabo a goofy smile and put down his guitar for the first time. 'Heath says to me: Jimi, that Commodore 64 of yours, it's ancient, it's like a million years old, you gotta try the very latest thing, it's outtasight – and it really is – and he says if only we had the innernet it would be unbelievable. You know about the innernet? It's some kind of instantaneous cosmic space communication.'

Jimi was blinking almost in slow motion as he spoke, and each time he opened his eyes he was looking at something else: at the pool, at his guitar, at River and Bruce, back at Gunzabo if he wished to put emphasis on a particular point. 'Anyhow, Heath's console... I'm addicted, totally hung up on it. And Bruce, he's got a repetitive strain from seven days straight.'

'It's too much, baby,' said Bruce. 'My eyes are rectangle. Human beings should not do such things.'

'River too. River's really digging this new video game scene, man. He's like, you know... a pacifistic killer. Put that controller in his hand and he's gone. That gentle herbivore, eating the ferns, it's gone, and he's a T Rex.'

Gunzabo looked round at River, sleeping on his sunbed, then back at Jimi. 'Is this why you didn't go to the party on Full Moon Island?'

'The other night? That was an East Beach thing. We stayed here.'

The waitress returned with Gunzabo's drink. He took a sip. It was very strong; he nodded approvingly and took a larger sip. 'You know why I'm here?' he asked.

'Sure we do,' said Bruce. 'You checking us out, seeing if we're the ones who did John.'

'I'm checking everyone out. It's nothing personal.'

Bruce narrowed his eyes. 'Well we were asleep.'

'Where?'

'Here.'

'You were all asleep together?'

'Yeah.'

'You weren't in your own houses?'

Bruce was sitting upright in his sunbed now, arms folded high across his vest, looking insolently at Gunzabo, shoulders back, chin raised.

'We were here. I just told you.'

'Here by the pool?'

'No, here inside. It's not difficult: we stay here in the daytime, we go in for the night time.'

Gunzabo took another sip of his cocktail. 'You were inside the house?'

'We were inside your ass.'

'Give him a break, man,' said Jimi. 'We all asked for him, if you remember.'

'We didn't ask for *him*.'

'Well, Christian said he's the best of the best. You know any other detectives?'

Bruce looked up and down the length of Gunzabo's tracksuit, grunted derisively, and lay down again. 'Someone call Ken and get me some Temazepam. I need maximum dose.'

'Don't mind him,' said Jimi. 'He's just like, you know, not digging it right now, on a highly negative come down. Makes him kinda moody. Makes us all like that.'

Gunzabo looked over at the house. 'Who's the artist?' The outer walls were covered in overlapping layers of sprayed graffiti: obscenities, tags, male genitals, anti-war motifs; all surrounding murals of black political leaders.

'Us, baby,' said Bruce.

'You live here together?'

'We hang out here,' said Jimi. 'You know, like cats do. Bruce jumps over the fence – well he used to – and River comes along, arching his back, spraying those pheromones all over. So does Heath sometimes. It's an open invite, like a beautiful, funky, freaky club the whole world belongs to. This place, this island, it's everybody's, every living thing in fact, so quite naturally this place, you know, belongs to us all. There's no strangers here, no riots, no crime – well, until now I guess... but it doesn't matter. Besides, we take our chances every day. Bruce can tell you about that.'

'You're not well?' asked Gunzabo.

'No baby, I am not.'

'Bad heart,' Jimi said. 'Getting old is such a drag.'

Bruce clenched his teeth and stared gloomily into the pool. 'I used to be capable of anything, man. I was like a dragon. There was no such thing as no.' He turned his head to stare at each of them in turn, jabbing at his chest with his index finger. 'They all used to wanna fight me, man, and they couldn't even lay a single punch. I'd fight them *without* fighting, any shape you can think of: steam from the kettle, cloud in the sky, water in the bowl. Untouchable.' He grabbed a beer, bit off the cap and gestured to his round belly and the loose flesh on his arms. 'Look what happened to me. I should not have come here.'

'You had no choice,' said Jimi. 'There was nothing else you could do.'

'There is always a choice, man. I could have handled the Triad. Or died trying.'

'So do it. It's never too late.'

'It's way too late, baby. All of us, my friend, are just waiting to die.'

'We already have, man,' said Jimi. 'We already have, ten thousand times over.'

Bruce grimaced, muttering bitterly, until he lay back on his sunbed and they all drank in silence. The waitress brought more cocktails. Jimi rolled a joint. He passed the joint across and Gunzabo sat smoking on his sunbed in the relentless heat, listening to the unseen creatures that called and chirruped beyond the confines of the garden, watching the insects flutter into the swimming pool and dance gently on the surface like a troupe of tiny black puppets.

The day was waning and Gunzabo could feel Didi getting restless under his tracksuit. After a while he said, 'I should do some detecting. Can I look inside?'

'Be my guest,' said Jimi. 'I'll come with you.'

They walked over to the house. Gunzabo looked at the graffiti as Jimi pointed out a particular image, covering the entire roof, of a crescent moon and a lion leaping, or perhaps falling, towards them, snarling with the claws on all four feet splayed open. 'That one was for Bob,' Jimi told him. 'I wish he'd have come here, man.' Gunzabo followed him onto the balcony and through some sliding doors.

It was stiflingly hot inside; his lungs burned with each inward breath. He glanced up at the dormant air conditioning units, where finger-like spider legs poked between the grills. Scores of stringed instruments hung on the walls: violins, violas, guitars, mandolins; all dark brown, damp and uncared for. At one end, two ragged sofas faced a flat-screen television. Between the sofas, on a low coffee table, was a record deck, surrounded by loose tobacco, plates, spent cans and bottles, and two great circular ashtrays containing a dead forest of cigarette and joint butts. A double-barrelled shotgun hung on the wall above the television: single trigger, straight grip.

'This is real,' Gunzabo said, putting his hand on the barrels: cool and dull, despite the heat.

'That? Oh yeah, I forgot I had that.'

Gunzabo sniffed the muzzle, twitching his nose like Didi: no aroma; but wiping it brought gritty, black powder onto his fingers.

'Yeah, it's real,' continued Jimi. 'We use these though.' He pointed to the controllers and plastic guns hooked up to the games console.

They moved away from the wall, back to the coffee table, stepping over the piles of vinyl records lying amid discarded military clothing. Jimi picked up an album at Gunzabo's feet, pulled out the disc and put it on a record deck.

Gunzabo looked at the sleeve: the stencilled face of a man,

hair billowing out like black fire. 'It's rare,' he said.

'Christian gets them sometimes when he goes to the mainland.'

Jimi picked a blackened, half-smoked butt out of the ashtray and lit it. Music began: a skittering drum beat, aimless guitar, a few mumbled greetings to a crowd.

'It's been a long time, man,' Jimi said, not looking at Gunzabo, closing his eyes as he sucked on the cigarette. The music began in earnest.

'Is this you playing?' Gunzabo said.

'Summer of sixty eight. Such a nice, long, beautiful summer.'

'I used to have this, I think.'

'Everyone used to have a piece of me, man.'

'They still do.'

They listened for a few minutes until the song ended to sporadic applause. Another song began. Gunzabo glanced at the shotgun. It had certainly been used. But as recently as three days ago? He turned to ask this question, but Jimi was staring vacantly at the record spinning on the deck, its red label taking his name round and round in black letters.

'I didn't think I missed it,' he muttered, pushing the cigarette butt back into the ashtray. 'You wanna take a look around?'

There were three bedrooms upstairs. The first was filled with records, old and rotten from the damp heat. The second room was a crumbling music studio, filled with cobwebbed keyboards, a partially assembled drum kit, guitars propped up against amps, and speakers mounted on stands; the floor was carpeted and mouldy, covered in a mass of pedals and cabling, which terminated in a huge analogue mixing desk.

'I used to live in here, as good as,' said Jimi. He picked some scribbled lyrics off the floor. 'Sleep and eat and urinate and all that, you know, making an album, a totally new kind of music. I wanted it to be like... like it would sound in the thin toxic atmosphere of Mars, or Venus or somewhere. I took a break though, I just got so very tired of it, left it in stasis, suspended in the air like a… a photograph of a butterfly, and Bruce was like, come on Jimi when're you gonna finish it, it's your life's work – this is when he cared, when he had focus – and River was saying that too. Well he was thinking it – I could tell, on a subconscious level – but he's too nervous to say – they were the vibrations he had anyhow – and now Heath's saying it.'

Gunzabo followed him into the last bedroom. A grubby, uncovered mattress lay in the corner; cockroaches crawled through piles of clothes and skittered into cardboard boxes filled with yet more clothing.

'You should get this place cleaned up,' Gunzabo said. 'Why do you want to live like this?'

'This is my home, man. It's not a hotel. Christian comes round sometimes and brings his people with their mops and so forth and then I have to tell him to go screw himself.'

'He probably does.'

Jimi laughed. 'No way, man. He's sexually in a complete mess, you know? Some chick – or some guy – musta put some crazy spell on him way back.'

They went back downstairs into the living room. The record was still playing.

'Christian said you were in a commune before you came here,' Gunzabo said.

'Yeah, that's right, man. We were there a year, or two, I don't remember how long exactly. It was beautiful. We were young and more cats kept turning up. Then we came here, came on this crazy boat. That was some boat trip, it took months, we stopped everywhere, all dressed up, partying in disguise with the Europeans, the Africans, the Asians, checking out every continental scene. We grew moustaches if we weren't known for them, shaved them off if we were. Janis went by the name of Ralph.' He smiled fondly at the recollection. 'Jack and Bobby made out they were sisters... that was one beautiful, freaky boat.'

They listened to the music for a while: a long, explosive guitar solo, followed by applause and screaming women.

'Why did you do it?' Gunzabo said.

'Do what?'

'Leave your life behind. You gave up so much.'

Jimi was reading the record sleeve. Gunzabo watched him closely, kept his eyes on Jimi as he frowned and his eyes became hard and he stared down again.

'I don't know, I don't remember. It was forty or fifty years ago, man, going on a million. Maybe it just all got too crazy, you know, maybe I did one too many Woodstocks, Isle of Wights, whatever. Maybe it was romance. Love. Or maybe it just seemed like the really freakiest idea you ever heard. Something you can't resist.' He shrugged. 'I don't remember, man. Probably it was love. But it was all a haze, a multi coloured haze. Not just one colour.'

The record had finished; it was an old fashioned turntable which carried on spinning and the needle stayed in the final groove; Jimi was watching it spin round, blinking slowly with each muffled click marking the next, empty revolution. Gunzabo looked at the mess covering the floor, as bad down here as it had been upstairs.

'Where did the others sleep?' he said.

'They've got their own places, you know, here on West Beach.'

'The other night, I mean. When John was shot.'

'Oh, the other night. We didn't sleep, we were up all night playing console. Shooting games, you know, that first person scene I was telling you about.'

Jimi wouldn't look at him. His body seemed to tense under his military clothes.

'You didn't sleep?'

'Not one second. What can I say, we're addicted.'

'Were you in the house the whole time? All three of you?'

'Yeah, that's right. We were in the house the whole time. All three of us.'

Gunzabo rubbed the wiry stubble on his cheek and looked closely at Jimi. 'Bruce said you were all asleep when the shooting took place.'

Jimi shifted about, still would not return his gaze. 'He did? We must have been asleep then. Those games, day and night kinda blend, you know?' He looked down at the record player, still spinning. A look of anger crossed his face; he pulled off the disc, snapped it in two across his knee; he tossed the pieces on the floor. 'That haze, it's coming back, man,' he said, walking away. 'It's coming back.'

They stepped outside. Gunzabo surveyed the garden from the top of the porch steps. It was evening now; the pool was still and the trees grew close to its edge on the far side. River was still asleep; Bruce was lying down with his eyes shut and a book on his chest.

'I might have a little sleep,' Gunzabo said.

'Sure, man,' Jimi mumbled. 'Hang out with the cats. I could use a rest myself.'

Gunzabo made his way to the sunbeds, lay down and stretched out on his back. 'Didi,' he muttered. 'Wake me in an hour, I'm having fifty winks.'

He ignored Jimi's mystified look.

'If Jimi nods off, wake me sooner,' he added, quietly this time, as Didi scampered off towards the trees.

He pulled his baseball cap down over his eyes and immediately fell asleep.

11

Didi was nuzzling his cheek. He opened his eyes to the throbbing evening heat. In his dreams he had been cold, but there was no car crash this time. Pomegranates hanging by a spiralling mountain road; his mother, looking sad, pulling one from a tree; then cutting into the dry, papery skin, which opened like a wound. He chewed on the seeds, which were cold from the November mountain air; and he too was cold, despite the shawl his mother had given him that day in Troodos. She used to knit him a shawl every year, even as he got older.

He felt Didi against his cheek again.

'What is it?' he said, voice cracking, his throat dry and sore.

'Just following orders, your worship.'

He sat up in the dark. The garden was alive with noise, as if the jungle had grown around him while he slept. He picked up a half-empty drink, took a swig, brushed ants away from his lips. Stepping forward, he bumped into a sunbed, tripped and fell onto something hard and sharp: teeth, which parted into a scream in his ear. He groped in the dark: long hair, small nose, clean shaven.

'Are there any lights?' Gunzabo said.

River lay under him, moaning with pain, until Gunzabo got to his feet and introduced himself, extending his hand into nothingness.

He heard muttering, more groans, then laboured movement, and a series of fairy lights came on, twinkling in the umbrella spokes like fireflies. Larger lights followed, inside the pool, shining ghoulishly through the filthy water.

River hobbled back onto his sunbed and gasped. 'Goddam, I keep forgetting my leg,' he said.

'Can I get you a drink?'

'Um, yeah, thanks. Carrot and ginger, no ice.'

Gunzabo looked around; the waitress appeared immediately from the darkness. He ordered the juice, and an Irish coffee for himself.

'Looks nasty,' he said. River's leg was a mass of purple bruising, ankle swollen and hurriedly bandaged.

'Comes from chasing these guys through the forest all goddam night, playing their freakin' war games.'

'Let me have a look,' Gunzabo said. 'I'm a trained physiotherapist.'

'Sure.'

Gunzabo knelt at the end of the sunbed, put River's foot onto his knee, removed the bandages and pressed on various parts of River's leg.

'I liked your movies.'

'Thanks, man.'

'*My Own Private Eiderdown*, that one I like very much. And *Mojito Toast*. Is that what it was called?'

'They weren't called that at all,' River said.

'I must be getting you mixed up with someone else,' Gunzabo told him. 'I was very sad when you died though. It looks as if you did this several days ago.'

'Yeah, three it must be now.'

River yelped when Gunzabo pressed his foot.

'During the night, you said.'

'Early hours of the morning, I guess,' River said, still grimacing with pain. 'I just wanted to play more video games, but we were smoking so much meth and Jimi just flips and makes us all dress up like we're in *Platoon* or something. We were out running wild with the beasts, man.'

'Is this the morning the shooting took place?'

'Yeah. Earlier though, like three am or something.'

'Where did you go?'

'Everywhere. We went all the way into the forest, through streams, over to the sea, back again. I kept saying, someone's gonna get hurt, I said Bruce you're gonna bust that ticker of yours, but he wouldn't listen, he's got that death wish of his. And Jimi, Jimi was caught up somewhere else, man. Another world. And he was shouting and yelling like it was Vietnam and we were tracking down the VC and they were just ghosts, always one step ahead. That was when I stepped in some rabbit hole, or snake's den or whatever it was. I didn't feel anything; luckily we had a few lines of ketamine before we went out. But I knew something bad had happened.'

'What did you do?' Gunzabo asked him.

'I just lay there shouting for them to come back, but they were gone, and then eventually Bruce came, brought me back here.'

Gunzabo started wrapping the bandages back round River's leg.

'What time did you get back?'

'Gosh, I don't know. But it was light and it was damn hot. Hey, Jimi. What time did you come back, man? You must've been an hour after us.'

Jimi had woken up and was lying on his sunbed picking out chords on the guitar.

'I just wrote a song,' he said. 'It just came outta my head in one piece, like a goddess or something. Don't you just dig that?'

'Cool, man,' said River. 'Gunzabo here was just asking what time it was we came back from the forest. You know, when I busted my leg.'

Jimi was biting his lip as he gazed out into the darkness. 'It was just a dream, wasn't it? It still is, man. I look at your leg there and it gives me that feeling when you're asleep, but like' –

he half closed his eyes to demonstrate – 'like you know you're asleep. It's like that.'

'I wish it was a dream, man. You nearly blew my head off.'

Jimi put his guitar down. He picked up a book from a pile under an ashtray, opened it somewhere in the middle and stared vacantly at the page. 'You told me about a thousand times already,' he muttered.

'Yeah, well, I've been thinking. We should give the box back to Heath. It's sending us crazy. I even started dreaming about hotdogs.'

Jimi gave him a look of irritation, tossed away the book and reached for a beer.

'Watch the library, baby,' said Bruce, waking up. He put the book back under the ashtray; it was Dante's *Inferno*. 'That's one of my favourites, man. Reminds me of this place.'

'So you returned to the house at what time?' asked Gunzabo.

River winced as he shifted position on his sunbed. 'We were out till seven am I guess, maybe eight. Bruce will know.'

'I don't remember,' said Bruce. He was lying on his back, looking across at Gunzabo with one eye open. 'We were out of it baby, but it was not that late I think.'

Gunzabo secured the bandages and lowered River's leg back onto the sunbed. 'You've been lucky, it's superficial.'

He looked at each of them in turn, his eyes resting on Jimi. 'You realise I am investigating two murders. It is very important that you tell me everything, and that you hide nothing.'

'Just leave it,' said Bruce. 'You're asking the wrong people the wrong questions.'

Jimi began playing his guitar again, and quietly sang the words of his new song.

'You left me, man,' said River. 'I thought I was dying, it was not cool. Where in hell did you go?'

'We did what we had to, that's all you need to know.'

'What did you have to do?' Gunzabo asked.

Bruce shrugged. Jimi stared past them all as he murmured his song. 'Tell me,' Gunzabo asked River, 'did you hear any gunshots while you were lying there on your own?'

River didn't answer. Gunzabo sat on the end of the sunbed, waiting for a reply. The lights were shining through the pool onto the edges of River's face, giving his still boyish features a certain gravity. Gunzabo did not take his eyes off him.

'I must ask you again. A man died on the morning you are referring to. Perhaps more will die if you do not speak.'

'Yes,' River said eventually. 'I heard gunshots.'

'When?'

'A few minutes after I fell.'

'Did you see anything?'

'No. There was shouting and people running through the forest. Then it was quiet.'

Gunzabo looked at the other two men, waiting for them to speak.

'We may as well tell him, baby,' Bruce said.

Jimi stopped playing his guitar and slipped the plectrum between the strings, high up the neck. He looked directly at Gunzabo for the first time since he'd woken up. 'We were trying to catch the Déjà Vu Killer.'

'Yeah, it wasn't us, if that's what you're thinking,' said Bruce.

'What happened?' Gunzabo asked him.

'We were near the beach, man, and we heard gunshots and John was down and we saw someone running through the forest. We chased after him, but I couldn't keep up, so I went back for River and Jimi carried on.'

Gunzabo turned to Jimi, who shrugged, and said, 'I lost him deep in the jungle. He was like a ghost, you know? A real fast ghost, who knew the jungle, like he was part of it, man. Then I came back to the house.'

'What can you tell me about the killer? Did you see his face?'

'I didn't see his face. He was dressed in black. You know, shotgun, balaclava, one of those standard, typical assassins.'

'His build?'

'Thin, medium height. Maybe. Thin, yeah.'

Gunzabo sat quietly for a few minutes, looking into the black space where the jungle buzzed relentlessly. He ran their story through his mind: Jimi and Bruce lurching through the undergrowth, out of their minds on crystal meth and ketamine and days of video games; River lagging behind, trying to make them stop, ducking as the shotgun was unloaded randomly into the trees; the morning still young as his ankle collapsed. They were hiding something of course. Everyone seemed to be. It was time to go.

'I'll see you later,' he said.

'Sure thing,' said Jimi.

'Take it easy, baby,' Bruce said. 'Want one for the road?'

'Why not.'

Bruce bit the cap off a beer and flicked it over in one motion, projecting the bottle swiftly with the faintest movement of his wrist. Gunzabo saw it shimmering towards him in the fairy lights, plucked it out of the air and took a swig. He walked a few paces towards the darkened beach, then stopped and turned round.

'One last question.' He looked at River. 'Why did you come here?'

'To Dead Star Island?' River thought for a moment. 'Because John and Jimi were here. They're my heroes. And Bruce, of course.' He smiled at Bruce, who scowled and opened a beer. 'I guess vanity came into it too. You come here, you become a legend. Like them.'

* * *

The heavens were black, filled with invisible, brooding cloud and he could almost feel the shape of the night-time heat as he walked across the sand. He passed the beach shack and peered in, saw the old man asleep on his back, candle flames swaying to the rhythm of his snores. He carried on along the beach, passed John's house and then Bruce's and stopped by some bushes, sighing as he emptied his bladder.

'They could have done it, couldn't they?' said Didi.

'Possibly.'

'It has to be one of the residents, anyhow.'

'Probably.'

'Who else could it be? Everyone else has an alibi, except Diana – who you've got a crush on, like every other female you meet.'

He grunted agreement and shook his penis in the dark.

'Which means if it's a woman we've got no chance,' Didi continued. 'By the way, why did Jimi and his mates go through all that rigmarole earlier on? Why be so evasive when they could have just told us straight out?'

'That is a good question,' Gunzabo said.

A figure in white hurried past him up the beach.

'Who was that?' Didi whispered.

A second figure flitted by, then stopped at one of the dimly lit beachside lamps. Gunzabo saw a skeletal face, glowing orange. He watched Tommy move away. 'Let's see what he's up to.'

He followed Tommy up the beach, staying near the treeline, back past Bruce, John and then Jimi's house. He turned a corner and stopped. Tommy was waiting under a tree. Gunzabo edged closer. The figure in white looked around, then turned into the jungle. Tommy was walking swiftly now, took out a torch and disappeared into the trees. Gunzabo followed. Rubbery leaves squeaked as he reached through and stepped onto a path.

'I came prepared this time, Didi,' he whispered, brandishing a torch.

He hurried along the path, keeping Tommy's strobing torchlight in view. Any noise he made was masked by the fevered din of the jungle, as he pushed his way through undergrowth and swathes of dead forest waste, zigzagging north for half an hour, until the light ahead became stationary. He crept forwards.

The white figure was standing in a glade. Gunzabo looked up: the moon was shining through a circular opening of sky. Directly below, in the middle of the clearing, delicate ribbons of light shivered on a circular pool. The figure was alert, but Tommy, standing in the entrance, made no effort to conceal himself, perhaps trusting his stillness and the fragile light. Gunzabo saw it was a woman but could not make out her face. She was moving her head around, as if somehow she sensed that she was not alone. She became still as a deer entered the glade, slender and beautiful. The deer dipped its nose into the water and drank, pushing the moonlight out in gentle ripples.

All was quiet, as if the jungle held its breath.

Gunzabo became aware of an intolerable itch on his shoulder; he reached up to scratch it. The deer lifted its head. An ear twitched in his direction. The woman looked over, saw Tommy and ran into the jungle. The deer had vanished. The sky closed, sending the glade into absolute darkness. Torchlight streaked across the ground as Tommy loped into the trees after the woman.

Gunzabo moved into the clearing.

'We're going to lose them,' Didi said.

He stopped at the pool. 'Leave Tommy to his white goose chase. I think she knows this place too well to be caught by an oaf like him. It's more interesting here.'

'Why?' Didi was perched on his shoulder.

'She stopped. We must be close.'

'Close to what?'

'Wherever she was going.'

He searched the edge of the glade, stomping through

vegetation, waving insects off his face and body.

'Do we have to do this, Gunzabo? I might get eaten by a snake.'

He wasn't listening. 'So this is why she was here,' he murmured.

He had come across a concrete structure: a hut, grey, unpainted, recently built. He shone his torch inside: a stove on the floor, cold; two clear plastic bags, tied up, full of rubbish; a pile of bedding, neatly folded in the corner. There was no one inside.

He examined the interior of the hut, shining his torch across the floor and walls, looking for graffiti, handwriting, clothing, anything that might hint at the identity of whoever lived here.

'Nothing,' he muttered. He opened the first plastic bag and checked its contents: food wrappers, tissue paper, empty food tins, bottles. He read every wrapper, every container and brand name, then checked the second bag: it contained eight empty, crushed beer cans. He stood and ran his fingers over the rafters and in the corners.

'Nothing,' he said. 'But someone was here recently.'

'Yeah, and he might come back. Can we go?'

He shook the torch. It was emitting a feeble orange glow, filament clearly discernible.

'What's your night vision like?' he said.

'No better than yours.'

'Mine's terrible.'

'So what are we going to do?'

The torch died. He had a peculiar sensation where he knew the walls were close, but the darkness seemed infinite.

Didi's voice came from somewhere on the floor. 'How do we get back through the forest in the dark?'

'We'll have to stay here.'

'You must be joking. This is the killer's lair.'

'Remember Diomedes of Thrace? He used to feed his victims' remains to the horses. I can deal with a celebrity stalker, Didi.'

'Do what you like, I'm going back.'

Didi bolted outside, and at that instant rain began to fall. It came heavy and fast and played bhangra on the metal roof of the hut. Didi came scampering back up his leg, soaked through.

'We'd better stay here,' she said.

'You don't want to brave the snakes?'

'I'd rather die in my sleep than with my eyes open.'

'I'll wake up before anything happens.'

'You sleep like the dead, Gunzabo.'

'With a bit of luck, yes.'

Gunzabo unrolled the bedding and lay on his back. Soon he was snoring loudly in the dark, adding a rhythm of his own to the pulsing rain outside.

12

He was dreaming again of the car crash. He saw nothing, heard everything: blaring horns as cars streaked by; his wife, pleading; the baby, crying inconsolably. The collision was a deep pulse which cut their screams short.

He opened his eyes: the ceiling was corrugated, new. Daylight leaked through perforations in the metal; a rhombus of light stretched across the open doorway. He lay on his back, staring upwards, mind empty now, barely registering the insects crawling through his hair and clothes. He did not know how long he stayed there for. He did not mind the insects, or the heat, or his hangover, or the smell of rotten food coming from the bags in the corner. But the loneliness was unbearable.

'Are we alive or dead?' Didi murmured.

'Neither.'

He staggered outside and back through dense foliage into the clearing. Every part of him was soaked with sweat. He noticed the pool, stripped off and plunged into icy water, grateful for the numbing cold which soothed his aching, missing arm.

'Do you think the killer does this each morning?'

He glanced up at Didi, who was balanced on his head. 'Not today.'

'Ian Fields. That's the name of the killer, isn't it?'

The scrap of paper in John's house. And on the back, that code. But he was feeling too morbid to give it any real thought.

'Maybe,' he said.

'Well what else could it be?'

He did not answer; instead he dropped into the water,

submerging himself fully, the sound of her voice suddenly cut off. He looked up through the surface of the pool, where Didi was shimmering in the world above. It seemed a great distance away, that world of heat, and down here in the icy cold, he began to lose all feeling, which he found comforting, pleasant even. Something inside told him to remain here, not to return, but dwell underwater for eternity. He wondered if that was possible. Didi was still speaking, small and distant, peering down with increasing concern. He came back up.

'We can't stay,' she was saying. 'What if he comes back?'

'From his latest killing spree?'

He stood up, pushed the water off his hair.

'It's not a joke. You may not care, but I don't want to die.'

'But why would anyone need to stay here?' he said. 'If the killer is a resident, he has a house. As do the villagers.'

'I don't know. Somewhere quiet to hang out, polish his trophies.'

'What trophies? Eight empty beer cans?'

He stepped up onto the short bracken of the glade. Didi ferretted around in the undergrowth as he put his tracksuit back on.

'What now, Führer?' she said.

'I'm going for a run.'

'You hate running.'

'With a passion.'

'I suppose it'll break up the drunkenness a little.'

Didi jumped off a tree onto Gunzabo's shoulder and he made his way back along the path, over ferns and roots and leaf drifts, until he could see the sky again: a pallid void which reduced the sand to the dead yellow of straw and robbed the sea of any colour.

As he neared the beach, three people walked across the opening: villagers dressed in their white uniforms. Dozens more came by in small, gender-specific groups. They looked at him and smiled and chatted among themselves as they filed past. He saw Lastri, dressed in a sari, white with gold trim. She stopped and smiled like a goddess.

'Good morning, Gunzabo.'

He stared back at her. He was staring at his wife.

'Are you alright?' she said.

He shook away the memories. 'Off to work, are you?'

'Roll call is in twenty minutes.'

'I need to speak to you. All of you. Part of my investigation.'

'It may be difficult today,' she said. 'We will be preparing all day and night for the talent show.'

'When is the talent show?'

'Tomorrow evening. Will you be performing?'

'Why not.'

'We'll look forward to it.'

He watched Lastri join a group of women and continue down the beach. His chest tightened as she walked away and now he was thinking again of Megara, when they first met on the beach in Skiathos: how they spoke into the evening until her friends dragged her off; the feeling in his throat when she looked over her shoulder and smiled back at him; sadness the next day while he waited on the beach, resigned to never seeing her again; heart bursting when she appeared, walking towards him, alone this time, across the sand. When they came back to Skiathos six months later he proposed to her on the same beach. She had smiled with such love and understanding all he could do was look at her in wonder.

'Are you going for that run then?' asked Didi.

Gunzabo blinked; the feeling died. 'I'm waiting for my running partner.'

He watched the villagers shrink, then drop out of existence, then he turned to see a figure approach from the north: an old man with skinny legs and white sideburns, dressed in electric-blue spandex shorts and matching vest, out on his morning run.

The man nodded briefly as he passed by, his breathing rhythmical, face lined and tanned and lean. He was still strikingly handsome, despite his age. Gunzabo did not often see this in a man, but he had a beauty still as rare as in his early years, though heavily lined by age and experience. Gunzabo ran after him.

'Mind if I join you?'

'Sure.'

The man slowed to let Gunzabo catch up.

'Elvis, isn't it?'

'Uh-huh.'

They ran south, past the residences and The Circles, running too hard for conversation, until they reached the jetty at the southern tip of the island and a table with a bottle of water.

'Are you the detective?'

He nodded. 'Gunzabo.'

Elvis picked up the water and drank whilst running on the spot.

'You find that guy who shot John.'

'I intend to.'

'Good.'

Elvis offered the water bottle, giving Gunzabo a stern look when he refused, then set off. Gunzabo ran hard again to catch up, and now he was alongside, running up East Beach with Elvis. The sand was coarse here, with patches of pebbles and rock, and for long stretches, the jungle came close to the sea. They dodged rocks and ducked under trees and took detours into the shallow water. They passed gated villas, set back like those on the opposite beach, then reached another star-point where the beach turned sharply to the left.

Elvis stopped. He took a swig of water. 'You're not in bad shape.'

Gunzabo was labouring for breath. 'Don't be fooled by the

tracksuit.' He took his baseball cap off and wiped the sweat off his forehead.

'Nonsense, you gotta stick at it, is all. Took me years to persuade John to get fit.'

Elvis looked out to sea, pressing his lips together. Then he turned to Gunzabo. 'Nearly done. Come on.'

They set off, back the way they had come: under the trees, around the rocks, through the clear shallow water. They passed the jetty, headed back up West Beach, past The Circles, Palm Grove and half a dozen houses. At the beach shack the old man turned up a thumb and smiled; he was naked, filming them on a handheld camcorder, and he ran alongside a short distance, his penis bouncing offbeat with his footsteps.

'Morning Jim,' said Elvis with a grin.

'You're a bit slower today, you know that?'

Elvis smiled but didn't answer. They left the old man behind and continued round a sharp corner under almost horizontal trees. The beach widened and they passed more houses, until Elvis stopped and began a series of stretches on the pale sand. Gunzabo was exhausted, his breath coming in short gasps. He noticed behind Elvis a magnificent villa, white as the sky, fronted with marble columns.

'Nice place.'

'I designed it myself.'

Elvis was clasping each knee in turn up to his chest.

'I want to speak to you about John,' Gunzabo said.

Elvis stopped exercising. 'I'm not sure I want to talk about it.'

'It is not an easy thing. But there is a killer on the loose.'

'I'm busy the whole day. Triathlon training, yoga, breakfast, therapy ten until eleven, then Chi Kung, then lunch. Gym all afternoon.'

'I only need fifteen minutes.'

'Maybe tomorrow. I always keep a slot free on Wednesday

mornings for spontaneity. I could do eleven fifteen. See you then.'

Elvis stripped down to a pair of speedos, gave a quick nod, and plunged into the sea. Gunzabo watched him swim smoothly away from shore and then wandered slowly back to the beach shack. The old man was looking out to sea, hands on hips, naked, sunburnt, and covered in sand. Gunzabo saw himself approaching in each mirrored lens of the old man's aviator sunglasses.

'Hey.'

'Gunzabo.'

'Jim.'

They shook hands.

'I wondered if it was you,' Gunzabo said.

'So did I, man. I'm always wondering that.'

Gunzabo looked down at Jim's round paunch, blistered and sandy, and his penis underneath, like a knuckle, tucked away in white fuzz.

'I used to have a T-shirt with your face on it,' Gunzabo said. 'When you wore those beads.'

'A picture of me? Why's that, man?'

'It's what people do now. To make a statement.'

'If they wanna do that they should try Socrates or something. He liked to make statements, man. Or maybe Plato.'

Jim inhaled deeply and ran his fingers through long white tangles of hair. A dead beetle fell out and landed upside down on the sand.

'I like to praise the sun,' he said. 'Do you?'

'Not usually.'

'Oh you should. I was contemplating a Sun Dance. You wanna join me?'

'Why not.'

'It's not a true Sun Dance, I should tell you that. It's more kinda...' Jim paused to think, and then continued, '...kinda improvised idolatry using artistic expression. Particularly poetry and dance. You could use any artistic form you wish, though. Certainly nothing should stop a shaman from expressing worship, much as a man should be free to speak his mind to any authority, be it higher, lower, or earthly for that matter. But for me, it's always nature. Nothing else is real.'

'It's a little cloudy.'

'Doesn't matter, man. He's still up there somewhere, waiting to be worshipped.'

Jim started dancing and chanting unintelligibly, swaying sideways and waving his hands around. Gunzabo closed his eyes, giving himself to the heat and the blank purity of the sky. The world drew distant, and he stretched his fingers to the heavens and began a chant of his own, falling to his knees alongside Jim as the chanting reached a crescendo. Then it ended and he lay still, curled up in the foetal position.

He slowly straightened his body and rose, sensing Jim doing the same beside him. He breathed softly with his face to the sky. The waves lapped at his feet; the jungle hummed behind. He opened his eyes, saw the sky, flat and white, but he could discern the outline of a glowing, perfect white disk: the hint of a break to the other side, a connection from this world to the one before. For a brief moment, he felt hope.

He turned and saw Jim on his knees, rummaging in the entrance to the shack; matted white hair protruded between his buttocks; his testicles showed pendulously below.

'I'm sure I have some spare goggles in here someplace, man. You wanna come for a swim?'

'Why not.'

Jim looked round and grinned, aviators replaced by an archaic pair of swimming goggles. He crawled further into the shack, his rear obscuring the rest of him, tossing around the debris inside as he searched for the spare goggles.

'You know, it's times like these when I realise what an asshole

I am.' His voice came out from somewhere beyond his buttocks. 'I gotta have a clear out one of these days. Somebody once said there's order in chaos, but I'm yet to experience that, man. Here they are.'

Jim held up a pair of goggles: modern, still in their packet. Gunzabo undressed and stepped into the sea with Jim. The water was shallow and warm, and rippled above a forest of dark green reeds. They swam out and came to a city of coral that lay in pastel shades a metre below. Jim pointed some out, telling Gunzabo the botanical names he'd given them, and did the same for the tiny, brightly coloured fish that darted in and out of sight.

'Christian said he'd get me a book, but I said no man, there's no need. It's kinda fun feeling like Darwin, discovering species for yourself. Or an ancient philosopher, describing the whole world from first principles. If I ever have a kid, I won't tell him anything. I'll just tell him to construct the world for himself, from the ground up, just the way he wants it.'

'Do you live in the shack permanently?' Gunzabo asked him.

'Pretty much. I go back to the house from time to time. Not very often, though. Charge the camcorder, that kinda thing.'

They were treading water with their goggles across their foreheads. Jim's white beard was spread across the surface of the water. Gunzabo rubbed the top of his nose, feeling the indents the goggles had made.

'Where you were at the time of John's murder?' he said.

'Just there, man, at the hut,' Jim said easily. 'I heard the shots. I came running to see what happened. By then plenty of people were already there.'

'Were you awake, when the shots were fired?'

'Oh, I was awake. I saw Elvis and John go by, like I do most days.'

'Was there anything different on this particular morning? Before the murder took place, that is?'

'It was just the same. They were running hard, they seemed happy, focussed. Everything was pretty customary.'

Gunzabo frowned in disappointment. 'Tell me, do you know of anybody who might have a reason to kill John?'

Jim started kicking back towards the beach. 'You're asking me to speculate on the intentions and motivations of my friends. I can't do that, man. You're gonna have to find that out for yourself. First principles.'

Gunzabo was now standing on the sand beside the hut. He handed the goggles back. Jim tossed them into the hut and squatted down to light a fire. Gunzabo sat down on the other side and watched him work.

'What about the night that Brian died.'

Jim mumbled a mantra as the wood caught light. 'I was with Brian most of it. I hold myself responsible.' He looked up at Gunzabo. 'Almost made me go back into therapy.'

'What happened?'

'We were up all night on ketamine. We thought we'd try it, seemed to be in fashion to do so. We'd been using DMT to travel the universe with our souls for months. Brian and I, we became like brothers. But he just wanted to take it easy that night, so I said, why not, but it went a little crazy, again, and then I said – it must've been dawn – I can't take this, I have to go back to the sea, back to where the fish live and the coral lies resplendent. I have to be with the sea in the morning.' Jim squinted and shook his head sadly. 'Next I hear, Brian's dead in his swimming pool.'

'Were you the last person to see him?'

'I guess. Unless…'

'Someone killed him.'

'Déjà Vu they're calling him,' said Jim. He twisted part of his beard that was less matted than the rest. 'I don't know, man. I always thought déjà vu was something in your mind, the manifestations of a chemical reaction.'

'Like DMT?'

'No, not like DMT. That's something else entirely. You take it, take the measure according to where you want to go, and it takes away the pieces of you that bind you here, bind you to this plane. The reason we needed that break, man' – Jim smiled as he recalled this – 'was the night before. We journeyed to the Land of the Harlequins. They were real, the Harlequins. We shot into space and ended up in some dark place. Black. I think it was black. We were out in space, with the planets. And these men, with pointy hats, tiny men, they were in lines going up and down. And they were laughing at us. Pointing their little fingers at us, telling us we shouldn't be there. They said we should go. And we did, we went further. And it was completely black. And we were still together, me and Brian.

'That was when we heard the Voice. It told us about the spirits, about death. About God. She said it was lies. There's nothing else, She said. Just Us. And we are Now. She said men teach that the soul is permanent and only the body withers and dies. But it's the other way round, She told us. And I knew at once: this was the most important thing anyone would ever say to me. Then we came to, and we had the terrible taste in our mouths, from the DMT.'

'This was the night before?'

'Yeah. It really made us think. About the continuation of the body and the impermanence of the soul. We were talking about this all day and I wanted to do it again, but Brian said, no, let's try some K. I said, yeah, if you want to. But it all happened again. Kinda. Except this time we went deep, the sand swallowed us up and we went down, as far as you can go. And it was light. But there was no light.

'Then we heard the Voice again. She said the same thing, word for word. Like a tape. The soul is impermanent, the body is forever. We musta nearly died, man. But someone down there

105

was watching us, and we came up again, up through the ground, through the sand, through our sunbeds. That was when I had to leave. The thing we shared, we couldn't even look at each other.'

'Whose quad bike was Brian driving?'

'His. He was always riding it around. Taking the villagers home, pissing off Christian. He had soul, man.'

The fire was established now, its lively flames dancing on the sand.

'One additional thing,' said Gunzabo. 'I know that many residents attend psychotherapy sessions with Diana. Are you one of those?'

Jim smiled behind his mirrored lenses. 'I went every day for five years.'

'Not anymore?'

'Not anymore.'

'Can I ask why?'

'You can ask what you like, man. I stopped going due to disillusion. I was a Jungian. I believed in the collective unconscious. But Jung, man, he let me down. I used to believe what I wanted to believe, without truly knowing, and then I found certain things out. And I disagreed. So I went back to... guess what?'

'First principles.'

'You got it.'

Gunzabo stood up. It was time for breakfast and a drink. 'Maybe we'll have another swim.'

'We'll praise the moon, next time. Or the forest, maybe. I'll see you later.'

13

Diana and the Bradleys were eating breakfast on the terrace at The Circles.

'Bonj,' said Mrs Bradley.

Gunzabo grunted and sat down. Tommy stalked off without a word, his food untouched.

'Oh, Thomas,' Mrs Bradley called after him, 'you are a misery guts.' She turned back to Gunzabo. 'He's upset about Kevin. We were on the internet with him this morning. Makes him all emotional.'

'I thought your son believes you're both dead.'

'Yes, but do I like to stay in touch. Dating sites mostly. He thinks I'm a Russian gymnast called Natalia.' Gunzabo glanced at Diana, saw her faint smile of sadness and pity, as she squeezed Mrs Bradley's hand. 'It's wonderful for his self-esteem. My Kevin was always so shy.' She bit her lip. 'I am a teensy bit worried, mind. He said he's booking a flight to Vladivostok.'

He ordered a beer and some fried eggs and bacon.

'A bit early isn't it, Gunzabo?' asked Diana.

'Helps me concentrate.' This was true. He couldn't do without it, but there was a definite art to getting the right balance. He looked away, his insides tight as he remembered the dream. He stared at the gardens and the sea, knew she was giving him that sad smile as she sipped her tea. His beer arrived. He drank half and relaxed.

'Which school of psychotherapy do you follow?' he asked her.

'Analytical.'

'Jungian?'

'Based on his ideas, yes. It's changed greatly since then.'

'You have many patients to see today?'

Diana put down her cup and smiled. 'I have my regulars. Would you like me to fit you in for a session?'

'As long as I can ask a few questions of my own.'

'Analysis is always two way, Gunzabo.'

He let the conversation lapse and drank his beer, looking at the angular path of the beach as it stretched north. He moved his gaze to the island interior, and the rising canopy. The hut was somewhere under there. He pictured the killer now returning, entering the glade, noticing where he had disturbed the undergrowth and the contents of the hut. He turned to Diana. 'What time do you see Elvis?'

She looked back expressionlessly. 'I don't see that's any of your business.'

'My business is to investigate the killings. And to prevent any more from taking place.'

He waited while she blinked repeatedly, in obvious discomfort. 'Ten o'clock,' she told him.

'How often do you see your clients?'

'Some weekly. Others from time to time as the need arises.' She had stopped blinking now. 'But I strongly recommend daily treatment, it's the only way to make true progress. I am fortunate to have some extremely committed clients with whom I work closely on this basis.'

'You don't run out of things to say?'

'On the contrary; there's never enough time.'

Gunzabo's breakfast arrived. He poured salt on his eggs, had the fork at his lips when he asked, 'Was John one of your regulars?'

Diana was sitting straight against the back of the chair, hands in her lap. She squinted up at the clouds from the corners of her eyes. 'He had intensive treatment for several years and then took a break.' She lowered her gaze back to him. 'More recently he resumed, though he was one of the as-and-when's. It is always the patient's choice.'

'What made him return?'

Diana blinked. 'He may be dead, Gunzabo, but patient confidentiality must prevail.'

Mrs Bradley started sobbing quietly. He saw Diana try to squeeze her hand, but Mrs Bradley wouldn't let her, shifting her large frame round the other way.

'He didn't say anything that might indicate who the killer is?' he asked.

'Certainly not.'

Diana paused for long enough to change the conversation. 'Have you had any therapy before, Gunzabo?'

'It didn't do anything for me.'

'Perhaps you weren't ready.'

His fingers strayed towards his missing arm. 'How about six o'clock this evening?' he said.

'Yes that's fine. See you later on.'

He sat on the terrace watching Diana leave, then turned to Mrs Bradley. She was still crying. 'Joan, what is it?'

'Oh bother, it's so hot!' She pulled an embroidered handkerchief out from somewhere inside her dress. 'He was so lovely,' she murmured, face downcast. 'He used to come up to reception for a cuppa most days. He'd tell me to go and have a lie down sometimes. Course I wasn't supposed to. They aren't supposed to go near our computers. Christian doesn't want them knowing about the internet. Oh but he'd flirt terribly, he was such a rascal. He was like a son, really. Even though he was older than me. Strange, isn't it?' She burst into tears again. 'Maybe that's why I'm so upset with her,' she sobbed.

He pulled her close. He could feel her breasts encompass him. He tried to ignore their amazing size and softness.

'Upset with who? What happened?'

'She broke his heart, that's what happened! She stole it from him, then she broke it.'

'Who?' he persisted.

But Mrs Bradley would not say. She pulled away from his embrace, her face flushed and wet with tears, and hurried off, dress bobbing like a gigantic flowery concertina.

He stayed in his seat, on his own now, watching the staff quietly tend to their duties. He finished his breakfast, then went inside, across the restaurant and up the stairs towards reception.

Didi poked her head out. 'Are we going where I think we're going?'

He glanced down at his sleeve. 'Yes.'

'Do we have to?'

'He asked for a progress report every morning.'

'That'll be a quick conversation.'

'The quicker the better.'

There was no one in reception. The silver tree stood lifelessly in weak daylight; the birds preened their sharp feathers near the ceiling; through the windows to the north, mist shifted in slow motion above the rising forest canopy. He wandered over to the reception desk, glanced at a spa brochure, flicked through a calendar, keeping his attention on the door to Christian's office. He took a chocolate éclair from a bowl, tossed the wrapper on the floor, skirted round the desk and sat down behind it.

'What are you up to?' asked Didi.

'Checking something.' He waved the mouse. A login screen appeared. He took the piece of paper that he'd found the day before from his pocket. *IAN FIELDS*. Turning the paper over, he reached for the keyboard and jabbed a string of characters with his index finger:

KB230574

The desktop appeared. Behind the icons was a photo of a young boy with fair hair.

'What was John up to?' he muttered. 'What was he looking at?'

'What you look at, I expect,' Didi said. 'Check the keyboard for pubes.'

He looked through Mrs Bradley's emails: unfiltered spam, updates from sewing forums, clichéd inspirational quotes forwarded on by Christian. Nothing of great interest. But John had been using this computer without her knowledge. That was definitely interesting. He logged off and wandered over to the window to wait for Christian to call him in.

'So, how are you?' asked Christian. 'Enjoying the weather, I hope. It's so nice to have you here.'

He didn't respond, just looked back at Christian in the cold gloom.

Christian flashed his grin. 'How are you sleeping?'

'Fine.'

'I'm so glad.'

They sat in silence for a minute. The Komodo dragon hissed soundlessly at Gunzabo in the twilight. He noticed three golden apples between its front legs.

'It was such a shame you couldn't join us for Scrabble last night.'

Christian was shaking his knee furiously under the table. Gunzabo looked him in the eye. 'Why was Thomas Bradley searching John's house yesterday? I presume he was acting on your instructions?'

'Oh, he was just tidying up. As you know, we're hopeful of getting a new resident sometime soon.' Christian smiled at him, an expectant look on his face as he waited for the next question.

'He wasn't tidying anything,' Gunzabo told him. 'I'm sure you are aware of this. And Christian, it's very tiresome – I'd rather not have to ask – but why do you insist on having me followed constantly?'

'Followed?' Christian looked confused. 'Why would I have you followed?'

Gunzabo frowned irritably. 'I found a hut in the jungle last night. Made from concrete. Do you know about this?' He saw Christian's eyes narrow for an instant. 'No? You may want to send Tommy. I'll draw a map for you sometime. Perhaps once you've got me that list.'

Christian resumed his pleasant expression. 'If you have nothing else, Mario, I really have a lot on this morning.'

Gunzabo stayed in his seat. 'I have something else. The villagers.'

'Aren't they wonderful? I call them my Oompa Loompas.'

'Are they from this island?'

'Oh no. This island was uninhabited. There are thousands, you know, in these seas. It's what protects us. I found the villagers... oh, hundreds of kilometres from here. They were a dying people. They led a backward, tribal existence, ravaged by malnutrition, malaria, passed over by society. I offered them paradise, another life, and they accepted.'

'Much like the residents.'

'Ha, *ja*, much like them.'

'When did they come?' Gunzabo said.

'They came before anybody else, preparing the island, making it a place worthy of our residents.'

'How many villagers are there?'

'Fifty-two,' Christian answered immediately.

'Do any ever leave, go back to their island? Off to the mainland?'

Christian smiled. 'Why would they do that? They have a

wonderful life here.'

Gunzabo looked back, steadily holding his gaze. 'Has *anyone* ever left this island, Christian?'

'Why would they?' Christian rocked back in his chair, silently laughing.

There was a pause.

'So, have you got a busy day ahead?' Christian asked him. 'I can recommend the snorkelling. The waters around the island are wonderful.'

Gunzabo was looking around the room at the menagerie of dead animals, eyeing them with distaste. 'Do sea creatures preserve well for taxidermy?'

'Oh, *ja*! I had a wonderful dolphin on the wall for many years. Poor Joan got ever so upset, so I keep it in my home now. It's a nice treat when she comes to visit.' Christian laughed heartily, speaking with more enthusiasm than Gunzabo had ever seen in him. 'But as you can see I do favour land fauna. I guess it's due to the… well, actually, it's the fur. I just have a thing for fur. It's so rich and clean and lush, like a… field of grass in the morning. Just look at them!' He gestured towards a pair of adolescent snow leopards. 'Aren't they beautiful? They're more beautiful now than they ever were before. There's no mischief, no dirt. I take something delicate, transient, and make it permanent. They're always here, in my room. Here for me.'

Christian shook his legs manically in the gloom. Gunzabo glanced idly round the room, scratching his chin. 'Christian, do you know who the Déjà Vu Killer is?'

Christian reduced his eyes to slits. 'If I knew that, why would I bring Greece's finest detective here?'

Gunzabo stood up, sick of being in the same room as him. 'I have no more questions.'

'Have a great day. See you the same time tomorrow.'

He did not answer, just walked out into the light, leaving the door open because he knew it would annoy Christian. But the light did not penetrate far into the office and The Director sat in the shadows, surrounded by his legion of dead creatures.

14

He made his way back up West Beach, past the locked gates, past the shack where Jim sat cross-legged with his video camera. He nodded into the lens as he strode by. He passed Jimi's place, Diana's locked gate, Elvis doing Chi Kung on his lawn, before advancing towards a tapering point and another beach. He did not know how far the village was. He increased his pace.

Halfway down this new stretch of sand a set of black railings showed between the trees, and another gate, padlocked, but without a nameplate. He looked through the metal bars.

The entire garden was taken up by an enormous playground, empty and pristine and painted in vivid colours: unused climbing frames; swings and trampolines; a motionless merry-go-round; seesaws mounted on metal cylinders in freshly dug soil. A railway track wound through the play area, as still as the python in Christian's office, and to the left a train engine stood in front of six child-sized carriages. The house was obscured by a tall bouncy castle; somewhere nearby a generator chugged noisily. There were no children and no adults. On the near side a tree-house lay on the grass, ready to be lifted into the branches of an enormous, ancient banyan tree.

He saw movement in the house, and a man stepped outside onto the lawn, pale and thin with tight black clothes and black hair. Gunzabo waved and called out, but his voice was lost in the noise of the generator. He could not see the man's features from this distance but he was quite certain of his identity: the oddly pale complexion, the black ringlets, the way he moved lightly across the patio, stepping on each paving stone like he was in a pop video. The man filled bird tables with water, feeder stands with seeds, then went back inside. Gunzabo moved on.

Further along, the beach narrowed to a sandy path which climbed upwards into the jungle. As he gained height the trees closed around him and a polyphonic hum filled his ears: the insistent calls of birds and mammals, the croaking of frogs and the rubbing of a million carapaces, all vibrating through every gap in the vegetation, as if in exultation at being alive.

'I need a rest,' he muttered.

He sat between two branches of a lychee tree, resting in a fork at its base. Clusters of plump, magenta-skinned fruit hung overhead. As he sat there eating lychees, savouring their sweet, fragrant flavour, a wild boar crossed the path, with greasy brown fur and powerful shoulders. It was limping. The boar glanced at him, snorted, and disappeared into the undergrowth.

'There goes Christian's next exhibit,' said Didi. 'We might see him come by with a gun.'

'He doesn't hunt,' Gunzabo said. 'He just waits for them to drop dead.'

Didi gave a sigh. 'What is it with you two?'

'What do you mean?'

'Well, I know you've got your history and all. But he did bring you here. Why all the suspicion?'

'You think he wants me to solve this mystery, do you?'

'Why wouldn't he?'

'I don't know,' Gunzabo muttered, standing up.

The path flattened and he carried on for ten minutes until he emerged back into daylight and stood on a rocky promontory overlooking the sea. Waves broke against rocks far below; the sea was turbulent on this northern part of the island. He saw the path easing down to an expanse of bare rock, and, further on, a group of some twenty huts formed a small, desolate village on the edge of the cliffs.

Didi scrambled ahead as he made his way down to the village. The ground was a mosaic of cracked mud interspersed with rock. A small child peered out of one of huts: a dark face with wide, pure eyes, immediately retreating as Gunzabo approached. The huts were unusual, their thatched roofs rising directly from the baked earth, each with a low, semi-circular entrance at one end.

He headed for the largest hut at the centre of the village. Smoke was drifting from its entrance. A crude fence marked the hut's perimeter and enclosed a small, well-kept garden, rich with flowers and a lotus-filled pond. Reaching the entrance, he leant down and called inside. A waft of smoke stung his eyes. He stepped back, and blinking away the fumes, saw an old man looking out at him, face the colour of dark chocolate.

'Can I help you, sir?'

Gunzabo introduced himself. The man came outside and stood up. He was tiny and round with a lime-green shirt hanging over the apex of his belly. He regarded Gunzabo with almost comic gravity.

'I am Rahmad. What brings you over here, sir?'

'I came to look around, ask a few questions.'

'I see, sir.'

'Call me Gunzabo.'

Rahmad lifted his shoulders the short distance to his double chin. 'Old habits die hard.'

'Can I come in?' Gunzabo asked him.

'Yes, of course.'

He stooped and followed Rahmad inside, who immediately began waving his arms, shouting, 'My God, woman, we have a guest. Look at the mess you are making, we cannot see a thing!'

An old woman was squatting in the middle of the hut, tending an open fire that belched fumes into the domed roof-space above them. She grinned through the fumes at Gunzabo, her face lost in wrinkles, now chattering in a strange birdlike language.

'My wife asks if you would like some food.'

'Why not.' Gunzabo stepped forward and introduced himself.

'Sukma,' said the woman in a raspy, high-pitched voice. She sat, crossing her thin legs; her feet were as tough and cracked as the hut's mud floor.

'Sukma is her name by the way,' Rahmad said. 'Forty years on this island and still she cannot speak a word of English. Hurry up woman!' He clenched his small fists in frustration. 'Why you insist on these antiquated methods! We have this modern technology' – he gestured to a refrigerator in the corner, turned now to Gunzabo – 'and all she does is use it to cool my slippers in the morning.'

Sukma laughed and gesticulated at her husband. Gunzabo stood by the fire while Rahmad shouted back in his native tongue and then broke into English, saying, 'What do you mean, nothing to do? I have Joko to look after and to educate. How will he learn English? How will he survive in this modern world? You and the other women would have him run wild, illiterate and naked, making arrows or suchlike.'

Sukma cackled, showing toothless gums and slapping her knee, as if her husband had just told a wonderful joke.

'You don't work with the others?' Gunzabo said.

Rahmad glared at his wife. 'We are too old now for such things. We stay here and die a slow death.' He sat down heavily in his wicker chair. 'Once you reach eighty years of age, they ask you to stop working. It makes the residents feel old, having us about, serving their beer.'

'You said you've been here forty years?'

'Since the beginning. And I have cursed myself every day since.' Rahmad was staring into the fire. 'We were seduced, now we are cursed. And so I curse myself. Only I can take responsibility for what has happened to my people. For our slow death. Oh, why does God hate us so? What did we do to Him?'

'Who is in charge of the village?' Gunzabo asked him. 'You?'

Rahmad didn't answer immediately. He closed his eyes and rubbed his forehead. 'No one is in charge,' he said eventually, with great bitterness. 'Other than God, who has His own purpose and who we trust will one day free us... Until then, we are treated like slaves. All the promises we were given have been broken.' He looked up at Gunzabo and his eyes widened as he realised his candour. He lowered his gaze. 'I should not speak of these things.'

'You should,' said Gunzabo. 'Someone should speak honestly for once.' He sat down in a homemade chair. 'I want to ask some questions about the murders.'

'I see,' said Rahmad as his wife looked up sharply from her cooking. 'But I do not know how I can help you.'

Gunzabo scratched his leg and studied Rahmad's face from side on: his cheeks were podgy and freshly shaved, with a slight dampness that shone in the orange flames; his hands rested on his belly as he watched his wife prepare the food.

'Where were you on the morning of John's murder?'

'We were here,' said Rahmad. 'We are always here. With Joko.'

'Joko?'

'Our grandson.'

'The little boy I saw just now?'

'Yes, surely.'

'Is there not a school?'

'A school?' Rahmad snorted. 'There is hardly a need. Joko is the only child in the village. He was the first baby in a decade. There have been none since.'

'Why?'

'I told you, we are cursed.'

Gunzabo considered this for a moment, then continued, 'The three of you were here in the hut?'

'Yes.'

119

'And who else was in the village?'

'Nobody. Everyone was at work,' Rahmad told him, still looking at the fire.

'As they are now?'

Rahmad turned now, sighing heavily, his face holding a dignified sadness that caused Gunzabo to forget the man's smallness and his ridiculous pot belly. 'Some are asleep, those who worked overnight. But everyone attends roll call, those who are starting and those who are ending their shifts.'

'How many hours does each shift last?'

'Officially eight. But my daughter usually works sixteen, as do the others.'

'It's a long day.'

'It is what it is,' said Rahmad, looking down. 'It is what we agreed to more than forty years ago.'

'You have much regret.'

'I have nothing but regret. But we have no choice, just as we had no choice back then. God provides, and thanks to God we have food and we survive.'

Sukma began speaking now in her high pitched voice.

'What did your wife say?'

'She said there was a choice, because some stayed behind. Her parents and mine. They will be long dead by now.' He turned to his wife. 'You are living in the past, woman.'

Gunzabo saw the bitter resignation on the man's face, and his wife looking back and laughing at Rahmad like he was an old fool.

'My wife, others like her, insist on living a traditional life, as much as that is possible,' Rahmad said, in a quiet, beaten voice. 'But there is no life. There are no children, there is no laughter. We are frozen in time, our numbers stay the same, never changing.'

'The curse?'

'Our men are like shadows. Our women are no longer fertile. All they do is work for the lazy foreigners.' He shook his head pitifully. 'Is lunch ready yet, Sukma? Just some chapattis to make? Alright, hurry up though, will you.'

Lunch was delicious. Sukma looked approvingly at Gunzabo as he ate on the floor with her, mopping up vegetable curry with a piece of charred flatbread.

'Tell me,' he said, when he had finished his food, 'what do you and your people feel about these deaths? If the residents die, you will be free.'

Rahmad looked down at Gunzabo from his chair, chin quivering with dignified offence. 'That is not a question I like, sir. You are saying that one of us killed John? I was asleep. My wife was here with my grandson.' He was about to remonstrate further when a woman appeared in the doorway. Gunzabo looked up. It was Lastri.

'My daughter.' Rahmad smiled fondly, forgetting the tension of the moment before. 'What are these for?'

Lastri was carrying eight cans of beer. She ignored her father, but then noticed Gunzabo sitting by the fire, and blinked in surprise before quickly regaining her composure. 'They're for you,' she said, smiling graciously. 'I thought you might be here. Will you have one?'

'Why not.' Gunzabo opened a can; the beer was warm. 'We were discussing the murders,' he said. 'Who do you think is responsible?'

Lastri gazed back at him expressionlessly. In his peripheral vision he saw her mother pour the remaining food into the fire, reducing the flames to a low flicker as Lastri's face became wreathed in shadow.

'I do not know,' she said softly. Only her eyes now showed. 'It's just awful. I do hope you find who is responsible.'

The child, Joko, ran into the hut. He wrapped his arms

around Lastri's waist.

'Hello there,' Gunzabo said, smiling. 'What a handsome boy.' He reached out and ruffled the child's hair. Joko edged away and peered at him from behind his mother's white sari. He had his mother's looks.

'May I ask who his father is?'

'He is dead,' answered Lastri.

All pleasure at seeing the boy evaporated. Gunzabo quickly rose to his feet in an attempt to escape the terrible sense of guilt that now filled his chest.

'It must be lonely for him,' he said, louder than intended.

'He does not find it so. He is lucky to be here.'

Gunzabo finished his beer, felt the metallic dregs wash away some of the sadness. Lastri passed him another can; he drank half and felt a little better. He picked some sleep out of the corner of his eye. 'You have no suspicions?' he asked. 'No thoughts about what happened to John?'

'I told you, I have no idea,' said Lastri. Her face was perfectly still, her gaze steady, but fiery stars danced across her placid, unmoving eyes.

No one spoke for a moment. 'Everyone loved John,' she said eventually. 'He was wonderful to us all. He took great interest in our lives here in the village.'

'In what way?'

'He was fighting for our rights.'

Rahmad snorted. 'Giving us more work to do, more like. Trying to make us dig another well.'

'He had our best interests at heart,' Lastri told him.

'Why did he not dig it himself then?'

'He offered. But you would not hear of it, father.'

Rahmad scowled, crossing his arms, wedging them between belly and chin. 'This is our village,' he said. 'It is the one thing that is our own. And it is *our* well.'

'Where is the well?' Gunzabo asked.

'It is half a kilometre away,' Lastri said.

'Why do you always find problems where none exist?' Rahmad's chin wobbled with anger. 'You are like your mother. We fill up tanks every few days. We keep them here.'

Lastri sighed. 'My father does not like change.' Gunzabo saw her look briefly at her mother as Sukma put the remaining beer into the refrigerator.

'In what other ways was John involved in the village?' he said to Lastri.

'He was petitioning The Director to build a school.'

'For one child,' said Rahmad.

'There will be more,' Lastri insisted. 'He was also campaigning for our hours to be reduced, and for statutory annual leave. He had many ideas.'

Rahmad shook his head in exaggerated despair. 'The only sensible thing he said was to stop sending Joko to Michael's house.' Gunzabo looked intently at the old man, who added, 'I would have punched him myself, if I had any strength left in me.'

Gunzabo suppressed a smile, saw that Lastri noticed and did not mind. 'What happened?' he asked.

'John had a fight,' she said. 'It was nothing.'

'With Michael?'

'Yes. I do not know what it was about.' She appeared upset and looked back with wide eyes, lips pursed tightly.

'Tell him, tell him,' Rahmad said. 'We have nothing to hide.'

Lastri mastered herself and was distant again. 'John threatened to kill Michael,' she said quietly. 'He didn't say why.'

'How did Michael react to this?'

'He didn't. He went back inside his house. I haven't seen him since.'

Gunzabo took a large gulp of beer, lifted the can and frowned at the unrefreshing warmth of the drink; it was an unusual drop in standards.

'When did the fight take place?' he asked Lastri.

'Two weeks ago.'

He sat in his chair, keeping his eyes on Lastri, waiting to see if any other emotion would reach her face. She looked back, showing nothing. He finished his beer, stood and nodded at each of them in turn.

'Leaving already?' Rahmad said.

'I have an appointment at five o'clock.'

Rahmad's forehead suddenly creased with worry. 'What time is it now? *Baywatch* is about to start! Quick, Sukma!'

Sukma pulled away a rug hanging across the far end of the hut, revealing a flat screen television larger than she was.

'Come on woman, it's started already!' Rahmad shouted as the screen burst into life. 'Are you sure you won't stay?'

'Another time,' Gunzabo said, ducking under the doorway.

'Goodbye Gunzabo,' Lastri called after him.

He didn't look back.

The air outside was hot but pleasantly clean after the dark smokiness of the hut. He scanned the village. No one was about. He considered walking further along the coast, but the village was surrounded to the north by impenetrable jungle, and besides, he didn't want to be late for his appointment with Diana.

15

He sat in the Spa reception, on the lower ground floor of The Circles, flipping through magazines but thinking about Lastri: the smoothness of her skin, the glow of firelight across the edges of her cheeks while he questioned her. The look of surprise when she first came in, carrying those cans of beer. There was something he was missing.

He glanced at the receptionist: the plump middle-aged woman who had brought him breakfast the day before. 'Can I get a drink?' he said.

The woman smiled and called over one of the instructors, a man of about thirty dressed in a navy blue tracksuit.

'You look like you'll be quick,' said Gunzabo. 'I'll have a cold schnapps.'

The man inclined his head and jogged off. He turned his thoughts back to Lastri, replayed the scene once again. But he knew he should stop, let his unconscious mind work on it, so he tossed away the magazine and walked over to the two closed doors on the other side of reception. The first door was to Diana's therapy room. He would be seeing that soon enough. He turned to the second door:

MEDICAL CENTER
DR. KEN L. WINTER, M.D., F.E.C.S., S.I.C.S.

He turned the handle and went inside.

The room was dark and silent. He switched on the light. Laminated posters of breasts, noses, foreheads flashed into existence, between framed prints of half-naked models climbing mountains. A low shelf held factsheets on dementia, arthritis, sexually transmitted diseases, incontinence. Didi dropped down out of his sleeve and he followed her to the polished teak desk which occupied one end of the room, glanced over a few papers, then moved on to the grey filing cabinet against the wall. The cabinet drawers were sparsely filled: medical notes on staff and residents, x-rays, MRI scans, a collection of death certificates which included John's and Brian's. Nothing controversial. Everything confirmed the explanations given during his investigation.

He went through a doorway into a large windowless room which served as pharmacy and operating theatre. It smelled mildly of disinfectant. In the middle was an operating table, cushioned in green plastic. Two floor-to-ceiling refrigerators stood on the far side. The first was filled with branded medicines and drugs. Glass chinked, pills rattled as he searched through bottles and boxes, examined capsules arranged in uniform blistered sheets. Nothing of interest.

He opened the second refrigerator. Bags of blood hung on metal rails. Each bag was marked by name, date and blood type, a rail for each resident. He inspected each bag. Six per person. Apart from John. Only two bags hung on his rail.

'What happened to John's blood?' he murmured.

Didi was inside the fridge, pawing at a bag like it was a carcass in a cold-room. 'Maybe they used it when he was shot.'

'He died instantly,' Gunzabo told her. 'They may have used some, I suppose. But why, if he was dead already?'

'I dunno, you're the detective.'

He shut the refrigerators and walked back into the consulting room, half expecting to see Ken grinning at him, feet up on the desk, smoking a cigar. But the room was empty. Back in reception, his schnapps was waiting on the counter. He knocked it back. Where was the receptionist? He was annoyed; he should have asked for the bottle.

'I hope you won't be attending our session in an intoxicated state?'

Diana was standing in the entrance to the therapy room. 'I'll get you some water.'

She reached down to a water cooler, filled a paper cup, handed it to him. The cup had a pointed bottom and he was forced to drink it all.

'It won't kill you, you know.'

'It won't bring anyone back to life.'

He followed her into the therapy room: spacious, minimalist, white; two chairs in the centre.

He sat down. 'No couch then?'

Diana smiled. 'No couch. One must be alert during therapy.'

She looked at him for several minutes without speaking. He shifted in his seat, itching himself in various places, cracking his toes, each foot in turn.

'You are a fidget,' she said. 'You're like a ferret. Have you always been like this?'

He resisted the urge to scratch his phantom arm. 'My mother used to tell me I did handstands when she was pregnant with me.'

'Were you close?'

'Of course.'

'Not everyone is.'

He reached down for a drink, realised there wasn't one. 'I had two mothers, you know.'

'Really?'

'Mine and Christian's.'

She raised her eyebrows. 'You mean our Director? How interesting.'

'His mother, Rhea, I loved her very much. We were very close.'

'And did you have two fathers?'

'Neither of us had a father. Christian's died soon after we were born. My father, he may as well have.'

'What happened?'

Gunzabo paused, looked at Diana sitting in her chair in front of him, hands in her lap, her attention constant, slightly coy but in control, eyes looking up between mascaraed lashes. It made him think of an interview he had seen years ago on television. What was the name of that journalist? Except the roles were reversed: she was questioning him. For now. She was waiting for him; he remembered her question.

'My father, Joseph his name was. He had his way, promised her everything, which my poor mother believed. He went to find work abroad and disappeared for fifteen years. He knew she was pregnant. She told him before he left.'

'That must have been terribly difficult for her.'

'To have an illegitimate child in Cyprus in those days? Yes it was. Lucky for her, Rhea and my mother were good friends. They were both pregnant, due dates almost identical. She took my mother in. When Christian and I were born we were proclaimed as twins. For years, I knew my mother only as the housekeeper. In this way, her reputation was saved. For a time.'

'So you and Christian grew up together.'

'When we were ten, he and his mother moved to the United States. My mother did not want to leave. She should have.'

Both he and Diana were silent for a while. Eventually he laughed. 'So, this is therapy, is it?'

'Yes, it is.'

'What do you do once your clients have told you everything? For how long can people talk about their parents?'

'Oh, years.'

'What's the point?'

She sighed, as if she had been asked this many times before, but knew it was part of the ritual. 'The point is, we so rarely speak of the most important things in our lives, the things that shape us. We have so little space to talk solely about ourselves, to free the many strata that cover our past... like so many layers of soil at an archaeological site.' She smiled sadly. 'You mentioned that your mother should have gone to America with Christian and Rhea?'

He stared at the floor. 'It became known about my background, in the village. My mother was treated as an outcast. She brought shame to the family, the few relations we had. They refused to speak to her, would have nothing to do with her.'

'How did they find out?'

'Someone told them.'

'Who?'

'Who do you think?'

Diana nodded. 'This must have affected you greatly.'

He looked up, made a gesture of indifference. 'My mother never recovered.'

Diana was sitting in front of him, waiting for him to speak. He felt her eyes on him regardless of where he looked. He wanted to leave, but knew he could not.

'What happened to her, Gunzabo?' she said quietly.

He looked back. The silence was terrible.

'Her body was still warm when I found her. She hanged herself with a shawl she'd been knitting. It was supposed to be for me.'

Diana gazed at him, her face still, eyes full of sorrow. 'How awful. What a terrible, terrible thing.'

He looked past her at the wall, moved his eyes up to where it met the ceiling. 'I was five minutes too late. Helping my cousins build a new house. They lost theirs when the Turks invaded. These were the ones that would not speak to her.'

'I'm very sorry Gunzabo.'

'I left immediately. Went to Athens.'

They sat quietly for a minute, until the silence was broken

by a man's voice outside, followed by laughter. It sounded like Ken. Gunzabo listened to the trivial conversation until the voices faded away and the room fell silent again.

'How did you get on, you and Christian,' she said, 'when you were growing up?' She was still gazing compassionately at him.

'We hated each other's guts. And faces and spleens and livers. You name it.'

'You were glad to see the back of each other then?'

'I didn't hate his back so much.'

She smiled at this. 'How do you feel about him now?'

'I feel nothing.'

There was a pause. Diana clasped her hands tightly in her lap and leaned towards him.

'So... how very interesting! Didn't you find it odd, that he should contact you to come here, after so many years?'

'Of course. But I needed the money.'

'OK. So you go to Athens. This is certainly going to take months by the way. I hope you're prepared for it.'

'One session will be enough I think.'

'One session? There's so much to explore, we've only just begun.'

He saw the great interest his story had aroused in Diana; she was almost glowing with excitement and curiosity; her eyes were shining and wide as if she was taking in every image of his confession for later analysis, reading something in every movement he made.

'I see you therapists are not so different from my line of work,' he said to her. 'My mother used to tell me the reason I always wanted to be a detective was I'm too nosey.'

Diana frowned disapprovingly. 'That is most certainly not the case as a therapist. I'm simply saying there are many, deep rooted, heavily intertwined issues here. It takes time – and hard work, from you – to unpick such things.'

'You think I want to?'

'I do think that, yes. Why would you be here otherwise?'

'I am investigating murder. That is why I am here.'

'And I am investigating life. But what I see, what I'm sensing, is a real deadness inside you, Gunzabo. An absence of emotion. You are so matter of fact about the awful things that have happened to you. Have you forgotten how to live?'

He looked straight back at her. 'I have not forgotten anything.'

'But neither do you feel anything,' she persisted.

He stared at her now. He had never considered this before. 'It does not matter,' he said. 'Those things I told you, they are gone. In the past.'

Diana looked at him thoughtfully. 'Yes,' she said. 'Your father's absence, your mother's death, there is much to explore there. But it's not the real heart of your darkness, is it? There's something else.'

He felt a rising sensation of anger in his throat, but didn't respond, pushed the feeling back down.

'You were telling me about Athens?' she said.

'You were asking. I wasn't telling.'

'So tell me then.'

He looked back at her. 'No.'

She looked disappointed for an instant, and blinked it away, the professional look of empathy back on her face. 'Tell me about your life now, then.'

'I lead a simple life. In England. Worthing. I teach tennis to bored women. I flirt with them, they indulge me, pity me whilst being a little scared. That's it.'

'You seem very dismissive of what you do.'

'I was the foremost, most famous detective in Greece.'

'And what happened?'

'That I will not tell you.' He said this matter-of-factly. The anger was now gone.

Diana looked back at him. 'Yes, you did say that. It is your right, of course. So can we go back to your childhood?'

'First I want to ask *you* a question.'

'This is your therapy session, Gunzabo,' Diana said. 'I am a neutral participant, a catalyst you might say. I cannot get personally involved.'

'That is my condition for continuing. Same rules. You do not have to answer if you do not want to.'

Diana looked at him, her eyes wide and blue. 'Yes, alright,' she murmured, looking down.

He smiled at her. 'Good. Did you kill John?'

'I... what?' she exclaimed. 'No, of course not.'

'Who did then?'

'I don't know.'

'Where were you at the time of the murder?'

'I was—' He saw fear in her eyes, a scared, vulnerable look. 'You've really put me on the spot. I can't think. I was in bed. Yes, I was asleep in bed.'

'You're sure about that?'

'Yes.'

'You weren't at roll call with the others?'

'No. I told you that yesterday.' She sat forward, recovering her composure. 'My turn now,' she said.

'Go on then.'

'Who do *you* think killed John?'

'That's not a very therapeutic question.'

'I think we've given up on that now, haven't we?'

He paused, then said, 'I do not know. But I know who did not kill him.'

'So who didn't do it?'

'The residents of East Beach. They were on Full Moon Island. The staff: six villagers on Full Moon Island, in addition to Thomas Bradley. The others were at their team meeting. Joan

Bradley was at the team meeting too, as was Ken. You were asleep. Alone?'

'Yes, alone.'

'In whose bed?'

She blinked, the trace of a smile on her lips. 'It's my turn now. What about Christian? Could he have done it?'

'Perhaps. He says he was off the island. We have only his word for that. Someone else could have brought him here I suppose, or even Tommy could have. Neither will tell me the time of day or night, let alone assist with my investigations.' He paused. 'Were you asleep in your own bed?'

'No.'

'Whose?'

Diana turned her face down, then gazed up at him, eyes vividly blue. 'Are we speaking in full confidence?'

'Of course.'

'I was asleep in Elvis's bed. I woke up late and by the time I left his house all hell had broken loose. It had all happened.'

'I see. He was out running with John, of course. So you are having a relationship.'

'Elvis and I are lovers.'

'For how long?'

'Seven months.' She smiled fondly.

'Is he still in therapy?'

'We meet in this room every day.'

'Isn't that unethical? Forbidden?'

Diana looked up at him, her head inclined slightly to one side. 'I tried, Gunzabo. But Elvis insists. Believe me, I thought long and agonisingly about it. But then I saw the simple truth: we love each other. That is all that matters.'

Gunzabo watched Diana's face redden with joy.

'I think it's my turn again, isn't it?' she said.

'Yes.'

She said, 'My question is this: you know you're stuck here, don't you?'

'Here on the island?'

'Yes. So you will come back for more therapy. Because you must.'

'If I solve this case, Christian will have no choice but to let me leave.'

'You'd be the first, Gunzabo.'

He ignored this. 'I have one last question for you.'

'And what is that?'

'Who is Iris?'

'Iris?' Diana's eyes widened. 'I don't know.'

'Yes you do.'

'What makes you say that?'

He watched her fidget in her chair, hands straying to her hair. 'Tell me about you and John,' he said.

'John had regular counselling sessions here, for several years, if that's what you mean.'

'It's not what I mean. You and he were lovers, weren't you?'

She looked back at him in fear. 'Yes,' she whispered.

'Does Elvis know?'

'No. And he mustn't. It would destroy him. Even now, even with John...'

'Dead?'

Diana looked disconsolately at the floor. Perhaps she saw her own reflection in the polished tiles. 'Yes,' she murmured.

'Is he a jealous man, Elvis?' said Gunzabo.

Diana's face softened. 'He is protective.'

'What would he do if he found out?'

She became serious, speaking firmly, 'He won't find out.'

'What makes you so sure?'

'John swore he would never say. Nobody else knows, just as they do not know about me and Elvis.'

'Why did things end between you and John?'

'Many reasons. Mostly though, because we made each other unhappy. John was never happy here, on the island. His therapy was compromised by our relationship. I must confess to this, it was a mistake, our coming together. He began seeing me again – on a professional basis, of course – in the last few months before his death.'

'What did you talk about?'

'You know I cannot tell you that.'

'Was he seeing anyone else? Is there another Iris?'

Diana crossed her legs and smiled. 'I think that's enough for one session isn't it, Gunzabo?'

He grunted, nodding at her as he rose from his seat.

At the doorway Gunzabo turned and said, 'I want to thank you, Diana, for your openness. It must have been difficult.'

Diana laughed, a full, unrestrained laugh. 'I see that you are right, Gunzabo. Our lines of work are much the same. Enjoy your evening.'

16

'So what happened?' asked Didi. 'I can't believe I slept through the whole thing.'

'It was quite good.'

'Quite good! Did you end up shagging her or something?'

Gunzabo did not answer. He felt different and he was trying to work out why. It was his insides: they felt lighter, less solid. Less dead. As if someone had taken a huge wooden spoon and stirred them into life. Feelings rose through his chest and across his throat in a prickle of sensation; the need to scratch and fidget was gone; his mind though was like a pan of boiling water: memories rushed to the surface in brief flashes of sound and colour, immediately gone.

'The gardens are beautiful today,' he said.

Didi gave him a quizzical look. 'They're just the same as ever.'

Entering a rock garden, he smiled as a butterfly settled on his hand, and he suddenly realised he could not remember the last time he had smiled without irony. It must have been years. He hadn't noticed the absence of feeling before, but it was clear to him Diana was correct. His mind was buzzing. It was impossible to concentrate on the case.

He stepped through a wooden portico heavy with peppercorn vines and entered the same herb garden he had come through two days ago. Ken was sitting on a bench, sipping champagne, smoking a cigarette. Ken turned round, made to stand but changed his mind, giving him a look of mild irritation.

'Expecting somebody?' Gunzabo asked him.

'No,' said Ken.

'I didn't know you smoked,' Gunzabo said. 'Cigarettes, that is.'

'I don't. Gave up.' Ken took a lungful of smoke and blew it out sharply. He topped up his glass and put the bottle back into an ice bucket. On the bench next to him a selection of silver dishes contained wasabi peas, seaweed crackers, golden-crusted gyoza dumplings.

'Have a nibble if you want. I need a slash.' Ken cleared his throat loudly in an attempt to distract Gunzabo as he pushed a second, clean glass onto the ground.

Gunzabo sat and ate dumplings while Ken urinated into an enormous basil bush.

'So what've you been up to then?' Ken asked.

'Continuing my investigations. I had a look around your office and the medical centre this afternoon.'

'Oh yeah. Find anything?'

'Maybe.'

Ken laughed ironically. 'Play your cards close, don't you? Maybe it's just as well poker got cancelled.' He threw his cigarette on the ground and sat back down. 'You can check out my bungalow too if you like. I'm past caring.'

Gunzabo watched Ken purse his lips and look around the garden. He seemed nervous and irritable, glancing at his watch, crossing and uncrossing his legs, darting his eyes around.

'It's easier if you just tell me,' Gunzabo said.

Ken looked at him, suppressed a frown, then said, 'What do you want to know?'

'How did you get the job? Here on the island.'

'Oh, that's a story, that is. I'll give you the short version.' Ken took out a cigarette but did not light it. 'I had this clinic, over on Hollywood Boulevard. One day, who walks in for an appointment? Christian. I didn't know him, thought he was there to get some work done. Well he was, just a different kind. He knew all about me, though. He didn't let on, but he must have. All the gambling debts, the wife, ex-wives, kids. I was being sued too. Some nutter who'd come in for her tenth nose job, claimed I botched it.'

Gunzabo waited while Ken lit his cigarette, took a deep drag and let out a lungful of smoke.

'Anyhow, Christian just sits there, we talk about mutual acquaintances while he grins and shakes his leg in that inane way of his. Then I get down to business, ask what he wants done. And he says, "If you give me one of your clients, I'll give you ten million dollars." Of course, I don't know what he's on about, but the money sounds great, so I just said, "Yeah, alright, what do I have to do?"'

'He took quite a risk.'

'Guess so. But like I said, he'd done his homework, he must have. Not that it was difficult, everyone knew the mess I was in.'

'You became his recruitment agent.'

'BDM, Gunzabo. Sounds a bit grander.' Ken was still distracted, scanning the entrance to the herb garden as he spoke. 'Two, I bagged.' He smiled now and eased back slightly in his chair, enjoying the recollection. 'Only person who's had more is Christian. That was early on, he had it easy in those days. Half of them were seduced by the money, they had such bad record deals, and the ones who could pay were so out of it, they just thought it would be a laugh.'

'Christian paid them to come here? Why?'

'He had to, just to get things started. They all pay him now. You wouldn't believe how much.'

'Who did you recruit?'

'River and Kurt.' Ken had stopped looking around now and he relaxed, nodding his head with satisfaction while he contemplated his cigarette. 'River was a good one,' he said. 'I was pleased with him. Meticulous planning, that one took. Get the right cocktail of drugs, make a good scene, whisk him off in the ambulance. Played his role perfectly. As soon as they said he was gone we had him out of the morgue, did the switch and he was straight off to the airport. Job done.'

'And Kurt?' Gunzabo asked him.

'Kurt was easy. Ripe for the picking. Did as he was told, just wanted out. Straight on the plane, he was here in two days. I could've had more, too. I had so many leads. You just have to drop enough hints about who's here. They all love Jimi, they're desperate to see him. And John too. Makes them go weak at the knees, the thought of hanging out with those two. Things were just getting too hot, though. So I came here too.'

Gunzabo gazed at Ken thoughtfully. 'Did you like the job?'

'Oh, I loved it. It was such a buzz. I didn't want to stop, to be honest.'

'Who's working there now? Anyone?'

'Oh yeah. I couldn't tell you who, though. I heard it was someone famous, someone who knows *everyone*. You know what Christian's like, loves his little secrets.'

Ken smoked the remainder of his cigarette and dropped it in the basil bush. Gunzabo sat there, following Ken's eyes out of the gardens, up into the meadow and towards The Circles. Something moved briefly across his line of sight: a figure, dressed in white.

'Brian and John's bodies,' he asked, still staring into the meadow, 'were they brought to the medical room?'

'Yeah. Made a right mess John did. Poor sod.' Ken was rubbing the tips of his fingers together, contemplating another cigarette.

'Did you attempt a blood transfusion?'

'No point. Died instantly.'

He looked at Ken closely. 'So why is John's blood missing?'

'Is it? I hadn't noticed.' Ken looked at his watch, glanced

again out of the garden. 'Eating at The Circles tonight are you?'

'Probably.'

'You should get going, you might pick up some interesting clues.'

'You think so?'

'I know so. Keep an ear out. You know how unguarded people can be after a glass of wine and a slap-up meal. Go on, off you go.'

Ken crossed his legs and lit another cigarette, waving genially as Gunzabo left the herb garden and headed back up towards The Circles. The gardens were filled with the noise of invisible creatures as dusk descended and lamps flickered into life.

'Gunzabo!'

He looked up, saw a messianic figure striding towards him: Jimi, dressed in an ankle-length cotton smock and battered leather sandals. An acoustic guitar was hanging from his shoulder.

'How's it going?' Gunzabo said.

Jimi shook his hand. 'Fine and freaky, man.'

'You're the first resident I've seen over here.'

'We usually stay clear, huh? I guess that's mostly true. This is all Christian's thing, you know, his own groovy scene, makes him feel big and all. I don't like it so much, it gets all, you know, very crazy. I get out of my comfort zone. It's a pretty small zone.'

A huge beetle flew across Jimi's face. They watched it buzz away into the evening.

'Oh, by the way, man, I don't know if you had any plans? There's a party out at the Commune tonight. You could come along, if you want.' Jimi smiled his shy, goofy grin. He shifted his guitar from one shoulder to the other.

'The Commune. Who's there?'

'Oh, those cool East Beach cats. They're all into free love, even more so than the rest of us, living in the jungle together, that kinda thing. Come over my place later on, I'll take you there.

It's not that simple to find.'

'Why not.' Gunzabo looked at Jimi's white smock. 'Why the change of outfit?'

'Oh, this? I woke up with a different feeling today. A beautiful, new feeling, like a second coming, or a third even.' Jimi blinked slowly. 'I don't know if I'll keep it. See you about ten.'

Gunzabo waited for Jimi to pass out of sight into the next garden, then quickly followed, careful not to be seen.

'What's going on?' whispered Didi.

'That's what I want to find out.'

Gunzabo peered round a bush, into the herb garden. He saw Ken stand up and nod a greeting to Jimi as they both left, heading towards the beach.

He skirted the bushes and shrubs, keeping the two men in sight, reluctant to risk coming close enough to hear their conversation. Ken was doing all the talking, on the beach now, animated and enthusiastic as Jimi walked alongside with his head bowed. They stopped by the water. Gunzabo moved lightly across the sand and watched from behind a starfruit tree as Jimi grabbed Ken by his lapels, pulling him close so their noses nearly met.

'Are you bullshitting me?' Jimi said, his tone angry and suspicious.

'No, Jim, never,' said Ken. He was looking a little scared as he stood helplessly, waiting for Jimi to release him. 'It's true. It's all true.'

'It better be. You know how much I hate that sonovabitch. But I'd go to him, you know I would.'

Their voices lowered again. Ken's voice sounded placating. He gave his jolly laugh as Jimi left and headed back along West Beach. 'So what do you reckon?' Ken called after him.

Gunzabo lingered at the starfruit tree, watching Jimi's smock darken and merge into the evening sky, saw him stop and turn and shout, 'I'm still thinking about it.'

Jimi carried on up the beach, as Ken called back, saying, 'Yeah, yeah. Don't think for too long, though.' Ken paused and then he shouted, 'You look like Jesus, you know that?'

'Yeah, I know that,' Jimi said, without looking behind him.

17

The Bradleys and Christian were eating dinner on the terrace. Gunzabo sat down, helped himself to the platter of rabbit paella and thought about the case, keeping an ear open while Mrs Bradley went through the final details of the talent show. Elvis wouldn't be doing his onstage cookery this year, she was saying. He was too upset about John, but he'd compère as usual. Ken was doing his magic act, Heath would be playing five simultaneous games of speed chess, she and Tommy would be doing a duet. She reached for her notes, was about to list the other performers, when Ken arrived. He nodded at Gunzabo and ordered a bottle of champagne.

'Kenny-Wenny-Bongo,' Mrs Bradley said. 'I was wondering if you were going to turn up. We were just talking about your magic act.'

'Were you now, Joan?' Ken said, sitting down.

'Makes me go all weak at the knees.'

'Maybe I should magic you round the back and give you a good seeing to.' Ken gave Gunzabo a nudge.

'I wouldn't if I were you. Not with the body odour I get towards the end of the day. It's enough to floor a rhino.'

Ken wrinkled his nose and lit a cigarette. 'So, is it all sorted?' he said, glancing at Christian. 'Do we have a show?'

Gunzabo saw Christian's look of irritation, his tight lipped refusal to answer. He had forgotten about those dirty looks. That was at least two people upset with Ken. He watched Ken eating paella, smoking a cigarette between each mouthful, laughing and flirting with Mrs Bradley. But his jollity seemed forced, he still seemed as on edge as he had been in the gardens earlier, waiting for Jimi.

'What about you, Gunzarby,' Mrs Bradley asked him. 'What are you going to do?'

Ken looked over. 'Yeah, what's your secret talent?'

He looked back at Ken. 'Solving murders.'

'We're yet to see that. Best kept secret in town that one.'

'Try asking Diomedes,' he told Ken, 'with his man-eating horses. Ask him how good I am. Or Stavros, while he was waiting for the firing squad.'

'Alright, alright, don't get touchy,' Ken said. 'I was only pulling your leg.'

'We all like to take part, you know,' Mrs Bradley said.

Gunzabo glanced at Tommy, who was staring blankly into the night sky. He was looking forward to that duet.

'Christian doesn't though,' Mrs Bradley continued. 'You're way too important, aren't you, love?'

Christian rocked back in his chair. 'I prefer to watch,' he said softly.

A waitress leaned over Gunzabo's shoulder to pour him a glass of wine. He put his hand over the glass, shook his head, and instead turned to the new dishes being brought out: braised octopus, tiger prawns flash-fried with chilli, chicken liver salad, chickpeas in a blood-red sauce. He ate slowly, ignoring the champagne being offered, only half listening while Mrs Bradley speculated on what his own act would be. He was more interested in the vicious looks of hatred Christian was giving Ken, and Ken's furtive, nervous glances back.

'Forgot to mention,' Ken said, fumbling with a cigarette. 'Jimi says he'll be playing this year.'

'Jimi? Are you joking, Kenneth?' Mrs Bradley gave him a shocked look. 'He hasn't played in fifteen years.'

Christian tipped his chair forwards so that all four legs were on the ground. 'How wonderful.'

'Don't worry, Joanie, he won't stand a chance against you,' Ken said.

'Well, I don't like to brag. But you'd better watch out, Gunzarby, I'm the one everyone wants to beat.' She sighed theatrically. 'If only my Kevin was here to see his mum.'

Tommy got up, his chair toppling backwards to the floor. Gunzabo watched him stalk off into the gardens and melt into the night. Then he sat back as waitresses placed a chocolate fondue in the centre of the table, and bowls of fresh fruit, cream, nuts, chocolate cake and a Victoria sponge. He sat and watched Mrs Bradley eat, while Christian vibrated his legs and Ken chain smoked half a dozen cigarettes. The staff waited patiently in the background. When finally Mrs Bradley had finished her third helping of cake and sat there panting and sweating with pleasure, cheeks as red as watermelon flesh, he stood up to leave.

'Getting an early night are you?' Ken said, winking.

'There's a party at the Commune.'

'That's right. I might see you there.'

He nodded goodnight and walked through the gardens to the beach. Someone was standing at the water's edge. As he drew near he saw it was Tommy, staring into darkness. He followed Tommy's gaze: broken pieces of lamplight glittered on the water in front of them; infinite, saturated black lay beyond. Gunzabo stayed a while next to Tommy, looking out to sea, feeling the heaviness of the food. He was feeling lonely again. The session with Diana, the lightness he had felt in the gardens afterwards, now seemed long ago. Somewhere deep in his abdomen he sensed black fingers creeping out of the buried gloom. He wondered what Tommy, alongside, was feeling, and a sudden insight came to him and he knew, with great certainty, that within Tommy was also a supreme sadness, a loss as great as his own. And this appalling loss had stolen away his senses, robbed him of speech.

'Take care of yourself, Thomas,' Gunzabo told him.

He continued up the beach towards Jimi's house. He needed a drink.

18

No one was ready at Jimi's place, so Gunzabo helped himself to a beer and sat on the porch. The late evening air was hot and filled with insects attracted to the exterior lights. Bruce was meditating by the pool; River was upstairs getting changed; Jimi was in his studio.

Gunzabo sat and listened to take after take of electric guitar, waving away mosquitoes while drinking his beer. His phantom arm was itching; the new feelings from earlier were a vague memory. He was finishing his fourth beer when Jimi walked out onto the porch in his Messiah outfit, looking stoned, but slightly troubled, with an air of nervous irritation. Jimi picked two beers from the bucket, took the tops off and threw one towards Bruce, who plucked it from the air with his eyes shut, smiled serenely and took a swig.

'You ready to party, baby?' said Bruce, opening an eye to look at Gunzabo.

'Always,' Gunzabo told him.

River came out onto the porch, dressed in black linen trousers and a black shirt.

'How's the leg?' Gunzabo asked him.

'Much better, thanks. Good old sister morphine.' River was walking easily, looked mildly sedated. 'Is Jim coming?'

'Yeah, he's coming, man,' Jimi said, and he yelled towards the darkened beach, then put two fingers in his mouth and let out a deafening whistle. There was a faint call in the distance. 'Yeah, man, he's coming.'

Gunzabo stood on the porch, looking into the night, and then he saw Jim, illuminated by the electric green of the swimming pool, bedraggled and tubby, naked but for a leather loincloth. He climbed onto the porch, and after they had all exchanged *hi's* and *man's* and disinterested nods, trying to outdo each other in their stoned complacency, Jimi took them round the side of the house and off into the jungle.

'Where're they at, man?' Jim said.

'The lovers?' said Jimi. 'Quite deep at the moment. Maybe an hour away.'

Within seconds the jungle was deep and thick and black. Jimi started cursing and sent River back for torches. Gunzabo sat on a fallen tree with the others while Jimi rolled a joint. The forest was hot and noisy with life. Shining insects and other, unlit invertebrates swirled around Gunzabo, darting and buzzing in hypnotic patterns around his head. Loud hoots sounded in the trees above, answered by distant echoes from afar. Creatures slithered through vegetation at his feet. Nobody spoke, and the only sign of human company in the black jungle night was the glow of the joint and a nudge on his arm as it was passed on.

River returned with torches. They moved on, through the vegetation to a path flanking a stream, which they followed on an upward course deep into the centre of the island. Moths flew crazily in and out of the torchlight. Gunzabo trod carefully; the path was damp and steep, and riddled with tree roots. It reminded him of his journey through the jungle the night before. Jim started up a Native American chant and everyone joined in as they walked uphill alongside the stream. When the chant ended, Gunzabo again became conscious of the ancient choral hymn of the jungle: the strange harmony of a billion insects which rose in waves to a pulsing crescendo and fell away to a foreground hiss; the calls of monkeys and birds; and the busy, fidgeting noise of unseen creatures on the ground and in the air, in holes and in the trees.

They reached level ground where the water gathered in a pool that wobbled almost imperceptibly under Gunzabo's torchlight. Here they stopped, opened beers, rolled joints and sat talking for ten minutes. They moved on. The stream widened; the roar of fast moving water sounded nearby. They reached a drop where the trees fell away and Jimi called out, 'Watch out, it's kinda treacherous.' Gunzabo edged across a narrow lip, holding onto a relay of tree branches as the roar of water grew louder, and now he felt the spray of a waterfall on his face, cascading from far above. He waved his torch across the falling water, causing a brief shower of sparks, extinguished as he moved the beam over another, larger pool which split in three directions: one smaller tributary snaked back down the way they had come; another led into the trees; another fell over a precipice into hidden depths below.

'Nearly there,' Jimi said, as he plunged into the water, swam across, and pulled himself up onto a rocky path on the far side. Jim did the same; Gunzabo waded behind River and Bruce. The path led down until they arrived at a lower pool and Jimi led them back into the forest. Progress was now slow; their route was merely a lower density version of the rainforest, where someone had hacked away the growth to force a way through. They trudged and pushed through vegetation for almost an hour, cursing and sweating in the hot night.

'You trying to finish me off, man?' Bruce called out. 'My tick-tock cannot take much more of this, you know that.'

'Two minutes, alright? Two minutes,' Jimi said testily.

'You been saying that all night. I gotta have a smoke.'

Jimi relented with a scowl and they took another break. Gunzabo urinated against a bush.

'Watch out for those creatures that swim up your wee,' Didi whispered.

They carried on, working their way through the vegetation,

until they came to a large flag hanging down in front of them: the Tibetan flag, hand-sewn, the sun rising on a white mountain with shards of light splitting the night sky; at the foot of the mountain two beasts held aloft a flaming torch.

'We'll let ourselves in,' Jimi told them.

They passed through the flag, into a clearing. Five people, dressed in crimson robes, were sitting around a fire, a white tepee behind them. Gunzabo saw they were meditating, their shaven heads gleaming in the firelight.

'Hey, people,' Jimi called out. 'Wake up.'

They turned and mumbled greetings as Gunzabo crossed the knee-high ferns behind the others.

'You made it then.'

A plump, white woman with a melodic, raspy voice was smiling at Jimi. She was the only member of the group without a shaved head; white hair fell down her back like a waterfall and mingled with the forest floor.

'Did you doubt it?' Jimi sat down next to her, pulled out a clear plastic bag filled with weed and cigarette papers, and started rolling a joint.

'You can't stop coming over here, can you?' she said. 'Finished your album yet?'

'Just the mastering now. You know how things are, quite naturally you keep listening back and imagining all those things you should have done... but that's it now, I'm done. Tomorrow. Tomorrow it'll be complete. It has to be. You can be the first to listen. If you like...'

'Yeah, sure Jimi.' The woman laughed, a full, unrestrained laugh. She paid no attention to Gunzabo or the others; she had eyes only for Jimi. 'There I was all these years thinking you'd taken a permanent vow of not-doing-music. Or seeing me. Like a good Buddhist.'

'You know how it is, and how it isn't,' Jimi told her. 'Some cats like to settle down for one thing. They've found their thing, they dig just that. But some cats like to flit, you know? Flit to this, flit to that, maybe a chick comes along and takes you to another place, then you emerge and you start all over. And so forth.'

She sat there next to Jimi, leaning back and grinning. 'Whatever you say, Jimi. At least you know yourself.'

Jimi pulled the wet smock over his head and tossed it on the ground. The woman glanced at his lean body shining in the firelight, then noticed Gunzabo.

'Hey, what do we have here? A newcomer. Well now, that don't happen every year. I'm Janis.'

'Gunzabo.' He shook her hand. 'You haven't changed a bit.'

She grinned at him. 'Oh, I've changed a lot! Thanks though, man. Cool name, I like you already. Sit yourselves down, I'll get you boys a drink each.'

He sat down with Bruce, River and Jim, nodding across the flames at the other robed figures. Janis brought fruit juices. 'No ice. Sorry 'bout that.'

'What about some vodka?' said Bruce.

Janis grinned. 'Well now, that's against the rules, ain't it?'

'You are gonna sing for me tomorrow, aren't you?' Jimi asked her.

'We haven't decided yet.' It was the woman sitting beside Janis who spoke. She smiled distantly, the flames making her robe vividly crimson. Her head was shaved down to grey stubble and she looked like an aged child.

'Well, I don't see why not?' Janis said to her. 'We're performing too, ain't we?'

'Yes we are, Janis,' the woman answered.

'So, we may as well help out Jimi. Else he's going solo. Course, you could do that, Jimi, we know that. You'd steal the show whatever. What're we doing by the way?'

'I'll tell you tomorrow,' said Jimi, absently loosening his soggy

Y-fronts. 'Come over at two. Something like that.' He nodded towards one of the men on the other side of the fire. 'You're coming too, right?'

The man bent forward in affirmation. Though his head was shaven, stubble indicated the early growth of a full head of blond hair. Gunzabo studied him across the flames, trying to decide who the man was, watched him adjust position, and show pale, skinny legs.

Janis laughed. 'You ain't gonna get a lot outta him. He will be coming though, right Ushnisha?' She said this to the woman sitting next to her.

'He hopes to, yes,' the woman said.

'Kurt's taken a vow of silence,' Janis said.

'Silence?' Jimi looked appalled. 'I want him on backing vocals.'

'One day shy of a year, he ain't talked. Didn't you notice, all this time?'

Jimi bit his lip and then said to Kurt, 'We still need you on bass, man. You're gonna have to make *some* kinda noise.'

'Don't get yer feathers all ruffled, Jimi, he wants to do it,' Janis told him. 'And I'll do backing for ya. So long as old Buddha here lets us. Haha!'

'It's not a case of anyone stopping anyone else,' the woman said. She smiled sadly and looked at them all in turn as she spoke, her brown eyes large and luminous. 'We all do as we choose, but must be mindful at all times. We should take Keith's example, over there.' Gunzabo looked across the clearing, saw an old man sitting alone, illuminated by a lamp hanging in the trees.

'What is old Keithy doing there, man?' asked Bruce. 'He gone crazy?'

'He has taken *rukkhamula dhutanga*,' the woman said, solemnly. 'Literally, to remain under a tree.'

'Remain under a tree?' Jimi said, and his eyes went hard.

'Keith's supposed to be playing drums.'

Gunzabo sipped his juice, waving away insects and watching Jimi's increasing frustration. He grimaced at the thin sweetness of the drink. It was going to be a long night. The joints were alright, but they slowed him down too much, made his brain foggy, detracted slightly from the murder investigation. The woman was giving a lecture on the great benefits that abstinence brings. Jimi sat brooding by the fire, saying nothing.

'Still, perhaps Keith may decide to break his *dhutanga*,' she said. 'It is his choice. It would be disappointing though.'

The conversation quietened, and for a while there was only the crackling of the fire and the noise of the jungle, until Jimi jumped up, muttering oaths, and strode across the clearing towards Keith.

The woman smiled sadly and turned to Gunzabo. 'You must be the visitor everyone's been telling us about. Welcome to our humble dwelling. I'm Ushnisha-sitatapatra. Call me Karen, though, if you find it easier.'

He nodded, seeing the resemblance now. He should have recognised her from the eyes. 'What's wrong with your houses?' he asked, indicating the tepee, the miserable fire, their dirty robes.

'Not one thing, man, not one thing,' said Janis, smiling broadly. 'We go back there from time to time. When the forest drives us crazy, becomes like hell.'

Karen smiled fondly at Janis. 'Yes, that's true. It does from time to time. We have only just returned to the forest in the past few days, for example.'

'You were at Full Moon Island, I understand?' said Gunzabo.

'Yes we were.'

'Isn't it a party island?'

'Yeah it sure is,' said Janis. 'When I'm there, anyhow. Haha! Those men, they don't know how to have a good time – or any kinda time – without a *real* woman about.'

'We go to these things sometimes,' explained Karen. She gazed at him and the fire gave her eyes extra zeal. 'It allows us to... I was going to say proselytise, but it's not the correct word at all. More to show the other residents a different way of living. A route to enlightenment, you might say.'

Gunzabo shifted his weight from one buttock to the other. 'When did you hear about John?' he asked. 'About his death?'

'Oh, John,' said Janis. 'Man, I can't believe he's gone. He was one of the good ones.'

A creature hooted, high in the trees, as if in agreement.

'We heard about it on the boat, coming back,' Karen told Gunzabo. 'It is a test for us all.' Her eyes shone. 'An examination of our ability to detach ourselves from the physical world.'

Janis shook her head ruefully. 'Well, I've failed this time, Ushnisha. I can't believe he's gone.' She looked at Gunzabo. 'You're gonna catch the cat who did this, ain't ya?'

'Yes,' he told her.

'You seem very certain,' Karen said. 'You realise that nothing is certain in this world? Other than the pain and suffering we experience, from which even death is no escape.'

Gunzabo looked at Karen with a steady gaze. 'My only concern is my job. To ensure that recent events are not repeated.'

'Everything is repeated, Gunzabo,' said Karen. 'I wish you luck. But for us here, it is all irrelevant. If it is ordained that we must die a violent death, then so be it. We simply return, are born again. It is why we work tirelessly here in the forest: to release ourselves from life and death. I hope the same may be true for everyone who has come here. But it takes a lifetime – many lifetimes – of great effort to reach the ultimate realisation: that this island is no different to anywhere else we have been. That still our lives remain exactly as they always were. And we can only escape life – and death – through great discipline and sacrifice.'

He looked over Karen's shoulder as she spoke, irritated by

the lecture, and saw Jimi and Keith chatting at the edge of the clearing. They were taking swigs from what appeared to be a hip flask. It looked quite good over there, under the tree. He thought he might join them.

Karen was still speaking in her soft voice. 'Take Mrs Bradley for example: she and her husband arrived some years ago, yet still she cannot let go of her previous life. John – before he passed on – knew this all too well. He was a Buddhist, though he didn't necessarily identify himself as such. Many times he told Joan to leave her son be. But she could not. She deceives the boy, causes him great pain and does not even realise.'

'What did John say to her?' asked Gunzabo, looking directly at Karen now. He scratched his missing arm, ignoring a beetle which rested on his head.

'John knew the danger of material attachments. People are attachments, of course. The ones we love chain us to this world. That is what he said. He was going to say this to her son also. He was determined to end the deception. Perhaps he did end it. He said he'd found a way to make contact.'

Gunzabo stopped rubbing his arm. The computer. He still had the scrap of paper in his pocket. But that did not explain who Ian Fields was.

'Still, enough of this.' Karen said, lifting her sad, shining eyes from where he had been pressing his arm. She smiled tenderly at him, then at the others. 'It is late and I will go to bed now. Goodnight everyone.'

Karen rose and went into the tepee. Gunzabo watched her silhouette move across the canvas as she got undressed. She was still beautiful, and he was sad when the light went out.

19

Bruce let out a whoop.

'Party time, people. You got your freedom back. Hey, Jimi.'

Jimi shook Keith's hand and came pacing sullenly back to the fire, lean and wiry in his Y-fronts. He grabbed a huge bag of marijuana, fumbled with the plastic lip, scattering buds across the ground at his feet. Swearing fiercely, he hammered the buds with the flat of his hand until they were crushed into the soil.

'What's eating you up, man?' Bruce said. 'Take it easy, try this.'

He handed Jimi an even larger bag.

'So where's the booze?' Bruce asked, turning to Janis.

'Booze, now ya'll talking,' said Janis. 'That'll snap you out of it, Jimi. Me too. I never can take more than a couple o' days of this ascetic nonsense. If Karen weren't so goddam cute, I'd be holed up in one of them villas permanently.'

Jimi gave a sharp whistle. Four villagers appeared, laden with crates, backpacks, wicker baskets. Everyone made noises of appreciation. Bruce skipped about, opening the containers, handing out bottles and glasses. Janis was now sitting next to Gunzabo, an arm across his shoulder, the other arm free to periodically remove Jim's hand from her upper thigh.

'What do you boys say to a nice tumbler of Southern Comfort?' she asked.

'Why not,' said Gunzabo.

Jim grinned as he took his glass. 'If you're falling off the wagon tonight, my little Sea-Oyster, then so am I.'

'Hey, I was only ever on it for the ride.'

'Be careful, I may take you for another one.'

Jim's hand was straying up her leg again.

'Jimbo, you behave now.'

'Janis here,' Jim said, smiling to Gunzabo, 'is the reason I came to this place. Did you know that?'

'You came for love?' said Gunzabo.

'Oh no. That was Jimi. We had our moments, though, didn't we, Oyster? Purely physical.' Deep inside his beard, Jim's tongue moved sensuously across his lips. 'No, the reason I came here was *preservation*. When Janis here died, it hit us all. Bummed us out, woke us up, like a... bathtub of cold water.'

'I have that effect on folks,' Janis said, beaming at Jim.

'It made me think, man,' Jim said. 'Made me think about the structure of reality and how it could be restructured along entirely new lines. Even now, a second, replacement structure would be greatly beneficial. My preference would be—'

Gunzabo grunted occasionally during Jim's discourse, but his attention was on Janis. She was looking at Jimi, who kept glancing back, and each time his eyes softened before returning to a sullen glower.

'Why did you come here?' Gunzabo asked Janis.

The fire was sparkling in her eyes as she turned to look at him, hair falling white down her back. She held her tumbler up to the flames.

'I guess I was tired of all the conflict,' she said. 'That and being alone. Sometimes it's nice just to belong, you know?' She shook her head and grinned. 'Me and Jimi, we thought we could make it. We knew we had no chance on the outside. Too much temptation, too many ladies. See, when I walk in a room, well I ain't the prettiest one in it. I always knew that. Jimi did too. But what I know now, what I never used to, is that everyone in that room, well they wanted *me*.' She looked straight into Gunzabo's eyes and grinned. 'Some girls they don't like that, I see that now,

157

I see why they did what they did and said what they said, my whole life.' She shook her head, downed her drink. 'Anyways, like I said, we thought we had a chance. So we gave it all up. Rolled the dice for love.'

'It didn't work out?'

She looked across at Jimi again, who was on the other side of the fire, opening a case of vodka.

'Oh it worked, hell it worked. For a time, anyways, specially before we came here. Then all we did was work, try and try like little trying things, hurting each other and hating and loving all on this tiny island, this silly little place, Lord knows where… It's like a goddam cemetery! Make a good song, wouldn't it? The Tropical Cemetery Blues.' She turned her eyes to Gunzabo; she looked beautiful. 'Well, we broke up and made up and destroyed and recreated so many times I couldn't tell ya how many. Poor Jimi, I remember him saying to me, "Jan, I'm getting like my daddy and I don't want that." So I told him we should break up for good. And we did.'

Gunzabo studied her as she smiled a crooked smile and looked at her empty glass. 'Did you make a mistake coming here?' he asked her.

She thought for a moment. 'If I did, then we all did,' she said finally. 'What do the others say?'

'I haven't asked them.'

'Well, don't ask them, man. I don't see everything the same as Karen, but she's right about one thing: if you ain't happy, you ain't happy anywhere.'

Bruce came over and filled their glasses with whisky.

'Oh, Bruce, thank the Lord!' said Janis. 'You've come to save us from introspection and regret! Leave that bottle here, will you? Leave yourself here too.'

Bruce grinned and they all clinked glasses and downed their drinks. Janis rocked back, laughing, a hand on Gunzabo's knee, the other on Jim's. 'Oh my,' she said. 'Oh me, oh my! We're gonna have a ball, ain't we? And we've got the talent show tomorrow. Are you looking forward to that, Gunzabo?'

He curled out his bottom lip. 'Not particularly.

'It's like that, is it, honey? Well I ain't much looking forward to my goddam Buddhist dance with Karen and the boys, truth be told. Jimi'll make fools of us all. Least I'm in the band too, though.'

Jim rubbed his chin and said, 'You know, Sea-Oyster, I don't think I can agree with you about that. This show, it's important for everyone, it's something we all look back on, and, I guess in some way we look forward to looking back on. It's really a quite valuable form of artistic expression, a, uh, manifestation of the living spirit of the island I guess you could call it.'

'Yeah,' said Bruce. 'You could also call it a whole restaurant of baloney.'

'Uh, yeah, you could call it that too. We can call it anything we like, actually. I mean, I always felt that language favours our forefathers so much more than the present generation. Why accept the given name of anything? That tree over there, for example. What is its given name?'

'I dunno, man,' said Bruce.

'Me neither,' said Jim. 'But that's the point. When men first came to a new land, and found a tree, they didn't know its name either. It didn't *have* a name. So why should it be any different for us? I mean, why should we feel foolish about such things? I think, sometime in the near future, people will come together and say, "We reject the past, we reject what our fathers told us to say, told us to think. We are the now." And they'll call this tree something else.'

'Oh, you mean the coconut tree over there?' said Bruce.

'Yeah, that one there, man.'

'But it's a coconut tree. Why you saying this, man? I thought you meant the one next to it. With all the crazy fruit.'

'It doesn't matter which one I was talking about. And it doesn't matter what it's called. That's what I'm saying.'

Bruce frowned, then laughed and pointed his finger at Jim in a sharp, quick movement. 'Hey, you make me laugh, man. You really oughta get out that shack of yours more often. Stop being a bum. Have some self-respect.'

Someone passed Bruce an enormous joint and the subject was dropped. Everyone drank and talked and Kurt crept into the tent and emerged with guitars. Janis and Jimi fetched wood, threw it on the fire, and the party became raucous and everyone more animated. Even Jimi smiled and joined in. Kurt started singing sea shanties, his vow of silence put aside for the night; Keith came over from his place under the tree. A second contingent of villagers arrived with great trays of food: salads and breads, blood-red steaks, racks of lamb, joints of pork, fresh fish in iced containers. The villagers offered to stay and cook, but Janis and Jimi waved them off and cooked it all themselves. Gunzabo watched Janis entertain them all, singing the blues and telling jokes and laughing loudly. She was shouting when she spoke, shouting above the guitars and the singing and laughing and the hiss of the fire and the jungle, while Jimi looked at her as if he was a young man again.

Later on, with the party at its peak and the island suspended somewhere else, Gunzabo was lying on his back, eyes closed, feeling the electrical charge of the party and the alcohol and narcotics coursing through his nervous system. He listened to the shouting and laughter, smelt the smoke and the cooking meat, felt himself leaving his body and witnessing it all – witnessing himself, even – and hearing the comments about whether he was OK, that he was OK, and he sure could take his drink; and Janis saying, 'He's havin' such a ball, I'll bet he wishes there's a murder here every month! Oh, I forgot, there is!'

He opened his eyes and suddenly the sound went and he was alone. He looked up into the black purity, blacker even than the surrounding darkness of ten thousand trees. Far away on the horizon, at the extremes of his consciousness, someone was having an argument. The distant shouts dissolved into the darkness of the world above, and as he stared into curving black, he saw it was like the impenetrable ceiling of an almighty cavern, and he wondered what was beyond that black screen, wondered where the stars were, where the sky was. He hadn't seen the sun since his arrival. Was he dead? Perhaps they all were dead.

He rolled onto his side and vomited, violently, the entire contents of his digestive system. It took a while, but when he had finished he felt wonderfully refreshed and clear-headed. He rolled onto the other side and lay there with his cheek against the ground. The earth smelt damp and clean; the ferns were soft and warm, like clothes from a washing machine.

'Hey, Gunzabo, you alright mate? Something didn't agree with you, eh?'

'Everything.'

He sat up, cleaned his face with his sleeve. Marc handed him a drink. Marc's robes were covered in sick and he pulled them over his head and sat naked on the ground with a guitar in his lap.

'Sorry about that,' Gunzabo said.

Marc tossed the robes in the fire. 'Don't worry about it. I needed some new ones anyway.'

Gunzabo heard a familiar laugh: Ken, on the other side of the fire, joking with Kurt and Keith.

'Look, it's Jim the Baptist.' Ken pointed at Jim, who was standing in his loincloth studying a fern leaf.

Keith tossed a half-eaten leg of lamb over his shoulder. 'It'll be *my* head on a plate if I'm not under that tree when Karen wakes up.'

'Why's everyone so damned scared of her?' said Ken. 'I don't get it. Be a man, for Christ's sake.'

Jimi had moved across from the barbecue. He stood with a bottle of whisky in his hand, still dressed in his underwear. He didn't take his eyes off Ken.

'She's just got this way,' Keith was saying. 'You end up doing stuff just to keep her off your back. Why do you think I chose that tree all the way over there?'

'You could always go back to your house,' Ken said.

'I spose. Boring though, innit?'

'Well if you're bored, I can always help you out. If I was you, Keith, what I'd do right, is—'

'Quit hassling him, will you?'

Jimi was staring at Ken, his eyes hard and fierce and bright. 'He can do what he wants.'

'That's exactly what I was saying to him.'

'No it's not.' Jimi took a step towards Ken. 'It's not *exactly* what you were saying. You don't ever say anything *exactly*. You've always got your agenda, your own scene. You go on about some-such-thing and some-such-person, and all you're ever doing it for is yourself. For your agenda.'

Ken assumed a look of innocent surprise. 'Well, I'm sorry if you think that, mate.'

'I ain't your mate.' Jimi's tensed arms gleamed in the firelight.

'Whatever,' Ken said. 'You do seem to like my agenda though, now and again, when it suits you. Anyhow, I'm not hassling anyone. Not Keith and not you. You're all of you free to do exactly as you please.'

'We are, are we?'

'Yeah.'

'Alright then!' Jimi said, thrusting forward and flinging the whisky bottle at Ken. It hit him on the head, making a loud clonk, then a thud as it landed on Ken's foot.

'Christ! What did you do that for?' Ken was holding his head with both hands, looking back with shocked pain, almost betrayal. 'You could have killed me!'

Jimi shrugged. 'Go fix yourself up, doc.'

Keith moved across and held Jimi's arm. 'Come on, Jimi. That was out of order, man.'

Jimi was still staring at Ken, violence in his eyes. 'It was the least I could have done.' He jerked away from Keith, who was trying to grab him again and received an angry shove in retaliation, fell backwards, tripped over Gunzabo's leg and landed in the fire. 'Aargh,' Keith shouted. 'I'm burnt, man! What the hell are you doing?' He lowered his head and charged. Jimi stepped aside like a matador, and Keith staggered around, swearing and shouting threats, until his anger turned to panic, as he looked down at the flames rising up his crimson robes and everyone was pouring their drinks over him and taking sides, and amid all the shouting and aggression Janis had picked up a guitar and was singing the blues at the top of her voice, howling above the pandemonium.

'What in hell is going on?'

Karen had come out of the tepee. For an instant everyone stopped. Karen looked reproachfully at Jimi. Janis had stopped singing. Nobody spoke.

Jimi went berserk.

He smashed anything that came to hand, upending crates and kicking bottles and plates and musical instruments into the fire, even moving through the fire to get more stuff to break. Shouting and grunting from the exertion of his violence, he destroyed everything, hurled objects into the darkness, smashed and stamped in a helpless primal rage. No one could stop him; everyone seemed to realise this and did not try; and all the while Janis sang the blues and Karen watched sadly and everyone else stood in awe at the carnage he wreaked.

Gradually, his rage lessened. Janis stopped singing and took Jimi in her arms. He was crying now, sobbing into her shoulder as she led him off, saying, 'There, there, baby.' Pushing aside the Tibetan flag, they disappeared into the jungle.

'Wow!' Bruce said. He was looking at the destruction around him, arms folded, nodding approvingly, as if he himself had caused it. 'Now, I have known Jimi a long time, man. And I have never, not ever seen him like that before! He's like a locust, man,' Bruce gestured sharply with his fists and chin, 'destroying everything in his path. One dangerous dude. And he never even had a single lesson from me!'

Gunzabo watched everyone standing there, their faces pale and sober; Karen was moving between them, tidying away the mess; Ken had an ice bucket to his forehead and was muttering to himself, 'I don't know. You just try and help, just try and do your best. Look what happens.'

As Gunzabo stood there in the clearing, watching Karen pick up empty beer cans and put them into a plastic bag, he was suddenly reminded of the night before: following Tommy and the mysterious woman into the clearing on the other side of the island; finding the concrete hut; searching the hut for clues. He watched Karen reach for another crumpled beer can, tie up the plastic bag, toss it next to a pile of empty food containers. His mind went back again to the previous night. How many empty beer cans had there been in the hut?

He realised what his unconscious mind had been working on. He made the connection: Lastri, in her parents' hut earlier on. She had come in with eight cans of beer, claimed they were for him. He hadn't questioned it at the time. But they weren't for him. He remembered the surprised look on her face, the way she had smoothly recovered. Was Lastri the woman in the jungle last night? Had she been on her way to visit the Déjà Vu Killer, bring him supplies? Or perhaps she was clearing up after him.

'Hey.'

Jim had come over; Bruce was next to him.

'I think it might be, uh, prudent to go back now. Besides, I miss my beach.'

'Let's go, baby,' Bruce said.

They left without saying goodbye. Gunzabo walked behind the two men, thinking about the case. Ken was plotting something, this was certain. He wondered if Christian knew. Jimi certainly seemed to. He pursed his lips in the dark and stroked Didi, who was still asleep in his tracksuit top. Jim was walking ahead in silence, waving his torch at the trees, while Bruce chatted happily, catching creatures in mid-flight and releasing them back into the jungle.

20

'So, you haven't answered the burning question.'

'What burning question?'

Gunzabo was sitting in Christian's office. He had come over to The Circles after breakfast in his room and he now looked across the desk, his revulsion a distant second to the pain of his hangover.

'Oh, I'm sorry, I thought you knew? Everyone's talking about it.'

'Talking about what?'

Christian smiled, both legs quivering under his desk. He could barely contain his glee. 'Why, about your performance this evening, of course. What will you be treating us to?'

'You mean the talent show?'

'*Ja.*'

Gunzabo stared back irritably. 'I haven't decided yet. Some traditional dancing, probably.'

'Wonderful. Did you have anything particular in mind?'

'No.'

'OK, let it be a surprise. I like surprises.'

Gunzabo stirred another sugar into his espresso. The Komodo dragon glared at him as it guarded its golden apples. 'I have a question for you,' he said.

'A burning one?'

He didn't answer.

Christian flashed his smile. 'Go ahead. Ask.'

Gunzabo took a sip of espresso. 'Did you authorise the systematic poisoning of the villagers?'

'You've lost me, Mario.' Christian's legs stopped quivering.

'It's certain that someone is contaminating the villagers' water supply.'

'Why, that's awful.' Christian smiled again.

'Sodium fluoride,' continued Gunzabo. 'It affects health, mental state, causes listlessness, sterility. Very useful if you have a tribe of fifty villagers who might overrun your island, demanding rights, rather than doing topiary and pouring drinks all day.'

'I'm sorry, what does this have to do with your murder case? You know, the one I'm paying you a million dollars for?'

'John was trying to put an end to it. He encouraged the villagers to dig a new well, one closer to the village. One that would be much riskier for Tommy to conduct his chemistry experiments on.'

'How very mysterious,' Christian said, eyes wrinkling behind his rimless spectacles. 'If you have no more questions I have a very busy day ahead.'

'I do have another question.'

'You seem all questions and no answers. Is that how they solve murders in Athens?'

Gunzabo looked steadily back at Christian. The disgust was catching up with his hangover. 'It's how we caught the Geryon Triplets. I questioned each one of them, every day for three weeks, until they confessed.'

He pushed his coffee cup to the side of the desk. It left a black trail on the veneer. 'How did the Bradleys come to live on the island?' he asked

'We found them. A little like the villagers.'

'How?'

'We have our ways.' Christian grinned, nothing in his eyes. 'I like to read the minor news stories in the US and the UK. There's always opportunities. Like Joan and Thomas.'

'Joan Bradley appears to be very attached to her son. It seems strange for her to leave him.'

Christian adjusted his glasses. 'We've all left something behind, Mario. Haven't you?'

Gunzabo didn't answer. He sat, motionless, gazing at Christian while prickling sensations coursed up his neck. 'What did the Bradleys do before they came here?' he asked eventually.

'Much the same as they do here. Joan was receptionist in the local school. Thomas was caretaker. It's how they met, I believe.'

'What was the story, that you read in the newspaper?'

Christian flashed a smile and showed his teeth. He looked back at Gunzabo, hands on the desk, waiting for the next question.

'What was the story?' Gunzabo repeated.

Christian's eyes gleamed in the half-light. His legs were vibrating manically but his hands were as still as the gloomy host of dead animals around him.

'That smell,' Gunzabo said. 'Are you making a new exhibit?'

'I am, *ja*. Oh, you must see him.'

He watched Christian spin his chair round and open a large crate on the floor, saw a tusked boar, on its side, dead, the matted hair on its neck dark with blood. Short, thick whiskers white against its brown face. It looked almost human.

'I've still got some cleaning up to do. Isn't he wonderful? I'm going to call him John. I think it's a fitting tribute, don't you?'

Gunzabo didn't answer. He sat gripping the edge of the desk, ignoring the need to rub his arm.

'This is all very pleasant, Mario. But I really must be getting on. There's so much to organise, so much to do!'

'The talent show,' Gunzabo said.

'Oh, that's taken care of.' Christian's eyes twinkled, and he doubled the intensity of his shaking legs.

'What is it, Christian? I can see you're desperate to tell me.'

Gunzabo saw him pause, narrow his eyes briefly, as if he

was calculating how much to reveal. He looked up and gave an unpleasant grin.

'I can't tell you any details right now. But we have a wonderful new client coming to join us in a matter of days.'

'Someone I know?'

'You'll have to wait and see.'

'Of course, you like surprises, don't you Christian?'

'*Ja*.' Christian breathed the word gently.

'Have you told him about the serial killer?'

'He won't mind.'

'Won't mind being murdered?'

Christian smiled. 'Funnily enough, that is how he has decided to leave the outside world. He has a taste for the dramatic, shall we say.'

'A bit like John, then.'

Christian looked fondly at the dead boar. '*Ja*,' he said.

Gunzabo got out of his chair, stepped over the python and reached for the door.

'Oh, and Mario.'

He turned round and looked at Christian.

'Have you thought about your life on the island? How you might contribute to the wellbeing of our residents? You must stay, once we're done with all this.'

'No.'

He opened the door and left. It was time for his meeting with Elvis.

21

'What *are* we doing in the show by the way?'

The day was white and close. Gunzabo was walking north with Didi perched on his shoulder.

'I haven't decided.'

'Oh, I don't suppose it matters. You'll get drunk, make a complete arse of yourself. Remind me to be asleep at the time.'

He ignored the prim look she was giving him, too tired and ill to argue. He was nearing the beach shack, where he could see Jim's feet in the doorway, toes pointing in the air from under a grubby sheet. Suddenly the feet began kicking out, jerking uncontrollably as if he was being strangled. Gunzabo sprinted across the sand. He knelt down, peered in. Jim was lying on his back, alone, his hands moving rhythmically under the covers. Grunts now turned into ecstatic moans.

'Groupies,' said Didi. 'Never one around when you want one, is there?'

Jim's movements were increasing in tempo.

'He's not letting it stop him,' Gunzabo said.

He continued north, and as the sand widened he saw the white domes and columns of Elvis's villa showing above the trees, and then Elvis, dressed in a black cotton gown, shadow boxing on the lawn. Gunzabo walked up the central path, gravel crunching under his trainers, expanses of lawn either side, gazing at the arches and pillars and domes of the main building, at the marble columns stretching skywards from the terrace, at the statues of ancient kings and gods and generals; and then he looked at Elvis, who grinned, directed a few mock karate chops at him and began a series of stretches.

'Hey, Maz. Come to bring me in, have you? Lay those cuffs on me, man, I might even like it.' He jumped back up athletically. 'Come on over, you're right on time.'

He followed Elvis onto the terrace, where they sat at a marble table with veins like blue cheese. Elvis was sitting opposite him, face flushed from exertion and glowing with satisfaction, white sideburns damp with sweat.

'You're a man of strict habits.'

'Yes sir, I am,' Elvis said. 'You just gotta choose which habits to cultivate: the good ones, or the bad ones.'

'I always choose the bad ones.'

'Man, well, that's the thing. Most folks here, they're in the same boat as you. Me too, for an awful long time. But I came to realise something: your past comes with you. Everywhere. There ain't no escaping it. All you can do is try and come to some friendly terms, wish it a good morning each day.'

Elvis grinned and sat easily in his wicker chair. He put on a pair of sunglasses with enormous dark lenses. 'Now, can I get you a drink, Maz? And be careful what you order, these premises are strictly tee-total. 'Cept for extra special occasions – and this ain't one of 'em.'

Gunzabo lifted his shoulders apathetically. 'Whatever you're having.' If there was no booze it hardly mattered.

'A man after my own heart. I like you already.'

Elvis called over a maid, who was lingering discreetly in the background. 'Hey, honey, would do me a favour? Fetch me my protein shake, a glass of ice water with lemon, my morning vitamins. And I'll have my spirulina now. Same again for Maz, here. Oh and a bowl of fresh goji berries, I'm as hungry as a hog.'

The maid inclined her head and hurried off. Gunzabo sat quietly in his wicker chair, rubbing the stubble on his cheek, looking at Elvis's dark lenses and the deep furrows on his tanned forehead.

'So, I guess you got a barrelful of questions to fire at me?'

Gunzabo glanced across the terrace and at the magnificent entrance to the house. There was a statue of Hadrian on one side, Julius Caesar on the other. He nodded absently, wiped some sweat off the back of his neck, and started picking at a scab on his chin.

'You'll scar yourself, just leave it.'

Gunzabo looked up, shrugged, then examined a piece of crusted skin which was caught in his fingernail; he flicked it on the patio. The lines in Elvis's forehead deepened.

'Well, shoot away man. What is it you want to ask?'

The drinks arrived. Gunzabo took a sip of his protein shake, winced and put it down. He ate a goji berry. He chewed on a vitamin capsule; it was the first time he had ever tried one and it tasted dreadful in his already parched mouth. He ought to get a hip flask for emergencies like this, ease the hangover. Elvis was watching him, lips now curling around his teeth, the lines in his forehead still deep.

'You better get started, I got colonic irrigation booked at twelve.'

Gunzabo looked up.

'How long have you been seeing Diana?'

'What?'

Elvis looked back from behind the sunglasses, his expression frozen.

'You've been in therapy for quite some years, I believe.'

'Oh. Yeah. Eight years I think now.'

'You must have formed close bonds, I imagine, in that time.'

'Naturally. It would be inhuman not to.'

'She must form strong bonds with her other patients.'

Elvis pursed his lips, still shiny with sweat from his exercises.

He put down his water. The glass rang against the table. 'I guess.'

'I believe she was seeing John even longer than you.'

Elvis did not immediately answer. He was sitting rigidly in his chair. His nostrils were slightly flared. 'She stopped,' he said.

Gunzabo ate a goji berry. 'Yes, that's right. She did tell me this.' He took a miniscule sip of the protein shake, shuddered, then relaxed back in his chair. He looked up at the marble columns climbing like fossilised trees into the empty white sky. 'Nice place,' he said.

There was no answer.

'Different to the others,' he added.

Elvis's lips hardly moved. 'This isn't a trailer park, boy.'

Gunzabo considered this and picked out another goji berry, chewed it carelessly as he looked across the gardens and fountains and outbuildings surrounding the main villa.

He turned back to Elvis. 'Do you miss him?'

'John?'

'Yes.'

'He was my best friend,' Elvis said slowly. The skin around his nostrils had gone white.

'Did you see the killer?'

'I saw him running into the trees.'

'Describe him for me.'

Elvis flicked his head up to consider this and Gunzabo saw the clean shaven underside of Elvis's chin, the aged looseness in his neck disappearing briefly.

'Carrying a rifle. Dressed in black. Black hood. That's all.'

'That's all?'

'That's all.' Elvis was looking back at him again. 'I was with my friend. Trying to save his life.'

'You were the last person to see him alive.'

'Yes, sir.'

'And the first to see him dead?'

'I don't like the way you're saying that.'

'Who was next to see him?'

Elvis's lip curled. 'What do you mean?'

'I understand others came. To the murder scene.'

'Yeah.'

'Who?'

'Ken. Some of the staff.'

'Do you remember who?'

'Lastri, I think. Some of the other ladies.'

Gunzabo took a vitamin from the bowl. He chewed the capsule and did not speak for a while, ignoring Elvis, who he knew was glaring at him.

Elvis broke the silence. 'You don't know anything, do you?' he said, contempt in his voice.

Gunzabo did not answer.

'It'll stay like that if you don't open your eyes.'

'What would I see if I did?'

Elvis eased back in his chair, crossed his legs the other way. His hand was following the clean shaven line of his jaw to where the white sideburns began. 'I know who did it.'

'Who did it?'

'And I can tell you, you're wasting your time. You'll never find them.'

'Them?'

'Them.'

Gunzabo waited for Elvis to continue, watched him lean forward, take off his sunglasses, put them on the table and look directly at him, lashes as black and full as they were forty years ago, despite the shock of white hair.

'Why do you think John came here in the first place?' Elvis asked him softly.

He did not answer.

Elvis leaned close. 'He was terrified, he had no choice but to come here.'

'Why?'

'To escape assassination. Same as Jack and Bobby. They let him come here. Let them all come. They know about this place, of course they do. They always have. They tolerate it, or at least they did up until now.'

'Who?'

'Three letters: C-I-A.'

Gunzabo considered this, then said, 'Why kill John now? Why wait so many years?'

Elvis wore a look of satisfaction. 'Now that I do not know.' He leaned back again.

'And why kill Brian?'

'Ditto.'

Gunzabo ate another goji berry. 'I like these,' he said.

Elvis ignored him. 'John was plotting something. He wouldn't tell me what, but he was up to something. It made them act. Disturbed the equilibrium.'

'What makes you believe this?'

Elvis was looking away, across the garden. 'He'd say, "Elvis, you don't want to know, man." He always said that. It was better I didn't know, he said. I was too happy, he didn't want to spoil it for me. That's all he'd say: I was too happy.'

Elvis span his glass of water on the table, lifting it up slightly as he span it. He was looking sad now, the tightness and contempt gone, his eyes dark and tired.

'It must be the therapy,' Gunzabo said.

'What?'

'Making you happy. Or is it love?'

Elvis fixed his eyes on him. The hostility was showing again, naked now his glasses were off. 'I don't know what you mean.'

'I mean you and Diana.'

'What about me and Diana?'

'Your relationship.'

'I suggest you watch your words closely.' Elvis spoke in a quiet, measured voice. 'What is it you think you know?'

'That you are lovers. That she stays here with you. Perhaps you stay with her.'

'Who told you this?'

Gunzabo shrugged. 'I am a detective. It is my job to know such things.'

'Well, know this, mister,' Elvis said, eyes flashing. 'This has nothing to do with anything. You understand? You leave her out of it.'

'I'm trying to find your friend's killer.'

Elvis was staring unwaveringly at him. 'I already told you what happened. The CIA killed Brian. Then John. Someone else will be next.'

Gunzabo gazed back. 'That is what I'm trying to stop.'

'You leave Diana outta this.'

'Everything we've discussed is in confidence.'

'You ain't no priest.'

'No, I'm not.'

Elvis put his sunglasses back on. 'You can go now,' he said.

'I have one more question.'

Elvis looked away. 'Get outta here,' he said derisively.

Gunzabo remained in his seat. 'Who do you think is going to die next?'

He watched Elvis turn his head round and show the fronts of his huge sunglasses.

'Get out!' he snarled.

22

'Maybe he's right.'

Gunzabo did not answer. His mouth was parched and his tongue hurt from too much talking.

'Maybe there is someone else here on the island,' Didi persisted, 'staying in that hut in the jungle?'

'I don't like conspiracy theories,' Gunzabo muttered back. He looked at the sea lapping at his feet. Maybe it would clear his head. Didi poked him in the cheek. He scowled at her and grudgingly continued, 'If the CIA always knew about Dead Star Island, why act now? Why not ten years ago? Twenty years ago?'

'Maybe it's not them. Maybe it's another organisation conspiring against the island.'

Gunzabo passed Diana's house, which was as empty as the horizon far out to sea. He was past caring.

'What now then?' Didi said.

'Lunch,' he told her. 'Then siesta.'

'Let's see what Jim's up to.'

'You really want to know?'

He stopped at the beach shack. No one was there. The bedding lay in a damp, crumpled pile; video cassettes were strewn across the floor. He continued south, past another house.

'Gunzabo,' Didi hissed.

He stopped, followed her gaze back towards the house. 'What?'

'Somebody's inside.'

He wandered over to the gate, read the sign:

JIM

He stepped into the garden, heading towards the open front door, where Jim, fully naked, was pacing in and out of sight, stopping occasionally to speak with emphatic gestures.

'Afternoon,' Gunzabo said, stepping inside.

'How're you doing?' Jim said, with a nod.

Jim was in his living room; his shoulders and the top of his large, round belly were covered in cracked, sunburnt blisters, and he looked as vacant and hungover as Gunzabo felt.

'You've met, right?' Jim said, indicating the man lounging in an armchair next to a gigantic flat screen television.

'Last night,' Gunzabo said, shaking Kurt's hand. 'So are you still speaking? Is the vow over permanently?'

Kurt was dressed in the same scarlet robes as the night before. Nodding, he leaned back in the armchair with a cigarette.

'Hey, uh,' Jim said. 'Did you stop by earlier?'

'Yes.'

'I was slightly, uh, indisposed. Having a little jazz breakfast.'

'I arrived in the middle of a difficult solo,' Gunzabo said.

'Huh-huh. I abstain mostly – spiritual reasons. But sometimes it's a matter of releasing the juices. You know, when the pressure gets intolerable.'

Gunzabo looked at the television: it showed a still image of Elvis and John running on the beach. 'What's this?' he asked, moving closer to the screen. Elvis was caught in mid stride in his neon spandex shorts and vest; John was bare-chested in tiny running shorts, beard sweaty and grey as he grinned into the room.

'It's my film,' Jim said.

'For the show?'

'For many things. The show is just the opportunity. Primarily it's for John. A celebration of his soul, I guess. I'm calling it *Death After Life*.'

Gunzabo took another step towards the screen. He scratched his head vigorously. His hangover was irrelevant now, his weariness gone. 'Can I see it?' he asked.

'There's still a lot of editing to do.'

'Whatever you have, I'll see it now.'

'Alright man.'

Jim reached for the remote control. The film sprang to life. Gunzabo stepped back now to absorb the full picture, as John finished his smile and made a face, and the camera wheeled a hundred and eighty degrees, lingering on the two men as they receded into the distance. There was a rough cut in the footage, then another shot of them running towards the camera, Elvis in a different shade of neon shorts, John barechested, making another face at the camera as they passed by. The footage continued. There was the occasional shot of Ken, then Tommy, stalking along the beach, steadfastly ignoring the camera; a few seconds of Brian's funeral at Palm Grove, before Elvis placed a hand over the lens; scenes where Jim turned the camera back on himself and mumbled observations and poetry; several instances of the villagers trooping along the sand to work each morning. But mostly there was the daily routine of the two men running towards the camera.

'How long were you making this for?' Gunzabo said.

'A few months, I guess.'

'What else do you have on film?'

'Mostly the view from the hut. It started off as a, uh, an account if you will, of life on the beach here. I wanted to capture the monotony, the beautiful dreariness of it. But I still need to edit. It needs to become more dreary if anything. I don't believe I've fully captured that yet.'

179

Gunzabo asked Jim to rewind a few weeks. It hardly varied at all; Elvis and John passed the shack without fail every morning dressed in their scant, tight running gear.

'The day of the shooting, did you film anything?' Gunzabo asked.

'I film every single day.'

He stared at Jim in wonder and rubbed his cheek repeatedly with his palm. Keeping his voice calm, he said, 'I want to see this immediately.'

'Yeah, sure. I'm gonna have to find it though. There's months of this stuff, man. I've kinda left it a little late to get this all done for tonight.'

Gunzabo waited as Jim rummaged through dozens of cassettes scattered on the floor, placing a cassette in the player, fast forwarding through, trying another, rewinding it to the beginning, speeding forwards, then repeating the process with the next cassette.

Gunzabo turned to Kurt. 'Are you taking part tonight?'

Kurt leaned forward to stub out his cigarette. He did not seem particularly interested in either the film or the show. 'I guess.'

'What are you doing?'

'I've got a few paintings, gonna put them on display later on.'

'What did you paint?' Gunzabo sat down on a sofa, accepting a cigarette and a beer which he drank while he listened to Kurt.

'The forest. That's the theme. I thought it would be kinda fun to reimagine it, you know, try out some different angles. I got one here if you wanna see. Finished it this morning. I came to show Jim.'

Kurt motioned with an unlit cigarette to a square canvas propped up against the glass doors, perhaps three metres on each side, painted in black and greys and white; and whilst the jungle was clearly depicted, somehow it evoked the urban sprawl of a huge unspecified city: Gunzabo could see cars within the patterned leaves of the trees, highways in their branches, tower blocks in their trunks. Faces peeked out of the darkness: some laughing, some contemplative, others with unfathomable expressions; but all somehow pained, all in some way hiding there in the tree-city-scape of the picture.

'It's very powerful,' Gunzabo said.

'It's fantastic, man, is what it is,' said Jim, in his steady Californian monotone. 'The vibrations this piece emits, it's like nothing I've ever seen before. I myself cannot wait for Christian to see it. Huh-huh. Maybe he'll have a little difficulty sleeping afterwards.'

Kurt smiled proudly and looked at Jim with his clear bright eyes.

'You think he sleeps well usually?' said Gunzabo.

'Huh-huh. Probably not, probably not. That's a valid point.'

Gunzabo addressed Kurt. 'When John was murdered, you were on Full Moon Island I believe?'

'Yeah, that's right.'

'With the others who live on East Beach?'

'Yeah.'

Kurt went to brush a strand of hair over his ear, smiled shyly when he remembered his head was shaved.

'Ken usually joins you, doesn't he? For the parties on the island.'

'Usually,' Kurt said. 'But it wasn't so much of a party. Ken promised all kinds of things. It was kinda boring in the end. We all wanted to come back, even before we heard what happened.'

'What kind of things did Ken promise?'

'Hell, you know,' Kurt said, smiling. 'Girls, beer, narcotics. Everything a good Buddhist needs for the weekend.'

'Did Ken give any reason why this didn't happen?'

'No, not really. Maybe just because he didn't come along. Anyhow, it seemed kinda off to mention it, what with John and all.'

Gunzabo turned to Jim. 'You told me yesterday about when John was shot, and about Brian's death. Not about the footage though.' He gave Jim a scathing look. 'What else can you tell me about the time leading up to the shooting?'

Jim looked up from his editing. 'Well, I was in my hut. It was Diwali actually, the day before, and I conducted a puja for much of it. I made some firecrackers, let them off on the beach, chased the dragon a little, on my own. I, uh, masturbated for several hours in the evening, cleaned up a little after. I got an early night. And, I remember now, that night I had this amazingly vivid dream. I can feel it now, man, you know the feeling that you've been taken somewhere? Usually when you wake it goes almost immediately, but it's still here now. Yeah.'

'What happened?'

'What happened was I went to see Jimi. He was asleep in bed, tucked in under the sheets. And he wakes up and looks at me, and he looks strange, there's something odd about him, but I don't know what it is, and he's grumpy, real grumpy – angry in fact – and I think to myself it's because he's woken up. I go to the window and open the shutters and when I turn round he's getting out of bed and I don't notice at first while my eyes adjust. But then I notice what it is, what it is that's odd. There's nothing under his chin. I can see the wall underneath. He's just a head. No body, nothing. And in my dream I know it's not right. You know how sometimes the craziest things seem normal? It wasn't like that.

'So I ask what happened to his body. I thought maybe someone took it without his permission. But he says he got rid of it and lots of people are getting this done, like an anti-materialist stance, except he had no stance as such. He'd just had enough of it all. He says it always pissed him off anyway, his body, it's only going to go wrong, get old and frail. And we're talking, there in his room, and his head is suspended in the air. I don't know what it was that kept it there, some kind of radical technology.

'He showed me underneath his chin, and I could see some kind of a socket, like an electrical socket, and he says that some people plug themselves in to another body, they swap them over, like, uh, outfits for the day. But he says he isn't going to do that. He'll just live forever, his head sustained through some kind of advanced energy pack. And we start talking about it, laughing about the ideas we're having, about plugging into a dog, or an antelope or something. But all the while I've got this feeling, and I tell him he's made a terrible mistake and someone's tricked him, made him believe all these things. Because I know he's gonna die, like we all are, and I tell him this, tell him whoever took his body away, they're coming for his head next and there's nothing he can do to stop them. And I say to him, "Just live man, live, while you still can."

'And he looks at me. Wide eyes, frightened. And he opens his mouth and screams. But there's no sound and when he realises there's no sound he screams more and his eyes are open as wide as they can open.'

Jim looked up at Gunzabo, nodded slowly and said, 'Yeah.' He was clearly moved by the recollection of the dream. 'That was when I woke. It was morning, perhaps seven, a quarter before. And it was hot, I remember that. The hottest day of the year. By far, man. I was so beat from the dream and the heat and I looked out, and I could see Elvis and John in the distance, coming towards me. So I got my camera out, and I filmed them, like I do every day.'

Gunzabo set aside his confusion over the dream, deciding it was almost certainly nonsense. 'How long were you filming that morning?' he asked.

'Till I heard the gunshot. No, until the second one. At first I didn't comprehend what it was.'

'I must see this footage,' Gunzabo told him. 'It is vital to my investigation.' A thrill of excitement made his shoulders judder. Then, frowning, he asked, 'Why did you not mention it the other day?'

'You never asked.'

Jim rummaged through the piles of tapes on the floor; there were at least twenty 8mm tapes, unlabelled and unordered. Jim sent Kurt to the shack to look for more, then mumbled frustrated accusations at himself as he resumed scanning through each cassette. Kurt returned with more tapes piled in his arms. Gunzabo sat and smoked on the sofa next to Kurt, took another beer and watched monotonous video for an hour: the runners, the beach, sunset, sunrise, mumbled poetry and running commentary. But then a different scene appeared: John and Elvis as usual, but this time the camera bounced along as Jim ran after them. Gunzabo dropped his cigarette into an ash tray. He leaned forwards as the runners accelerated, grinning over their shoulders. Suddenly a figure intercepted them. It was Mrs Bradley, charging across their path, her face angry and red and streaming with tears. She grabbed John, began screaming at him.

'When was this taken?' Gunzabo said.

'Couple of days before John died,' said Jim. 'Old Joanie was going crazy about something or other.'

The camera now caught up.

'How dare you!' Mrs Bradley was screaming. 'You stay out of it! What have you done? I'll never see him again!' She lost control and fell to her knees, a blubbing wreck, saying, 'You leave my Kevin alone... he's a good boy... don't make him go away,' and John knelt beside her, tried to hold her face to his chest, but she pushed him away and screamed for him to leave. Elvis took John's arm, gently unfurled his fingers, then after one sad, desperate look of grief, John ran off with him. The camera panned now to Mrs Bradley, zooming in until she noticed the camera and screamed to leave her be. The tape ended.

'What happened after this?' Gunzabo asked Jim.

'I left her alone, like she said.'

'Did John mention this at all? Do you know if they spoke afterwards?'

'I don't know, man. Two days later, John was dead.'

Gunzabo stood up. 'I have to go,' he said, 'Make sure you finish the film.'

He left his beer unfinished and strode out into the garden. He needed to pay a visit to the Bradleys.

23

Gunzabo hurried along the sand in the heavy afternoon heat, passing by the West Beach residences, then turning up, though the gardens, towards The Circles.

'What's more important?' Didi said. 'Seeing Mrs Bradley going mental, or seeing the shooting?'

'Both. Jim must finish that film, it could provide a vital clue. The killer will certainly strike again.'

'Well he hasn't got long to finish it. Dinner's at six, then it's the show.'

Gunzabo arrived at the terrace. Across the tiles, under Lastri's direction, dozens of staff were moving tables and glasses and crockery, carrying them out of the restaurant and round the side of the building. Tommy mutely supervised a group of men as they carried the components of a PA system. Mrs Bradley flapped around ineffectually. There was no sign of Christian.

'You know, I was thinking,' said Didi.

'It's about time,' Gunzabo told her, not taking his eyes from the scene over at the restaurant.

'Whatever, big nose. I was thinking about the Bradleys' son.'

'So was I,' he said.

'What if he isn't actually living in England at all? What if he's here?'

He nodded thoughtfully, still watching the movement over at the restaurant.

'It could be him, living in the jungle, couldn't it?'

'Yes, it could.'

Gunzabo continued watching the movement over at the

restaurant, waiting until the Bradleys and Lastri had followed the sound equipment round the side of the building. Only a few staff remained now, and Gunzabo moved diagonally across the terrace, then followed the curving glass wall of the main building until he came to an orchard of tropical fruit trees. Passing through the trees, he came to an outdoor swimming pool, then tennis courts, a basketball court and finally a bungalow, much like his own, though larger. A selection of giantess-sized bras hung on a washing line out the back. He tried the rear doors, slid them open and slipped through.

It was dark inside the bungalow; the windows were shuttered and the patio doors admitted only traces of light through the underwear outside. He shuffled round a bed, moved into a corridor, then into another room, carpeted like the first, even darker. He reached around until he found a light switch. In the dull orange glow he saw a second bedroom: a child's bed, freshly made with red duvet and pillows; posters on the walls of footballers dressed in red with frizzy mullets and dark moustaches; trophies on a chest of drawers: lightweight, small mock-metallic footballers on wooden bases that read:

Sportsman of the Year – Runner up – 1979
Mid Sussex U10 Cup Winner – 1980
Melford FC – Player of the Year – 1981

He looked through drawers full of boys' clothing: clean, fresh, neatly folded. Turning to a chest-high wardrobe he opened flimsy white doors, pushed aside trousers and white polo shirts and grey school jumpers. At the bottom he found a cardboard box filled with assorted belongings: playing cards, football stickers, penknives, a pencil case scrawled with childish graffiti; elastic bands, loose Opal Fruits and Chewitts; a sheaf of drawings in blue biro of Judge Dredd.

He went back into the corridor and through a doorway at the far end. He clicked on the light, found himself in a living room: brightly lit, scrupulously tidy, with a wool carpet and a three piece suite. What interested him were the walls: hundreds of photos, all framed, all of a boy, either on his own or with the Bradleys – looking much younger – or with a corpulent elderly couple, perhaps the grandparents. Each wall was fully covered with photographs. He walked across the carpet to a mock fireplace and a life-sized photographic portrait of the boy in school uniform. It was dated 1981.

He moved to a dresser, quickly scanned more photos of the boy, then a wedding photo of a slightly slimmer Joan Bradley holding the arm of a fractionally less skeletal Tommy. He carefully replaced the photos, then knelt down and opened the cabinet doors. Dragging out a pile of family albums, he noticed an envelope tucked underneath. He opened the envelope, pulled out a greeting card: a scrawled caricature in black ink, of a man with long hair and round spectacles and a long, unhappy mouth. Inside was a message:

Joan & Thomas
Words cannot express how sorry I am. The last thing I
wanted was to hurt you. But I know I have and I hope
that in time you will come to forgive me.
Love and peace,
John x

Gunzabo put the card back into the envelope, then sat at a glass-topped dining table looking through the photo albums. Each book was filled with photos of the Bradleys: in their late twenties with a baby; their thirties with a young child; photos of the same boy as he became older: playing on a pebbly beach; hanging from a tree; smiling on a BMX bike; squatting on the halfway line with a football team of ten year olds. The fourth album was only half full. The final photo was of the boy in a Liverpool top, holding a signed, framed team photo; he was sat up in a hospital bed next to a smiling man in a suit with black, curly hair. Gunzabo vaguely recognised the man. The boy was smiling despite his gaunt, sickly face and the tubes running out of his nostrils. The rest of the album was empty.

Gunzabo closed the book, sat at the table and cried. For a while he lost control and forgot where he was, or even that he was alive, he felt so full of grief. Then he came to, opened his eyes and numbly watched his tears land on the clear glass of the table top and form flat discs of water. The covers of the albums were scarlet and blurred in his peripheral vision. Didi didn't say anything. She was crying too.

'Oh John,' he said softly, 'yes, you should have let them be.' He looked about the room, which he saw now was the very opposite of a living room, and with a heavy heart, he murmured, 'But I cannot.'

He gathered the albums, solemnly put them back into the cabinet, wiped away the tears from the glass table, and let himself out of the bungalow. He walked back into the gardens, his mind in a daze, his sight blurred from tears, went across the lawns and streams and arrived at his bungalow. There he kicked off his trainers and went straight to sleep.

24

He opened his eyes, clenched his teeth to stop them rattling.

The air conditioning was on maximum, as if someone was attempting to freeze him into a permanent sculpture. He got up, shivering as he went over to the patio doors. He slid the doors open and a wave of heat rolled in, warming the outer edges of his chilled numbness and carrying with it the drone of insect evensong. He looked out: the sea was darkening to black as it sucked the light from the evening sky.

'What was that all about, Gunzabo?' said Didi. 'I felt unbelievably upset, but I don't know why.'

He still shivered despite the evening heat. 'Their son is dead, Didi.'

Didi looked up at him sadly. 'A dead child. So that's why you were so upset.'

'I don't know what you mean.'

She gave him a stern look, then said, 'So he's not the killer then.'

'It's what the English call ironic. Everyone else on this island fakes their deaths. The Bradleys fake a life. She is a fantasist. Now I see why Tommy storms off whenever she mentions him.'

Didi ran up Gunzabo's leg and sat on his shoulder. 'So she's invented an imaginary personality to cover the loss of her child, avert the terrible anguish, maybe without even knowing it?'

Gunzabo glanced at her sourly, then squinted into the distance, his sorrow as deep and dark as the far edges of the sea.

'John tried to make her see the truth, didn't he?' Didi said.

'I believe so.'

'So that's why she went mad at him. It could be her, couldn't it? She had a reason.'

'I don't want to talk about it.'

He stepped outside and walked towards The Circles, ignoring Didi's concerned looks. The lamps were glowing in the gardens. He could hear orchestral music, becoming louder as he approached the complex. Didi strained forward on her hind legs, willing him to go faster. 'Here we go, then,' she said.

The terrace was full of residents chatting in small groups, while half a dozen staff glided around serving champagne and canapés. Jim came bouncing over. He was dressed in a crumpled linen suit, white shirt, aviator glasses and sandals; his hair was brushed into a matted parting; a layer of white powder dusted his moustache.

'Finish the film?' Gunzabo asked him.

Jim grinned. 'You bet. It's looking pretty neat, man, pretty neat.' His monotone was faster and more animated than usual. 'These kids are gonna love it.'

'Am I going to love it?'

'You too, man. It's gonna be awesome. I have a feeling it could be recognised as a vital landmark in the history of cinematography. I cannot wait.'

Jim fidgeted and hopped around and then dashed off, flapping his hands and downing every drink he came across. Gunzabo joined Diana and River, who were standing nearby, quietly sipping champagne. They were both dressed in black.

'How was your day, Gunzabo?' enquired Diana.

'It was alright.'

'I have a space tomorrow afternoon, if you would like another session.'

'I don't have a space.'

Diana smiled at him. 'I do hope you change your mind. You're a very interesting case.' She sipped her champagne delicately. 'And how is *your* case going?'

'Not particularly well.'

'Oh dear, I'm sorry.'

'Nobody else is.'

Diana did not respond. Gunzabo noticed River's hand twitching as a tray of steak tartare canapés passed by. 'Where's Christian?' he said.

'I expect he's finalising the arrangements for this evening,' Diana said. 'It's ever so important to him.'

He grunted derisively. 'Who else is missing?' he muttered, glancing around. 'Marilyn, of course. Is Michael coming?'

'Michael? That is one strange cat,' Bruce said, joining them. He was dressed in a powder blue suit, with matching shirt and a black string tie. 'Like he dropped off the moon or something. Nobody ever sees him.'

'He came last year. Everyone comes, even Marilyn,' said River.

'I never understood why,' said Bruce. 'It's the same every year. Like a goddam funeral.'

'Well why do you come, man?'

'For the booze, man. And the after party, man.'

They stood in silence for a few minutes. Bruce picked some scallop ravioli off a passing tray, ate one and flicked another into Gunzabo's mouth.

'Anyway, people,' said Bruce, 'this conversation is pretty flat. You better do something about that before I get back. I'm gonna go find some other cats to speak to. See you later.'

Bruce walked over to Jimi on the other side of the terrace. Keith and Kurt were with him, and Jimi was holding court in his white smock, playing air guitar, then bass, then drums. Gunzabo watched him mime the whole band's performance, mouthing words and taking them through the song he had planned. As Bruce joined them, Jimi's stoned smile was replaced by a momentary look of guilt, but then he grabbed Bruce and took him in a fierce hug.

'Ladies and gentlemen.'

Gunzabo turned with the other guests to face Lastri. She looked suffocatingly beautiful: ivory-white sari, like a wedding dress; black hair coiled above her head and decorated with sapphires.

'Dinner is served.'

She bowed gracefully, moving aside as the guests stepped through a cast iron, lily-studded gate. Gunzabo stared at her, devastated by her beauty, and then made his way along a path strewn with petals and palm leaves, under porticos fragrant with jasmine. He entered a garden behind the main complex, which was open and brightly lit, and beyond he saw the amphitheatre, also spectacularly lit. Passing through the garden, he descended an aisle between the amphitheatre seats and stepped into the arena.

A collection of paintings were on display on the gravel; guests mingled, hugged Kurt and told him how wonderful he was. Gunzabo wandered through the exhibits with the other guests, then moved into the centre of the arena. This was laid out with round tables, each surrounded by hand-carved teak chairs cushioned in gold fabric. In front of each chair were sets of silver cutlery, crystal wine and water glasses, bone china plates, stiff cotton napkins, butter in antique silver dishes, party poppers and Christmas crackers.

Staff appeared from the darkness at the edges of the arena. A plump, middle-aged woman in white guided Gunzabo to an empty table nearest the stage. He sat and watched the other guests being seated, saw the staff glide under the floodlights, which shone so blindingly from above it was as if the sun had finally appeared. Janis approached his table. She was with Jimi and they were holding hands, fingers interlinked, Jimi being pulled along like a teenager, almost embarrassed by their togetherness. She sat next to Gunzabo and grinned at him.

'So we're sitting with you, Mr Detective,' she said. 'Well that's fine! You recovered yet?'

'Not yet,' he answered.

Jimi smiled absently at him, before looking into the darkness at the edge of the arena. The rage from last night was absent, but he looked tense, nervous even.

'I hear you're performing tonight,' Gunzabo said to him.

Jimi continued staring beyond the lights as he answered. 'Yeah, that's right. It's something I decided not so long ago. A simple notion which grew into a beautiful possibility.'

Janis looked at Jimi, smiling with a mixture of fondness and pride. 'You're gonna be great, baby.' She took his hand from the table and put it in hers. 'It's time someone shook this place up, brought back the old times a little. You're gonna raise hell! Oh, Gunzabo, you should hear this album of Jimi's, it's like nothing you've ever heard.'

A waitress poured each of them a glass of champagne. Gunzabo saw Janis squeeze Jimi's crotch under the table.

'One last roll of the dice?' he said.

Janis turned to him, her face beaming. 'Sure is. Just the thirty years between rolls. Time to make up for lost time. Ain't it baby?'

Jimi looked at her now, gave her a trace of his goofy smile and kissed her tenderly on the lips. Gunzabo watched them thoughtfully while she whispered assurances to Jimi, until she turned back to grin at him.

'What about you, Gunzabo. You got anybody special, back in reality?'

'Nobody. Nothing,' he answered.

'Well, that's a real shame, that is. I just hope you do, sometime very soon. You know how it is when you find love. You just want everybody else to catch the bug.'

Janis looked quickly at Jimi, leaned over and kissed him.

'You never had children?' Gunzabo said.

'Nope.' said Janis. He saw a look of pain cross her face, dismissed with a flick of her white hair and a grin. 'We tried an awful lot, though. I guess it's probably what did for us in the end, way back. It's not easy when you both want something and you can't have it, and then you fight like tomcats and rip the life out of each other because of it.' She paused to down her champagne. 'Nope, we didn't have no kids. Don't matter now. Some things get easier when you're older, don't they?' She smiled ruefully. 'What about you?'

'Me?' answered Gunzabo. He had been looking at Jimi the whole time, watching him look into the dark, as if he was casting his attention further even than the confines of the island. 'No,' Gunzabo said, and a shiver passed through him and he shook his head, more to shake the feeling out of him than to respond to Janis's question. Janis was looking at him and she moved closer, her eyes searching his.

'What is it, Gunzabo?'

He sighed heavily, sat up, pressed his missing arm. Janis was still looking at him. Eventually he said, 'I always wanted a daughter. A little girl. They grow up, of course, I know this, but I always wanted one to grow up a little, then stay a certain age. When they're old enough to answer you back, but still a child and they need you for everything. I never had that.'

'You wouldn't have wanted me,' Janis said. 'I'd have driven you to madness and beyond.' She smiled her crooked grin. 'I guess I was cute. Terribly lonesome, though. How I wish I could go visit my young self, just give her some company, tell her not to mind the others. Tell her she's gonna end up with the greatest man there's ever been!'

Gunzabo looked at Jimi again, saw him looking into the distance while Janis laid her head on his shoulder. Gunzabo looked around to attract a waiter for another drink.

'Gunzarby,' said Mrs Bradley, leaning over from the next table. 'Oh Gunzarby, Gunzarboose, I'm drunk. Ken's been plying me with fizzy stuff.'

Ken was on one side of her, Tommy on the other, mostly hidden by his wife's enormous frame. Next to Ken was Christian, who flashed Gunzabo his grin, then looked out across the tables, wrinkling his eyes in all directions and shaking both legs under the table. Ken glanced quickly at Jimi, trying to attract his attention, when he noticed Gunzabo watching him. He shook his head and made a cutting motion across his neck. 'Look who they've put me with,' he said. 'Want to swap?'

'Shut it, Kin-Kan-Kenny.'

Mrs Bradley shoved him with a meaty arm and reached for a bread roll. He gave her a nasty, contemptuous look, and in that instant Gunzabo saw him without his mask, saw bitterness and repugnance etched on his features. Ken glanced again at Jimi, then turned to his companions, put a grin back on his face and made a joke.

Gunzabo turned to face his own table again. 'There's something I wanted you ask you,' he said, addressing Jimi.

Jimi looked at him, blinking as if he'd woken from a dream. 'What was that, man?' he murmured.

'You and Ken. What were you discussing yesterday, on the beach?'

Janis lifted her head quickly to look at Gunzabo's face, alarmed by the question, looking at him as if to discern his motive for asking it. Gunzabo noticed her hand gripping Jimi's thigh under the table.

'That and this, you know, this and that,' Jimi said. 'The purpose of life, where and how we want to spend the rest of our lives, and suchlike. It's not important really.'

'What exactly did he say?'

Jimi didn't look at Gunzabo as he answered. 'He says, we're all boring now, you know? Even him. Everyone here. That's what he was telling me, how we're all absolutely completely like zombies. The unliving, walking dead, you know, like an extinct galaxy, still shining there in the sky even though it died a billion years ago.'

'He said that?' Gunzabo asked dubiously.

'Yeah, just like that, that was exactly the way he said it.' Jimi gave an echo of his goofy grin, but it was gone immediately and he lit a cigarette and smoked, barely heeding Janis as she put her arm round him.

'Why were you so angry with him last night, at the party?' Gunzabo said.

Jimi looked at him now. 'Didn't you hear what I said to him? It's the agenda. Actually, no, it's the lies. That's all we have here now. Lies and deceit and so forth. But it's not for me to bring it all down, take everyone out of their particular dream, you know. The unliving lives they've fashioned here for themselves, the dead constellation they've hung themselves in.' He drew forcefully on his cigarette, breathed out smoke across the table and frowned. 'But it doesn't mean I have to like it.'

'Hey, baby.' Janis raised her hand to his clenched cheek, gently turned his face. 'You made your decision, baby. We made our decision. It's as good as done. So smile. Smile for me, baby. For us. For a new beginning.'

Gunzabo could not see their faces now; they were veiled behind Janis's hair. 'What decision?' he asked.

But then all the guests stood and began to applaud and he also stood, looking around to see what was happening.

25

A man had appeared.

The man was pushing Marilyn in a wheelchair. The residents cheered as the man smiled shyly but proudly, keeping his head down to let Marilyn receive the adulation. Marilyn gave a weak, dignified smile as she waved a hand at the guests, the other gripping the arm of her wheelchair. Behind, two nurses pushed a trolley of medical equipment.

They made their way to Gunzabo's table. The hubbub died down as everyone returned to their seats and resumed their conversations.

'Marilyn! My, is it good to see you,' said Janis. 'I ain't seen you in years, honey. I didn't think you'd make it. You're looking a billion dollars.'

'Thank you, nurse,' said Marilyn.

The man laughed. He was taller than Gunzabo had expected him to be. 'You silly birdie, Marilyn. This isn't your nurse, it's Janis.'

Janis did not return his smile or even look at him. Instead she gave Marilyn one final grin, then returned to Jimi and the privacy of their regained love, her white hair cocooning them from the world.

Michael turned now to Gunzabo. 'Hi,' he said.

'Gunzabo,' said Gunzabo, extending his hand.

Michael did not shake his hand, so much as brush it delicately with long white fingers. 'Pleased to meet you. I'm Michael.' He inclined his head, smiling timidly.

'Yes, I know.'

'And this is Marilyn.'

'We met the day before yesterday,' said Gunzabo.

'You did? How wonderful.' Michael looked at Marilyn with mock reproach. 'Marilyn, why didn't you tell me this? We share everything, don't we?'

Marilyn's eyelids drooped. Moments later she was asleep with her head back. A nurse leaned over and placed a mask over her face.

'She's so wonderful, isn't she?' said Michael. He took her hand. 'So beautiful. She has the most wonderful heart.'

'Did she mention my visit?'

'No, she didn't mention it at all. You must have missed me by a minute, I was there all day and night.'

'She's forgotten, I suppose,' Gunzabo said, hiding his relief.

Michael laughed like a child. 'She's so funny.'

The first course arrived: trio of rabbit with quail eggs, a delicate herb salad and lemon dressing, accompanied by a crisp, dry champagne.

'Aren't you sad, seeing her like this?' said Gunzabo, once he'd cleared his plate.

Michael put down his cutlery. 'How could I be? It's such a treasure, spending time with her. We talk so much, and about so many different things.' His eyes shone. 'It's like a window, a way back to a time long ago, a better time, a golden age. It's a really special thing.'

Gunzabo finished his champagne, put the glass down. 'You know why I'm here on the island?' he asked Michael.

'Yes, of course.' Michael looked back at him with a face like a wooden doll.

'Where were you at the time of John's murder?'

'I was with Marilyn.'

'You are sure of this? It was rather early, seven or thereabouts.'

'I'm sure,' said Michael. His eyes gleamed and each shed a

single tear. He wiped the tears away. 'How can any of us forget? It's so sad.'

'What time did you arrive at Marilyn's house?'

'Oh, I was there all night, at her bedside. She was asleep most of the time, but I like to be there. Guarding her sleep, I guess you could say.'

'Did you hear anything? The gunshots, any commotion?'

'Oh no, it's a way over to Marilyn's place from there. A mile or more. And her room, with all the instruments and pumps, it's noisy in there. Though I don't notice it anymore.'

'Can anyone testify to your being there at this time? A nurse who was on duty?'

'I don't think so,' Michael said. 'I sent the nurse away. I do that sometimes, particularly if it's night and Marilyn's asleep. I guess I want her all to myself.'

He looked at Michael intently. 'Did you kill John?'

Michael gave a despairing smile. 'How can you ask such a question?' he said. 'No, of course I didn't. I mean, how could anyone do such a thing? There's so much pain in the world already.'

'You had a fight though.'

'No! Not a fight. A misunderstanding. We've always been such great friends.'

Gunzabo finished his wine. A waiter came and refilled the glass. Michael looked at Marilyn, smiling fondly as he stood.

'Excuse me,' he said, 'I have to go and use the little boys' room.'

Gunzabo watched Michael walk between the tables and disappear between the blazing lights at the edge of the arena. Marilyn stirred and looked across the table.

'Has he gone?' she asked.

'Who?'

'The man. The one who's always there.'

'Yes.'

'Oh good.' She closed her eyes again.

Gunzabo poured himself a glass of red wine while waiters cleared the dishes, and another troupe of waiters brought each guest a rectangular plate with a line of four white eggs of decreasing size. Each egg contained a different type of caviar and released a bouquet like a sea breeze, its aroma subtly different to the others, as if borne on the wind from a separate part of the globe: silver beluga in the goose egg; another beluga, velvety and black with grains like peppercorns in the chicken egg; tiny glistening orange buds in the duck egg; and in the quail egg an amber caviar which shone golden under the lights.

'Oh, my,' Michael said, returning to the table. 'I don't think my stomach can take all this rich food. I wonder, should I wake Marilyn?'

Gunzabo gestured meaningfully towards the nurses; they moved forward to check she was still alive.

'Would anybody like my fizzy?' said Michael.

Gunzabo accepted the champagne, drank half and resumed eating. Michael nibbled the accompanying bread, but mostly he held Marilyn's hand and smiled fondly at her as she slept. Gunzabo looked round at the other guests: Bruce was flicking caviar into Kurt's mouth; Jim was holding each grain up to the light before eating it, as if searching for a hint of the beginnings of life; Karen, Keith, River and Marc were eating vegetable sticks and houmous in silence; Heath and Ken stifled yawns next to Elvis and Diana, who were talking earnestly while they drank sparkling water from crystal tumblers; Mrs Bradley was tucking into her husband's food; Ken, next to her, was looking bored; Christian watched everyone with a look of glee and rocked back in his chair, legs vibrating under the table.

The waiters brought more champagne and a coconut sorbet served in a coconut shell. After this came the main course: baby vegetables, a sweet, dark sauce and a quartet of lamb: a rack, rare, sitting on pureed celeriac; loin of lamb; sweetbreads; slow cooked neck. The plate was decorated with tiny fragrant leaves.

Nobody spoke at Gunzabo's table. He ate his food and drank red wine and champagne while Janis talked animatedly to Jimi, Marilyn dozed with her head slumped forward, and Michael picked delicately at his vegetables. Gunzabo turned as Mrs Bradley, still holding her cutlery, came over.

'I've never been so full in my life,' she said. 'That was blinking lurverly.' She looked at Marilyn, then at her untouched meal, saying, 'Do you think she'll want any of that?' She reached over to plunge her fork into the rack of lamb.

At that moment, Marilyn woke. She looked at Mrs Bradley, leaning across the table, her enormous breasts swaying like a pair of seals, and then at the silver fork with the piece of meat on the end of it. 'Thief!' she cried out. 'Stop him. Taking my jewellery. How dare you.'

Mrs Bradley stood there in shock, balanced over the table as the lamb leaked juices onto the tablecloth.

'Give it back, thief,' Marilyn said, weakening slightly in her anger.

Michael took Marilyn's arm, whispered soothing noises in her ear.

'Don't worry?' Marilyn exclaimed. 'How can I not worry when this person is making off with my jewellery box? And it's all covered in gravy! Someone, quick. Help!'

Everyone was now watching the commotion. Lastri arrived at the table. Mrs Bradley looked across to where Ken was sitting. 'Isn't there something you can give her?' she hissed.

Ken shook his head. 'She's up to her eyeballs already. Besides, I've only got happy pills on me, and I'm saving them for the party.'

'Pills? They're trying to drug me,' said Marilyn. 'Stop them!'

She flailed weakly at the people around her. Michael and Lastri uncurled her fingers from their clothing, released the brake on her wheelchair and ushered her off, followed by the nurses and her equipment. Background music came on. The diners returned to their drinks and conversations.

'She's worse than I thought,' said Mrs Bradley. She looked at the rack of lamb still attached to her fork. 'I've lost my appetite. Do you want it, Thomas?'

Tommy glared back at her. She started crying.

'Now *he's* got the hump,' she wailed. 'I just want to die.'

'Don't say that too loud, Joan,' Gunzabo said. 'There's a killer on the loose.'

She burst into tears, blew her nose on a napkin, and left to go to the toilet.

Gunzabo watched her leave, then moved into her seat, next to Tommy, who was alone at the table, Ken and Christian having gone to mingle with the other diners.

'Evening Tommy.'

Tommy was so still and vacant he might have been dead.

Dessert was served. 'Palm sundae, sirs,' said the maître d', and she stepped aside as waiters brought a bowl, handmade from palm leaves, filled with ice cream, raspberry coulis, candied pecans and a white chocolate cylinder. The dish was topped with spun sugar and garnished with sprigs of mint and shavings of coconut flesh. Gunzabo sat silently at the table while the ice cream melted, studying Tommy and thinking about the case.

Eventually, he said, 'I went to your house earlier.'

Tommy did not speak, or move, or even blink in response.

'I saw your son's room. And the photographs. In the albums.'

Gunzabo watched him closely, looking for any sign of life.

'I know what happened to him, Tommy. That he no longer lives, and that John did something to upset you both.'

He couldn't be sure, but perhaps there was a tiny tremor in

Tommy's lips.

'I won't speak to your wife about it, she seems to have recovered herself, renewed the fantasy. It is her right to hold on to whichever version of the past she wishes.'

He paused, and now, as he looked at Tommy, it was as if no one else was there in the arena, that only the two of them existed as he continued his one-sided conversation:

'Look at me.' Still no response. 'I know what it is to lose a child. I will not ever ask you this again, either of you. I know how much it must hurt you, the terrible feeling…'

His voice trailed away as emotion rose in waves through him, from his abdomen into his chest, concentrating in his throat. He forced the feelings down, determined to finish his speech.

'I have to ask you something. I must. Is your wife involved in John's death? Did she want him dead, Tommy? Is the pain sharp enough to do this?'

Tommy's face jerked towards him. Eyes, watery blue, were now fixed on Gunzabo. For a moment they stared at each other, eyes locked in mutual understanding, until Tommy's face convulsed and his jaws moved from side to side, and he squinted and screwed up his face and eyes as if in spasm; he scratched at his cheeks with sharp claw-like fingers, again fixed his gaze on Gunzabo, opened his mouth wide as a faint sound of laughter came out, coming in wheezes from his thin chest. But in his eyes there was no laughter; there was tortured loss and injustice and guilt and the accumulated, layered pain of decades of unprocessed torment; and perhaps there was the added misery accrued from all the souls he had ferried across to this dead star island – like Charon himself, boatman of the dead; only unpaid, rendered dumb, separated forever from the one person he would have given anything to have in his boat, but would never see again.

Gunzabo stared back, his heart full of pity and sadness as he watched Tommy get up and stagger away on his skeletal legs, teetering into the darkness outside the arena. Gunzabo sat there and turned his head from side to side, as he again tried to shake away his own terrible feeling of loss; he cursed, and again, with more force now, trying to jerk it out of his head.

The cheese course arrived, followed by coffee with *petits fours*, but he did not eat anything, and would not for the rest of his time on the island.

26

Staff were buzzing around clearing glasses and dishes. Gunzabo, feeling rather drunk now, turned as the lights dimmed and Elvis made his way to the low stage at the front of the arena. Elvis took a microphone from its stand and grinned, enjoying the attention as the diners called out and clapped and whooped with excitement.

'We've had a fine, fine meal,' he said in his deep, rich voice. Everyone murmured in agreement. 'It's wonderful to see you all here. It's not often we get together as a community.'

There were more whoops and hollers. Elvis raised his hand and became serious.

'Now, as we all know, way too well, there are people who couldn't be with us tonight, good friends who lived here for many years, and who I like to think are still with us. Our dear friend Brian, may he rest in peace.' He paused, looked around solemnly. 'And our very dear friend John. Let's be quiet now for a minute, and pray to whichever power watches over each of us.'

The arena was silent; even the surrounding jungle seemed to quieten to a distant throb. Gunzabo watched the guests sitting round their tables with heads bowed and the staff standing silently and respectfully alongside. Christian was rocking on the back legs of his chair, also watching, his eyes twinkling with pleasure. He glanced across and flashed his teeth at Gunzabo.

Elvis looked up, smiled in appreciation. 'Thank you, my friends,' he said. 'Now, we have some very special acts ahead of us tonight. And let's start with our newest guest: Gunzabo.'

Gunzabo looked back in confusion, then, realising he had not misheard the announcement, stood up, waited for the floor to stop spinning, then staggered onto the stage. At least he would get it over with quickly.

Facing the drum kit, his back to the audience, he pushed aside his thoughts and the background conversation and the dizziness. He took a deep breath through his nostrils, focussed on the air filling his lungs, then turned around and squinted into the lights. A waiter brought a napkin and a tumbler of water which he placed on his head. He closed his eyes, and now, standing with the lights shining through his eyelids, he suddenly realised how very intoxicated he was. His mind rolled and span like the sea. Was he standing still, or swaying from side to side? He could not tell. He concentrated on the weight of the tumbler of water on his head and blinked open his eyes as the opening chords of Zorba the Greek sounded.

Raising his good arm and his phantom arm either side of him until they were horizontal, he stood for a few bars and, as the bouzouki played its first two notes, he took a step to the side. Then back again as the notes were repeated. He skipped forward onto one foot, nearly fell over he was so drunk, but somehow pushed himself up and the glass stayed on his head. He stepped back with the music, then to the side, and back, skipped forward and this time he felt water splash his temples, but the glass stayed in position and he heard a smattering of applause.

The main theme began again, this time with a second bouzouki and he repeated the routine, embellishing it with taps of the hand on the bottom of his trainer and more pronounced skips and sidesteps across the stage. The music picked up now, became faster and more urgent and he span with his eyes shut and his arms outstretched, but still slowly and languidly, keeping his breathing regular, finding an andante pulse behind the urgency of the bouzoukis. He knelt down, slapped the stage floor, felt the sting of the wood, then rose and span as the tempo increased again and his breathing quickened and now he was lost in the music, taken back to Athens and his wedding, and as the bouzoukis became ever more frantic, there was Megara watching him dance. The wedding guests were behind her: family and friends and acquaintances – all hers – five hundred people he cared nothing for, most of whom he had never even met. But nothing mattered, everything was alright because Megara was there, and they looked at each other across the room, with that simple understanding only two people in love can have. He smiled, and as she looked back, he saw her place a hand underneath the folds of her wedding dress and against her swollen belly. Her face was shining with joy, eyes full of love. He thought his heart would burst.

The music raced in circles around him and through him and he was no longer conscious of his body or the dance or of his drunkenness. He let out a yell of exhilaration as the notes swirled like electrons. He looked into the lights and the light raced through him; his heart surged as he saw Megara again, but then he felt something was wrong: his feet were entangled and he found himself stepping over a succession of objects. The song ended. He thudded into something hard and black. Cymbals went crashing to the floor as the tumbler fell off his head and smashed into glittering pieces across the stage. He stretched his arm out to keep from falling, put it through the floor tom, collapsed on top of the drum kit.

Everything stopped. He looked up. Someone was standing over him. He saw it was Lastri. She smiled, pulled him up, looked at his arm and he followed her eyes, saw that it was cut and bleeding. 'You'll live,' she said, leading him off the stage and back to his seat, where a nurse came and bandaged him up.

'Dear me, Gunzarby,' Mrs Bradley said. 'You nearly lost your other arm there.' She stood up. 'Wish me luck,' she said.

'Just going to get ready.'

He blinked, trying to reunite the two floral dresses into one person, gave up, and stared at the shining glasses and coffee cups in front of him. He was hot and groggy and his head hurt, but his arm had no feeling; there was just an arm-shaped numbness that matched the hollow sensation on the other side. Gradually his head slumped onto his collarbone and the noise and the harshness of the lights and the smell of coffee and cigars dissolved into dreams.

Gunzabo woke as the final note of the Bradleys' duet sounded. He shook his head, came to a little more. The sleep had done him good, but he suddenly panicked: how long had he slept for? He cursed himself for not checking the running order; he could not afford to miss Jim's film. Ordering a brandy, he cheered the Bradleys, thumping his hand on the table and glaring at the other diners' polite applause. The lights went out and Gunzabo was left with the image of Mrs Bradley standing there in tears while Tommy awkwardly touched her shoulder.

The gathering became quiet in readiness for the next act.

A projector screen flashed on, vividly blue: the barely moving surface of a lake. Music started: trancelike Chinese classical music, which became louder as a candle-flame appeared in the air. One by one and at shorter intervals tiny flames sparked into life across the stage. A gong sounded and with its crash Bruce appeared, cross-legged in the lotus position.

Gunzabo watched Bruce's act and drank his cognac. Bruce was standing now, holding a huge sheet of white paper, began folding it, quickening the folding as the music increased in volume and tempo. Though Gunzabo's eyes were on the stage, he was still worrying about the film. The case was going nowhere without it. He tried to cast his mind back to the clips he had watched that afternoon, convinced he may already have seen a clue, but instead he found himself back in the Bradleys' bungalow, at their dining table, staring at the tiny round pools formed of his tears, the walls around him crammed with images of their son, like icons in an Orthodox church.

He sobbed drunkenly, coughed to mask the emotion. He looked up as the audience began clapping, and saw Bruce holding aloft his finished piece: a lotus flower on a short stem. Bruce bowed, attached the flower to a fine thread, and left it suspended in the air. The flower hung in front of the screen as if it was bobbing gently on blue water; its delicate shard-like petals reminded Gunzabo of the map in his room. Bruce now took a lighter from his pocket, lit the lotus stem, stepping aside as it fizzed and burnt up towards the flower head.

The music stopped. All was still for an instant.

Suddenly the flower erupted in a shower of multi-coloured sparks and exploded.

The lights came on. Bruce stood next to the charred remains of his origami lotus, looking defiantly at the spectators.

Elvis returned to the stage. 'Bruce, ladies and gentlemen. Give him another whoop and a holler folks. That was quite something, wasn't it?' He waited for the applause to die down. 'Next, I'd like to welcome to stage, a wonderful filmmaker, who will be telling us about his latest movie.'

The lights went out. Gunzabo leaned forward in anticipation, as the words DEATH AFTER LIFE: A MOVIE appeared on the projector screen. He had been waiting for this all evening.

Elvis handed the microphone to Jim.

'Uh, well, this is my film,' Jim mumbled, moving his weight nervously from one leg to the other. 'It needs no introduction from me, or anybody for that matter. All art – and that includes cinematography – should speak for itself, so I will let it speak for itself, and just say, for me, working in this medium, well it's been revolutionary. And revolution is a word, a, uh, concept, that I do not use lightly, as many of you know. Thank you.'

Gunzabo joined in the applause, staring intently at the screen, as Jim took a seat onstage and the film started.

The opening scene was a slow, lingering shot of the sea. The camera panned up to reveal a single cloud. The cloud floated slowly across the screen. A series of short sequences began, almost identical, of sand blowing on the beach and the waves arriving and receding as two figures approached the camera; they started as specks, barely discernible from the dark fringes of jungle, now clearly recognisable as they neared. Time and again this scene was repeated, early morning, then in the evening, then another scene and another, with Elvis in his spandex outfit and John in his running shorts.

The film now changed to night and shots of the beach shack, a fire outside, bats flapping in the air, Jim mumbling into the camera in video diary style. He talked about his day and the mundane things he'd done, about religion, philosophy, recited a poem he had just written. Then another night and the same again. At one point a parrot flew over and there was a two minute section of Jim having a one-sided conversation with the bird and feeding it scraps from a frying pan.

Mrs Bradley leaned over to Gunzabo. 'The suspense, it's killing me,' she whispered.

He did not reply, did not take his eyes off the screen, which was pure white: a close-up of the early morning sky. The glow reflected off the darkened faces around him. Now another shot, the same as the opening: the sea and the beach and two figures approaching on their morning run. Elvis was resplendent in his neon spandex; John was in his running shorts and a long-sleeved top. They smiled and waved at the camera as they passed and the camera span round and the two men became smaller until they disappeared round a curve in the beach.

There was stillness again and silence and the emptiness of

the early morning beach. It was so still the film might have been paused.

Nothing moved.

A gunshot sounded, a high-pitched crack, and then more shots, and a distant scream, a muffled oath from Jim, images of the sand and Jim's feet bumping around as he ran along the beach to where the shots had come from and the camera swung up, pointing ahead, jolting up and down and there was Elvis on his knees and John lying in the shallow, bloodstained water, a huge red patch on his top, tangled hair dancing gently in the waves, half a dozen people around the body.

'My God, he's dead!' someone cried out, and someone else said, 'Look – in the trees.' The camera span round, hurriedly focussed onto the jungle, and at first there were just trees and dark green and darker vertical patches in between, but then the camera jerked to the right and there was the gunman, running into the jungle, unidentifiable, gone in a second. The camera swung back to the murder scene. Ken was there and said, 'Turn that thing off, you sicko,' then the wails and shouting were cut off and so was the video as the film ended.

27

Nobody in the audience made a sound.

Gunzabo scratched his neck and carried on gazing at the now dark screen. The lights came on. Elvis climbed back on stage. He was in tears.

'I'm lost for words, Jim. My God. That was powerful, man.' He cleared his throat and in a stronger voice, said, 'Jim, everyone. *Death After Life: A Movie.*'

There were a few isolated claps. Gunzabo was still looking at the screen. He had expected more. Disappointed, he looked about him: the residents were talking in hushed tones, their faces tense with worry; the staff brought drinks and cleared tables.

'He's here among us, isn't he?' Didi was poking her head out from his sleeve. 'The Déjà Vu Killer,' she added.

'Probably.'

He ordered another brandy, ignoring Didi's look of despair.

'My money's on her.' Didi twitched her nose towards Diana, who had begun a freeform dance interpretation of Enya's greatest hits. 'She's protecting Elvis. Wanted to do the job right, knew he'd have messed it up.'

Gunzabo remained silent. He was missing something important from the film, he was sure of it.

'It's definitely a woman, anyhow,' Didi continued. 'This whole mystery, it has a woman's hand in it. Mrs Bradley, still reckon it might be her?'

'Fifty people support her alibi. Tommy wasn't even on the island.'

'Of course there's Lastri – old dream-girl over there. But she was at roll call too, wasn't she?'

Gunzabo rubbed his cheek thoughtfully. Lastri, certainly, was involved in *something*. What exactly he still did not know. But he was more interested in Jim's film. What was he missing? He cast his mind back to the start of the show, to the screen, which now stood grey and empty, and that final scene, but again the edges of understanding fell away. He frowned, brought his mind back to the present as Jimi came over to the table and sat down.

'When are you on?' Gunzabo asked him.

'Last, man,' Jimi said, with a stoned blink.

They both turned as Diana left the stage clutching a huge bouquet of flowers, and Wagner's Ride of the Valkyries began blaring out of the speakers.

Ken strode on, hair slicked back, wearing a black tuxedo. He bowed low, ran lightly across the boards, and dramatically pulled off his cape to reveal Lastri as his assistant.

'You made up with Keith, then,' Gunzabo said, loudly over the music.

'Yeah, we stamped out those flames.' Jimi's eyes were almost closed. 'Sometimes people fall out, stop digging each other... fall back in again, like lovers.'

Lastri had climbed into a box shaped like a coffin, which Ken was wheeling round the stage. Her head protruded from end of the box, her feet from the other.

The music had become even louder. Gunzabo shouted into Jimi's ear, 'Are you going to the after party?'

'Sure, man.'

Gunzabo switched his gaze back to the performance, saw Ken looking over at them as he pushed the coffin around the stage. Ken had been smirking at Jimi. He was sure of it. There he was again, stealing a quick glance this way, raising his eyebrows with a knowing look as he span the coffin round.

'Where is the after party?' said Gunzabo, watching Jimi shake his head good-naturedly and try not to smile.

'Elvis's. It's always there.'

Ken brandished a sword, chopped a pineapple in half to demonstrate its sharpness.

'What made you decide to take part this year?'

'Something I gotta do. Swan song.'

Gunzabo edged his chair back slightly, so that he could see both men at once. 'Who do you think the killer is?'

Ken placed the sword firmly into a slit in the top of the box, then thrust it down until it showed underneath. Lastri made a face of flirtatious pain.

Jimi stood up and shrugged. 'I'd say it was Ken.'

Gunzabo also stood, so as to keep his eyes fully on Jimi. 'Somebody else is going to die, aren't they?'

'Probably,' said Jimi, glancing back at him. His eyes were glassy and impenetrable. He headed backstage and Gunzabo watched him as he passed Ken, saw another look between them, and this time Jimi grinned openly as Ken put another sword through the coffin.

'Looks like Jimi's been making up with everyone,' Didi whispered, scurrying back into Gunzabo's empty sleeve as Mrs Bradley returned to the table.

Ken was putting a broad, flat guillotine through the middle of the box. Lastri carried on smiling, even when Ken separated the box and wheeled her upper half to the other side of the stage.

'He does the same thing every year,' said Mrs Bradley. 'I reckon it might count against him.'

The music stopped and the lights went out. There was a loud scream. Gunzabo stood, alarmed.

'Relax,' Mrs Bradley whispered. 'It's always like this.'

She pulled him back into his seat. The lights came on and the box was empty. Ken bowed to the audience, everyone clapped and then Ken skipped off the stage, came over to Gunzabo's table, where Lastri was sitting on the other side of Mrs Bradley. Ken took her by the hand and they went back on stage and smiled and bowed and accepted the crowd's appreciation.

'They do this every year, you say?' said Gunzabo.

'Well, Kenny does. But always with someone different. He chopped me up a couple of years back. I'm sworn to secrecy. Reckons he learnt it straight from old whatshisname. Nicholas Nickleby, that's it.'

Karen, Janis, Heath and Marc arrived on stage and began a traditional Buddhist dance.

'Who chooses the winner?' said Gunzabo.

'The villagers, love. They have a vote at the end.'

Gunzabo watched as the Buddhists walked in a circle, clapping their hands in time with the music. A waiter brought him another glass of cognac. He was at the point now where his brain was fine, or at least he thought it was, but he had very little control over his body.

'Who are they?' he asked, indicating three women standing with Lastri at the edge of the stage.

'They're the sisters.'

'Lastri has three sisters?'

'You are quick Gunzarby, aren't you?' Mrs Bradley burped loudly. 'Oh dear, I'm busting for a pee. Back in a tick.'

Gunzabo sat on his own at the table. He was starting to feel morbid again and he downed his brandy so it would burn its way down, burn away the lonely feeling. It seemed to work and he could feel the line of fire working down into his chest. He watched the band setting up on stage. Elvis took the microphone.

'Our very last act of the night, ladies and gentlemen. Coming out of retirement, and I'm sure you're just as excited as me...'

Elvis continued talking while the band tuned their instruments, banged drums and adjusted microphone stands. Guests hurried back to their seats and staff passed by Gunzabo's table, making their way to the back of the arena to stand and watch the show as Elvis raised his voice and stretched an arm back towards the band.

'Give it up for... Major Tom!'

The band were still; everyone watched and waited in silence.

Jimi strode onto the stage with a white electric guitar. He was wearing a silver all-in-one jumpsuit, silver boots laced up to the knee, collars flaring out across his shoulders, buttons open half-way down his chest.

Turning his back to the audience, he began playing an arpeggio in six-eight time, so quietly Gunzabo strained to hear it. Keith joined in, with a brisk military beat, gradually increasing in volume with the guitar as Jimi continued playing an open E minor. There were subtle deviations and flourishes, but each time he returned to that same chord and the same arpeggio, and when the sound had increased enough to completely fill Gunzabo's ears, the bass added its own deep, plaintive melody, and the band began their song together.

They moved through four chords now, a bar for each, then back to the start of the cycle. The music was familiar, but Gunzabo could not place it. He watched Jimi, who was still in the same position, head bent down, his back to the audience. Again the music rose in volume; cymbals were introduced as the notes from the guitar became more angular and piercing, then increased again in resonance and volume, as did the drums and bass, and now each guitar note hurt the ears. Finally Jimi struck a single note high up on the neck. He held the note with his ring finger, while the drums and bass continued on a six-eight pulse, moved close to his amp, introduced feedback to the same note still ringing out, then he turned round, pushed his mouth onto the microphone as if nobody else in the world existed and sang the opening verse of *The Final Countdown*.

It was nothing like the original; it was the blues, with the tempo and feel of *House of the Rising Sun*, and it reached into Gunzabo and pulled something out, up through his chest and neck, leaving behind a sad, tingling sensation. Jimi was looking at the microphone as he sang in a plain, deep voice, guitar resting silent against his upper body, his jumpsuit sparkling in the lights. At the chorus he took his guitar up again, returned with that same arpeggio, full of controlled, restrained power, like a stallion pressing against wire at the edge of a field. The chorus ended; the time signature became four-four; the tempo increased; and the bass, loud and distorted, drove the music forward. Jimi began the second verse, singing with more feeling, his eyes closed, hitting the guitar strings with his plectrum gripped in a closed fist. A spotlight revealed Janis on stage beside him; she echoed the lines he sang, her voice somehow endowed with a tainted purity that complemented Jimi's perfectly; between them they seemed to connect every living being in the amphitheatre in a grid of energy.

The chorus returned, this time longer, though faster and louder than before; and only now did the main musical theme of the song appear, played on the guitar, while Jimi and Janis sang in angry harmony. Their voices became howls as they finished the final line of the second chorus, the band returned to E minor and Keith played a drum solo, a flurry of arms and sticks, nodding his head violently and raining sweat on his drum kit, until he picked up a steady, urgent beat and the guitar solo began.

Jimi played a barrage of complex improvised passages with ecstatic ease, his head raised to the black sky, as if in praise of the night, and the notes intertwined into a single scream that stopped being a note and was just a feeling, and then the note diverged into a waterfall of sound, became a scream again, and another one, even higher pitched. The main melody came back and Janis took the lead now to sing the chorus and Jimi echoed her on the guitar and they repeated the melody louder and faster until finally the song climaxed and they all improvised in a mad cacophony that met and parted, met and parted and came back to fuse permanently as the song ended. Jimi hurled his guitar to the floor; Kurt swung his bass by the neck into one of the monitors; Keith kicked over his drums; Janis screamed with her hands stretched to the sky, as if to say 'Look what you've done to us!'

Jimi's violence was unmatched. He picked his guitar up and plunged it into the face of his amplifier, pulled it out, rammed it back in; the second was a mortal wound: the distorted wail of the guitar abruptly ended as he threw it aside and put a foot through the bass amp, grabbed a microphone stand and used it to destroy the drum kit, the monitors, the onstage lighting, the projector screen, and the spare instruments at the side of the stage.

Gunzabo sat and watched the carnage taking place. At first, it seemed to him a repeat of the violent end to the party from the night before. But this was different, he realised: last night had been the product of a primal, uncontrollable fury; this was part of the act, a very different Jimi, a destructive finale on the last night of a farewell tour. Jimi was on his knees, pouring something flammable onto the pieces of his guitar, which he lit with a match and he knelt at the flames, urging them to rise and spread, the folds of his spacesuit shimmering from the fire.

Then he stood, turned to the audience and looked at them for the first time.

'Thank you,' he said, and he turned and disappeared into the darkness.

The audience erupted. Gunzabo stood and cheered with everyone else. There was no point calling for more – the stage was a smoking, broken wreck – but he called out anyway. Only Christian remained seated, his small eyes hidden by the lights shining off his spectacles.

Gunzabo moved to the next table as the villagers disappeared to confer on the winner.

'He smashed it, baby,' Bruce said. His fists were trembling

with emotion. 'He broke my heart tonight. He tore it out and then he did it to everyone, one after the other, feinting like *this* and like *this*, and then the other way, like *that* and then landing a punch, and another one, then a jab to the eye...'

'Bloody amazing,' Heath said quietly. 'I'll never see anything like it again.'

Minutes later the villagers trooped out from behind the stage. One of Lastri's sisters walked over to Christian and whispered in his ear. Christian smiled and nodded, looking over at Gunzabo from across the arena. Then Elvis came onto the stage, thanked everyone, announced that the judges had made their decision, reminded everyone about the after party, then raised his voice and said, 'And the winner is...' He paused dramatically. 'Gunzabo!'

Everyone clapped, turning to Gunzabo as he looked around uncertainly and shuffled onto the stage. He was extremely drunk now, but a lucid drunkenness from drinking spirits, where his mind was clear but his body lagged way behind. He stared at the trophy – a shining silver likeness of Dead Star Island – and began a mumbling acceptance speech, but after a few halting sentences, realised nobody was listening and he wasn't making any sense so he stopped talking. He noticed Jimi standing in the darkness on the far side of the stage, outside the circle of light cast by the rig. Ken was talking animatedly into his ear, while Jimi nodded, sober and expressionless, like a boxer taking instructions at the start of a fight.

Gunzabo stood on the stage, clutching the trophy to his chest, oblivious to Elvis's good natured banter with the audience. Something was happening; something was being planned. He was certain someone else was going to die, but knew he would be too drunk to prevent it. He came to suddenly, as Elvis clapped him forcefully on the back. He fell off the stage. The trophy snapped under him as he hit the gravel.

He lay there, stunned, for what seemed like hours. The sky

was infinitely black, yet close and impenetrable, like the inside of a coffin lid. He wondered what was beyond the solid, all-consuming shadow, wondered where the stars had gone. Perhaps they were no more. Perhaps the universe was gone and all that was left was the island, a lone star hanging in the dead cosmos, frozen in time and space.

Lastri and her sisters were standing over him, looks of concern on their faces. They knelt down, sat him up and made him drink a pot of herbal tea. Jim came over.

'Hey man,' he told them. 'You should not be doing that. That stuff is dangerous. I doubt it's even organic.'

He produced a joint the size of a parsnip, poked it into Gunzabo's mouth and lit it. Gunzabo took a drag and inhaled deeply. It did not taste like cannabis; he did not know what it was but it felt strong and dangerous and ripped the life out of him. Everything went black.

28

Gunzabo emerged from the depths of unconsciousness. Somewhere, deep down, he had the strange, receding sensation of dancing harlequins. He sat up and blinked. The staff had finished clearing up and were sitting on the lower steps of the amphitheatre. Jim was cross-legged beside him, in his creased suit and black aviators, smoking a fat, badly rolled joint.

'Welcome back,' Jim said. He exhaled a huge plume of smoke and turned his head to Lastri. 'I told you it would work, honey. He's reborn, a new man.'

Lastri sighed, shook her head and left with a large group of women. A dozen or so male villagers remained, sitting quietly on the low steps with their knees under their chins.

'Adinda, we'll take those beers now.' Jim took two pills out of his shirt pocket. 'These are from Ken,' he told Gunzabo. 'For the party. These little princesses will keep you going all night.'

The party was in full swing when they arrived at Elvis's place. Jim strolled in with his arm round Gunzabo's shoulder, calling for drinks as he high-fived the other guests. 'And don't forget the boys, here.' He indicated the male villagers behind them.

'Sure thing,' River called out.

'It's the least you can do, man,' said Jim. 'They've been wiping your asses all year. Elvis, I forgot what a dump this place is. You should get yourself a nice hut on the beach.'

The villa was magnificent: its floors were intricate mosaics picturing scenes from Greek myth; bookcases lined the walls; velvet-cushioned chairs and settees were positioned alongside tables filled with fresh fruit and simple Mediterranean dishes;

marble statues of Greek gods and Roman emperors encircled the party goers.

Elvis was talking with Diana. After clapping Jim on the back, he turned to Gunzabo. 'I may have been a little impatient with you, Maz,' he said. 'You're just doing your job, I see that now.'

Elvis glanced at Diana as he said this. She smiled at him approvingly, nodded at Jim, then offered her hand to Gunzabo. 'Congratulations on your victory.'

'I don't remember much,' Gunzabo said.

'Just as well, Maz,' said Elvis. 'Just as well.'

They sipped their drinks.

'You'll have to excuse us,' Elvis said. 'I have some, uh, new soft goods to show the lady.'

Diana gave Gunzabo a meaningful look, reminding him of his promise to keep quiet.

'Young love,' said Jim, when they had left. 'Wonderful, isn't it? New and pure, untainted by external desire.'

Everyone stopped talking. Gunzabo turned, saw that Jimi and Janis had arrived. They stood holding hands as the room broke into loud applause, Janis in flared jeans and a billowing, frilly white blouse; Jimi was in his jumpsuit, holding a silver helmet with a black visor. Bruce rushed up to embrace them both, then everyone else thronged round and took turns to hug Jimi and shake his hand, while Janis clung on, looking up adoringly. Gunzabo could see her face reflected in Jimi's metallic suit.

'Love him, don't they?'

Gunzabo glanced around; Ken was standing next to him.

'You'd think he was twenty-seven again,' Ken said. 'Got your trophy, have you?'

Gunzabo took the broken pieces out of his trouser pocket. Ken smirked. 'Oh dear,' he said, 'you look a mess. Have one of these, this'll sort you out.'

Ken handed him a white pill, which he swallowed with the

rest of his cocktail. 'I'm amazed I won,' he said.

'Well you did. Congratulations.'

Gunzabo looked across at Jimi, who was talking amiably with the crowd still around him. 'Jimi should have it,' he mumbled. 'I'll be back in a minute.'

Ken took his arm lightly, but didn't let go. His smile had gone. 'Gunzabo, don't take this the wrong way.'

'Take what?'

'I'm telling you this so you don't make a fool of yourself.'

'What?'

'How can I put it? There's never a winner of the talent show. Only a loser. Too many egos, see. The first year – before my time of course – apparently Janis won. All hell broke loose.'

Gunzabo looked at the broken trophy in his hand.

'Sorry,' said Ken.

'I knew that,' Gunzabo said.

Ken didn't say anything.

'I was the foremost detective in Greece.'

'Yeah, course,' Ken said.

'For over a decade.'

'Yeah.'

'They thought no one would ever catch the Geryon Triplets.'

'Course not. Those elusive triplets, I bet they took some catching.'

Music started; the crowd around Jimi thinned out; Janis and Karen began dancing while the villagers and male residents stood drinking at the edges.

'Look, old A-Dolph's here,' said Ken. 'Now the party's really started.'

Christian had slipped into the room; he was standing on his own, sipping a glass of mineral water between statues of Poseidon and Zeus.

'Why'd you call him A-Dolph?' asked Kurt, who had just

joined them.

Bruce leaned across. 'Cause that's his name, baby.'

'Christian's his middle name,' Ken said. 'Joan told me a few years back. Had the hump with him about something, let it slip. He doesn't like using A-Dolph. Can't think why. Isn't that right?' Ken directed this at Gunzabo. 'You're his mate from way back.'

'It's true,' Gunzabo told them.

'Why would anyone call their son that?' asked Kurt.

'She liked the name,' said Gunzabo. 'And the uniforms.'

Kurt laughed. 'Hey, she had a point. I always wondered how those Nazis could have lost the war, being so finely dressed and all.'

'They should have spent more time fighting, man,' said Bruce. 'Less time starching shirts and polishing those jackboots.'

River came past with a tray of mojitos; they each took a glass.

'Old Major Tom over there,' Ken said, indicating Jimi in his spacesuit. 'He likes a uniform, doesn't he?'

'That was our song,' Gunzabo murmured, scratching his upper arm.

'What, *Space Oddity*?'

Gunzabo nodded. 'It makes me want to weep.'

The opening lines popped in his head, and he remembered how Megara would sing it to him, when he was at home, and he'd been thinking about a case for hours. It would make him surface briefly, make him smile.

'More of a Spice Girls man myself.' Ken leaned in towards them all, three pills cupped in his hand. 'Here's a protein pill for you. Keep you going all night these will.'

'What is this, man?' Bruce said suspiciously. 'Not one of those sex pills, is it? The last one nearly finished me off.'

'Nothing like that. Anyhow, you never listened to what I said. I said to have a quarter. You had six of them.'

They each took their pill from Ken. 'Right,' he said. 'I'm

gonna bolt. Things to do, people to see.'

Gunzabo chewed on the pill and watched Ken wander past Christian, greet him cheerfully, then shake hands with Heath and Marc and drop a pill in each of their drinks. Someone turned up the volume and everyone moved into the centre of the room, linking arms as they shouted along to the music. Janis appeared from the melee, a flirtatious grin on her face, as she grabbed Gunzabo and Bruce and pulled them in, and now Gunzabo was shuffling unrhythmically with the others, while Bruce swayed and pirouetted and darted about with his mouth open like a chameleon to catch loose splashes of drink. Gunzabo shouted along with the others as Black Lace came on, roaring with almost animal exuberance at the ceiling before being pulled back into the revelry, from which only Christian remained apart: alone by the door, as silent and distant as the statues flanking the room. An hour later, when Gunzabo was back at the bar, he saw Christian slip out of the French doors. As he was closing the doors behind him, Christian stopped for a moment, looked back longingly into the room at the merriment inside, before disappearing into the night.

'Almost feel sorry for him, don't you?' Ken had joined Gunzabo at the bar.

'No,' Gunzabo told him.

'He's got to be up in the morning, anyhow.'

'Why?'

'Going to the mainland. Important business, apparently.'

Gunzabo didn't respond.

'Old Brucie's enjoying himself, isn't he?' Ken said.

They watched Bruce down the remains of a bottle of rum while the crowd cheered him on. 'Way of the bottle these days, innit?' said Ken. 'Who's serving anyhow?' He tried a few of the dozen or so empty bottles littering the bar. 'That's the problem with inviting the staff, service goes out the window.

Right, nothing else for it, time for some Ken Winter specials.'

He stepped behind the bar, slammed a selection of spirits on the thick granite.

'Cinzano, Gunzabo?' he said.

'Why not.'

'I've been wanting to say that for days.'

Gunzabo leaned heavily against the bar. Revellers came and went as Ken mixed drinks and handed out pills. Fifteen minutes later, River appeared with two cases of champagne.

'Chelsea!' Ken yelled out, and a cheer went up as he opened each bottle, one after another, putting one into each outstretched hand along with a small white pill.

Later on, when everyone else was staggering around inside, drinking and shouting, roaring songs around the piano, Gunzabo found himself on the veranda, mumbling to Karen about his admiration for her and the wonderful career she'd had, and how everyone had agreed what a pity it was when she died. He stopped talking. She was looking back at him with a compassionate smile.

'I see such sadness in you, Gunzabo,' she said.

He looked into the darkness in an effort to steady his vision.

'What happened to you?' she asked him.

He turned to her and she looked so heartbreakingly sorry for him, and her shining, sad eyes seemed to gaze so piercingly into his soul, he almost sobered up.

'Do you know the story of Heracles?' he said.

'Remind me.'

'He was a Hero. Greatest of all the Greek Heroes. Even as a baby, he performed wondrous acts.' Gunzabo paused to check she was listening, then stared at the ground and took a deep breath. 'He committed a terrible crime. He killed his family. For this he had to perform twelve labours. The final labour, he descended to the Underworld, taken by the ferryman of the dead, Charon, across the Styx, to where no mortal may set foot.'

He paused as the world fell away and all he knew was a terrible thickness in his chest.

'What about you, Gunzabo?'

He glanced towards the voice, but saw nothing, breathed deeply as he tried to dispel the constricting, all-consuming tightness in his entire upper body, but his voice was steady now as he spoke.

'We were married two years only. I was so happy. My career was flourishing, I had forgotten everything that happened in Cyprus, so I thought. The baby came, my wife grew distant. I drank too much, she didn't like it, we fought. I had a short temper in those days. One day, I came home, I had been investigating a difficult case and I was drunk. I carried on drinking. Everything that was in the house, I drank that night. We had another fight, a terrible fight. I said things to her that a husband should never say to his wife. She took the baby and said she was leaving, she was going to her mother's house. She already had the bag ready, and when I saw this I became furious. She tried to leave, but I would not let her and I hit her in the face. I can still see the fear in her eyes. The silent helplessness, the sadness at the passing of our love.

'At first I would not let her leave the house. But when I saw how determined she was, suddenly I did not care and I told her I would take her. She wouldn't come with me, said I was too drunk. I didn't listen. I forced her into my car. She was holding the baby, our little girl, she was holding her so close, sitting in the passenger seat as I drove to Piraeus, keeping the baby as far away from me as she could. She would not say a word. I only became more angry and I drove through the late night traffic, shouting at the cars in my way. The road cleared, and I remember the feeling of satisfaction that I could drive much faster now and scare her.

'She started speaking to me, told me to stop, then she started pleading. She said to let her out, think of the baby. I looked at her, opened my mouth to tell her what I thought of her baby, what I thought of her, but she wasn't looking at me. She was looking ahead. She screamed and she said, "Mario!"'

At the edge of his vision Karen was gazing at him, tears running down her cheeks as she listened.

'No one else was killed. We hit a traffic light. Neither of us were wearing seatbelts. She and the baby died instantly, they told me. It was a miracle I lost only my arm.'

He stood in silence now as Karen came close and pulled his head into her bosom. Everything was black as he cried uncontrollably against her robes. He did not know how long for. He was not even there: he was looking into a chasm and he could not stop crying, and everything which he had inside him, everything that filled him, all that defined him, came in a great outpouring, came through his eyes and his mouth and his ears, out through the centre of his chest and the top of his head, until finally his mind slowly returned to the world, and he became aware of his face against soft material. He left her embrace, looked at her, smiled with gratitude, utterly spent. She smiled back. He heard noise as the doors slid open.

'Karen, what're you doing out here, honey?' It was Janis. 'Come on, dance with me.'

Karen shook her head, not taking her eyes off him.

'Go,' he told her.

'I don't want to leave you, Gunzabo. Let's take you home.'

'I'll be fine,' he said. 'Go and dance.'

Karen moved up to him. She looked him in the eyes, said nothing, then kissed him, fully on the lips, wiped the tears from his cheeks and his eyes, smiled and let herself be taken inside.

He watched them briefly through the glass: Janis was stamping gaily as Karen nodded her shaved head to the *Ghostbusters* theme. Then he walked into the depths of the garden where it was as black as the sky. Unbearably tired, he lay down, cheek against grass, huddled like a foetus in a womb. Somewhere at the edge of his senses, fragments of jokes and laughter and the occasional shout reached him, hollow, dreamlike echoes, and perhaps a flash of light, faint but probably very bright at its source, like a distant supernova. Then something changed and there was only sensation and Gunzabo couldn't tell which sense provided it: something gently stabbed his body, hissed quietly in the ground at his ears, was thunderous high above; now foulness in his mouth, but also purity; it extracted a new smell from the ground; it blinded him and washed his eyes clean. Gunzabo was soaked in seconds as he lay in the rain. It came in a torrent, flooding the ground and it was warm and shallow, like lying in the sea at the edge of a beach. He was asleep now, hair dancing gently in the water while the rain, softer now, splashed against his open lips.

He woke. The rain had stopped. It was dark, but maybe less so; dawn was approaching. The villa was dark and quiet; water dripped from the trees. He closed his eyes, floated in nothingness, opened his eyes again, and with that simple act felt instantly recreated, reborn into the world. He blinked, wondered where Didi was, and then, as he stared up at the sky, a single image projected onto his mind.

A still from Jim's film.

John, looking into the camera on the morning of the shooting.

Suddenly he realised what was wrong, what it was he had needed to see. He did not have the answer, but he had the question. He smiled into the darkness. There was no relief, just simple understanding that the answer was now coming. He left the image and the knowledge behind as his mind became elevated and his thoughts hurtled into space in a thrilling burst of energy.

Suddenly there was hope. And not just for the case, but for his past. Was there somewhere out here, a place for his wife and his daughter? Jupiter flashed by. Was there truly a renewal of life, way beyond Earth? His mind surged further, past Pluto, through fields of stars, to the outer reaches of the Milky Way; then beyond, into the void between galaxies. He hung there in nothingness, looking for them. *Where are you?* he shouted soundlessly into the vacuum.

Nothing.

Gradually the energy dissipated, the hurt returned.

Enough. Back to the film.

Back to the question. Yes, the question! Finally something to work with.

The answer would come. His mind rose again as he returned to the edge of the universe, waiting, staring; until finally he turned and looked back to Earth, which now came rushing towards him and as he fell he saw millions of people: also waiting; also mourning; and staring, but at screens, at magazines, at books, at machines; assuming that there is never an end; passively surrendering to false promise; alive but somehow dead.

He blinked open his eyes. His mind and body ached with exhaustion. Craving his bed, he stood, moved to walk across the garden towards the beach, but tripped on something soft. A body was lying in the grass. He felt a stab of fear. The killer. He had forgotten the killer. He prodded flesh. It grunted. He sighed with relief, saw it was Jim, who rolled onto his back and began snoring. Standing up, he saw more bodies on the grass: Marc, Kurt, Keith, and villagers, all passed out on the sodden ground. He checked them all, made certain they were alive, then made his way onto the sand and back to his bungalow.

As he lay naked in bed, before entering pure, grey, dreamless sleep, the question appeared before him one final time. Yes, he thought fuzzily, the question. Forget the rest of it, all that philosophical nonsense. The question, that was the key to it all.

Why was John wearing a long-sleeved top on the hottest day of the year?

29

The room was hot and bright. He lifted his head, saw the doors to the veranda were wide open. Insects buzzed outside. He clamped his hand round his forehead to ease the pain. He remembered the outpouring from the night before, that final release. He felt like death.

After a while, he picked up his clothes, folded them over his arm and walked down to the beach. The damp heat pushed against his bare skin. The pure whiteness of the sky was intolerable.

Leaving his clothes on the sand, he waded into the sea and swam out until the water was cold and he could look back to take in the whole island. As he trod water, he watched the tranquillity of the beach, saw the yellow sand become thinner as it angled into the distance, with the forest behind, green and dark and flowing in waves up the mountains. There was wind out here and he lay on his back, bobbing over waves as he watched the island; it seemed far below him, strangely inverted, and winked in and out of existence as waves flowed over his head. He vomited. Particles of food floated around him. He vomited again.

Somewhere in the distance an engine started. A wave rose up behind him as he was retching and took him deeper. The sound of the engine was more acute underwater, but still distant, and he could not tell where it was coming from. He surfaced and the world became vivid again. Seawater rattled in his lungs, and he tried to cough it out, but another wave came just as he was thrusting his arm towards the sky, then more waves, and each time he was taken down, until he stopped fighting and let the waves take him under, release him, then pull him back down again. His mind became clear now and he saw the world fall away from him and the roof of the sea swirling above his head, growing wider as he went down. The roar of the water had stopped; it crashed high above him soundlessly. He turned and stared into the depths of the ocean, felt himself being drawn ever down, saw how deep it was, as deep as space. He knew suddenly that it was here that he would see Megara, that she would come to him and he would see something in her face, a signal of some kind, one final message. He waited. *Please my darling*, he mouthed in the water. *Please forgive me.* But there was only sea, clear and pure and deep – and his insides were now equally as clear and deep – as a sudden realisation came to him: she was gone forever. Only one person could forgive him. He decided to live.

There was still no sound, just the sea filling his ears and his nose as he kicked with his feet and thrashed his arm until he neared the surface; one last burst of energy and briefly there was the roar of splashing water as he broke through, but waves crashed over him, forcing him down, and his strength was now gone. He heard the buzzing noise return; it passed through his ears, as he hung now without moving, suspended in the water. His mind grew still. All he knew was that insistent buzzing, which became louder and louder, and then he came jerking back into his skin and the sea was cold and noisy and there was a boat and arms hauling him up and out of the water.

'Mario. *Εντάξει φίλε μου;* Are you alright?'

Gunzabo opened his eyes. He was lying on the deck of a boat. Someone was thrusting their fists into his chest. He expelled water and was sick again.

'Don't get up, Mario. Just stay where you are.'

He saw Christian gazing down at him: rimless spectacles covered in watery brown vomit.

'So it was you,' said Gunzabo, eventually.

'We were just leaving. You've got Thomas to thank. He saw something, we came over.'

Gunzabo grimaced and lifted his head. Tommy was guiding the boat back to shore. He sank back onto the deck as Christian leaned over him again.

'You weren't trying to escape, were you?'

Christian flashed his teeth and grinned. Gunzabo muttered something that even he didn't understand.

'Don't be upset. I was only joking, Mario. Do you still not understand my humour? Of course you weren't leaving, where would you go? *Why* would you go? They *all* want to come here, you see. Did you know that? The prospects we have, it's such an exciting time. And I can see your loyalty, how you've come to love being part of our family. I'd like that to last forever. I'm so glad you're safe, so glad you're in one piece. Are you awake? You've been through so much, I know that Mario. That's over now, the future's taken care of. I'm going to tell you a secret. Would you like to hear it? I just can't keep it to myself, everybody will know by tomorrow anyhow when I make the announcement. We have a new person! I know, it's wonderful. Someone new coming to stay with us: David. He's going to be here soon, we'll have his house ready, make him welcome. It'll take time to acclimatise, it always does. He'll have some regrets, they always do. But he's on his way.'

Gunzabo lay silently on the deck with his eyes closed.

'You can teach him tennis, Mario. I believe he's an aficionado. Won't that be wonderful?' Christian whispered fiercely now. 'I'm so glad we can move on from this, this frustrating, awful treachery, this... time we've been having. It's over now. I'm so glad I brought you here, Mario. You're like a brother to me. You *are* a brother. Do you play table tennis? You could coach that too. You see, there are so many opportunities here.'

Gunzabo felt the boat slow to a halt. It floated on the water as the engine idled. They were at the jetty where he landed four days ago.

Christian flashed his grin. 'Here you are.' He spoke in his normal voice now. 'You have a nice day and get some rest. I have to go now. There's so much to do. Some of us can't party as hard as the rest of you.'

Gunzabo staggered onto the jetty and watched the boat until it merged into nothingness at the horizon. Something brushed his ankle. He looked down, saw Didi.

'What's up?' she asked. 'Been playing strip poker with Tommy again?'

'Nothing that exciting.'

'Where did A-Dolph go?'

'To the mainland.'

'Getting more gifts for everyone is he?'

Gunzabo squinted out to sea. 'Something like that. Come on.'

'Come on where?' Didi asked, scrambling after him.

'We finally have our chance,' he said.

'What chance?'

'To see Christian's house.'

'Don't you want to get some clothes on first?'

'There's no time.'

He waited for Didi to climb onto his shoulder, then hurried through the gardens, blocking out her continual questions. Nothing mattered except getting to the house in the hills. At The Circles, staff were arriving for the morning shift. He ignored their bemused stares as he strode past.

'Good morning sir,' they called after him. 'Going anywhere nice?'

'Off to ransack Christian's house for clues.'

'Very good, sir.'

He reached the amphitheatre, which was empty – no sign remained of the festivities from the night before. Didi raced ahead, skipping over the sandy floor of the arena, but he pressed on, into the jungle, by a narrow path which snaked upwards through thick foliage. Occasionally the path twisted and freed itself of vegetation and he could see Christian's lone white house in the green hills above.

'What do you think we'll find there?' asked Didi.

She was perched on his head in her meerkat pose.

'Nothing. I always expect nothing Didi. You know that.'

'I can't decide if you're being all mysterious, or you just haven't got a clue what's going on.'

'Both those things,' he told her.

He emerged into a clearing. Didi jumped down, racing the remaining thirty metres to the front door of Christian's house.

30

The house was a small, two storey cement cube, painted brilliant white. He stopped at the door, turned to look at the view: choppy, colourless sea stretching out to the horizon; seamless white cloud overhead, almost close enough to touch; dense vegetation running steeply below and reflecting every shade of green.

He turned back to the house. There was no patio, no garden, not a single chair outside, just neatly clipped grass, a concrete perimeter and the house with its flat roof and white walls and brown front door.

He pushed at the door; it was locked. He walked around the house. The windows were shuttered and bolted.

'I could try and get us in,' said Didi.

Picking up a large rock, he walked over to one of the shuttered windows. 'On this occasion I prefer breaking and entering,' he said, and proceeded to smash the wooden slats to pieces. He pulled the sharp remains from the frame, tore aside the mosquito netting, and climbed into the house.

Didi was waiting inside. 'I picked the lock, stupid-head,' she said. 'You could have saved all that trouble.'

He was in a simple, bare reception room which also served as the dining area and contained a small square table with a single chair against it. At the rear was a kitchen, functional and well stocked with crockery, utensils and ageing appliances. The kitchen walls were finished with cheap ceramic tiles. A single picture hung on the wall: a photograph of a stern old woman dressed in black, sitting in an armchair.

'Look, it's mummy,' said Didi. She wrinkled her nose at the picture. The woman stared back disapprovingly.

'Rhea,' Gunzabo said.

He left the kitchen and went back into the reception room. On the far side was a locked door. He put his shoulder to the door, which flew open and he stepped into a living area: a single leather armchair facing a home cinema, and underneath, games consoles, a laptop, a satellite phone; on a low, deep shelf at the back of the room was a coffee machine, two servers, and various unidentifiable boxes of electronic gadgetry with flickering green lights.

'It's like Marilyn's bedroom in here,' Didi said, taking a nip at the cabling.

There was nothing much to see upstairs: two ordinary bedrooms, plain and tidy, a wardrobe and a chest of drawers which he soon tired of rifling through. 'I'd forgotten how boring he is,' he muttered.

'Hadn't you better cover your tracks?' asked Didi.

'The mess will infuriate him. Even more than the intrusion.'

He looked at the clothes lying on the floor, then down at his bare flesh. He picked out a tracksuit: golden brown, with a hooded top. It was a perfect fit. He stood admiring himself in the mirror.

Didi blinked at him. 'When you said Christian was bullied at school.'

'Hmm.'

'It was you, wasn't it?'

He looked back at Didi. 'It was everyone. Don't feel sorry for him. Even then, he was torturing small animals like you, turning them into exhibits.'

He continued the search, checking the shower, the wall-mounted bathroom cabinet, the toiletries and sachets of hair dye under the sink. He went downstairs, back into the reception room. One door remained, also locked. He forced it open: darkness; the aroma of chemicals. He groped in the dark until he found a light switch.

'The workshop,' he said, gazing across the room disdainfully.

There was only one exhibit: a preserved dolphin on its mount against the far wall. On the other walls shelves were neatly filled with hardback books, empty glass jars, bottles of colourless liquid. A wooden seat was pushed under a plain desk; alongside was a high wooden bench, two metres long, leather straps folded across the top. Everything was tidy and scrupulously clean.

'Even his workshop is so dull it puts you to sleep,' Gunzabo said. He looked around. 'Didi?' She wasn't there. He hurried back into the reception room. 'Didi?' he called again, a slight unease in his spine. There was no answer. 'Did you get bored of my moaning?'

She was in the kitchen, sniffing at the floor level units. 'There you are,' he said.

Didi didn't answer. She nudged open the door to one of the units and scuttled inside.

'Are you hungry?' he asked her. 'I don't suppose he'll have any beer.'

Gunzabo opened the refrigerator. He frowned sourly at the contents: fruit juice, milk, salad vegetables, alfalfa, natural yogurt, various fresh fruits and cheeses.

A *click* sounded from inside the cabinet Didi had entered.

'Found something?' he said, shutting the fridge.

There was no answer. Squatting down, he looked into the cabinet, pulled out cereal boxes and packets of muesli, then leaned inside.

The interior was larger than he expected. The floor was raised at a slight angle. 'What have you found, my little beauty?' he murmured.

He reached to the back, felt a metal ring, which he pulled up and towards him. A trapdoor opened, hinged in the middle. It unfolded with a crash onto the kitchen tiles. Steep, dimly lit steps led down into darkness.

Gripping the kitchen worktop, he swung his legs onto the steps and made his way down. The stairs twisted in a dogleg at the bottom. He peered into a low, unlit passage. The air was cool down here and the concrete walls felt damp against his hand. He followed the passage until it turned ninety degrees, where he stopped and listened. Music was playing quietly nearby. A door was partially open at the other end, revealing the golden glow of lamplight. Didi was waiting for him.

'You've got to see this,' she said.

'See what?'

'Just come and look.'

Gunzabo pushed open the door. It swung silently on its hinges, revealing a large, red-carpeted, low-ceilinged room, bathed in soft light as gentle and comforting as the final glowing embers of a winter fireplace. Cocktail bar jazz tinkled in the background. He saw people, positioned at various points in the room: seated on a sofa, standing in the corner and at the bar; and in the centre a man stood waiting for him with a broad smile, leaning against a white baby-grand piano, arms open ready to greet him. Gunzabo could not see any faces in the twilight, but he knew everyone. He moved towards the host. Nobody else paid any attention, contented and sheltered as they were in this subterranean bar. The soft piano music chimed its endlessly intricate patterns and eradicated time itself; the carpet was luxuriant underfoot; the drinks sparkled in each guest's hand.

He moved forward, extended his hand to the host. But the man was looking beyond Gunzabo, ready to welcome someone behind him. He whirled round. The passage was empty. He turned back to the room, where the guests remained indifferent, unmoving. Yes of course! How had he not predicted this? He gazed at each guest, scanned each motionless figure, frozen in an instant, captured between the ticking hand of a clock and two beats of one man's heart. He knew that nobody would look over; no one would utter a single word of greeting, nor enquire as to his health, demand why he was here. Each glass stayed resolutely from each pair of lips; each face remained fixed in twinkly-eyed jollity.

'So this is what he does to them,' Gunzabo said, waving his fingers in front of the host's face. There was no change: a fixed smile into space. A placard hung above the man's head, suspended from the ceiling by a fine metal chain. Gunzabo pulled it towards him.

STEVE
This piece evokes the warmth and kindness of the man,
still remarkably vigorous in his twilight years; it was
made in the summer of 2003 at the Dead Star Island
workshop, and is widely acclaimed as Christian's
finest work.

He turned to a man sitting nearby, cross-legged on the floor.

BRIAN
A complex, many layered piece, it hints at the tragic
manner of the subject's passing: passionate and with
abandon, much as he led his life. It shows humour,
but also Christian's great affection for the subject;
most importantly it speaks of the continuation of
the physical, juxtaposed with the utter effacement of
the self.

Gunzabo moved around the room, studying each figure and its placard hanging above: a man and woman with dark skin, sitting regally on the sofa, a space ready for him between them; at the bar, two white-haired old men glanced round with jovial smiles and placards which read *Jack* and *Bobby*. He touched their faces and hands and hair, felt their perfect, soulless bodies.

'So where is he?' Gunzabo muttered.

'Who? Christian?' said Didi.

'Of course not. Think. Why are we here?'

He went back to the centre of the room, to the figure marked *Steve* by the piano, pulled the glass out of Steve's hand and took a sip. Real vodka. He downed it.

'Who then?' said Didi. 'You could just say, instead of all these riddles.'

'Christian is a master,' he said, gazing in wonder at the room and its occupants. 'I take back everything I said about him.' As his eyes passed over the piano he saw something glimmering in the air, and twisted his fingers round a fine chain which was dangling from the ceiling directly above the piano stool. There was no placard, just a metal chain.

He looked at Didi. 'See?' he said.

'What?'

'Where is he?' he asked her.

Didi was looking back at him blankly. 'Who?'

He sighed. 'John. Where is the body?'

A muffled shout came from somewhere above them. Didi scampered between Gunzabo's feet.

'Someone's here,' she said. 'We've got to get out.'

He hurried back along the corridor, heard another shout, urgent and high pitched, almost feverish.

'Who is it?' whispered Didi.

Gunzabo didn't answer. He poked his head out of the kitchen unit and listened. The voice shouted again. It came from the front of the house.

'Sir! Sir!'

'Something's happened,' Gunzabo said, pulling himself up.

He ran into the reception room, towards the front door, where a male member of staff was standing, eyes wide open, breathing ragged.

'Sir, you must come now!'

'What is it?'

The man was clinging to the doorframe, still catching his breath.

'Tell me, man. Quickly.'

'Something terrible has happened, sir.'

'Yes, yes. What?'

'Sir.'

'Go on, go on. Spit it out!'

'It's Jimi.'

'Yes.'

'He is dead.'

31

'We found him in his bedroom, sir.'

'When?'

'Thirty minutes ago, sir.'

'Who found him?'

'The maid, sir.'

They were hurrying down the path, through the forest, back down the mountain.

'Was anyone else there?'

'No, sir. She raised the alarm and we all rushed there, sir.'

'What about the residents? Was anybody else staying in the house?'

'I don't think so. But they sent me here immediately for you.'

'What's your name?'

'Gusti, sir.'

Gunzabo did not speak further until they arrived at The Circles. Staff milled around on the terrace, dazed and directionless. 'Where is the body?' he said.

Someone pointed dully inside the building.

'They must have taken him downstairs, sir,' Gusti said. 'To the medical centre.'

He took the stairs two at a time. Lastri was outside the medical centre, consoling Mrs Bradley, who was wailing into her sari.

'Who is inside?' he said.

Lastri looked at him slowly with red eyes. 'Only Ken. He insisted it might not be too late. He only just stopped trying.' She looked fondly at Mrs Bradley. 'There was nothing anyone could do. He has gone now.'

'Oh no, oh God,' cried Mrs Bradley. 'My boys. They're all dying. I just want to go home.' She began swinging her arm around and wailing. Her face and neck were scarlet. Gunzabo spoke softly to her, telling her she may do herself harm if she didn't calm down, that it wasn't what Jimi, or John, would have wanted. Gradually she quietened down. She nodded between trembling sobs and finally agreed to let Lastri take her upstairs for some air.

He went inside, through the office and into the operating theatre.

Ken was standing with his head in his hands. Behind him, Jimi was stretched out on the table, pale and lifeless. A sheet covered the body; feet and face showed at either end.

Ken looked up. 'I can't believe it,' he said, in a flat voice. 'It's happened again.' His face was haggard and pale; his eyes were bloodshot. 'I tried everything.'

'What was the cause of death, in your opinion?'

'Suffocation. Choked in his sleep.'

'Overdose?'

Ken shook his head despairingly. 'Can't say without a full examination.'

'What time was the body found?'

'Seven fifteen, this morning. He was dead when the maid found him.'

'Estimated time of death?'

Ken pursed his lips. 'It's not my field, but two hours before that, maybe.'

'You still tried resuscitating him when he was brought here?'

'Yes.' Ken dropped his head. 'I tried there, at his house, and then I had him brought here, tried again. It was hopeless, I knew that. But he was my mate.'

Gunzabo looked at the body, at the almost white face, and

for a moment he was taken back to Christian's mausoleum and the dressed corpses with the placards hanging from the ceiling. 'I want to be present at the post mortem,' he said. 'Will you be conducting it this morning?'

Ken lifted his head sharply. 'You think I'm an amateur don't you?'

'I'd also like a few minutes to examine the body. We must assume murder and it is essential I—'

'Gunzabo!'

He turned, saw Lastri in the doorway. She had lost her usual composure: her face was white and lined with worry and her voice shook as she said, 'I'm so sorry to interrupt you. It's Mrs Bradley. Please come.'

Reluctantly he followed Lastri down the corridor. 'She was asking for you,' Lastri was saying. 'She is almost deranged with grief. She said you're the only one who understands.'

Mrs Bradley was sitting in an armchair on the terrace. Her face was maroon and she was breathing heavily, but she seemed by now to have calmed slightly. He asked her how she was.

'Oh, I'm alright, love,' she said quietly. 'It's just such a shock. I don't think my heart can take much more of this.' She mopped her face with her handkerchief, then looked him in the eye. 'When are you going to catch him?'

'I don't yet know it was murder,' Gunzabo told her.

'Of course it is,' she sobbed. 'First Brian, then John. Now Jimi. Who knows, maybe Steve was bumped off too. Oh, what a mess!'

'Look, Joan,' he said. 'Stay here, have a whisky. Let Ken give you something. You'll feel better for it. I have to go now.'

He stood up.

'What are you going to do?' said Mrs Bradley.

'I'm going to examine the—'

'Nobody is going to do anything!' a voice snarled.

Christian strode past, knocking Gunzabo over the arm of Mrs

Bradley's chair and headfirst into her lap. It was like being stuck in an enormous beanbag as he grasped at flesh, finally pulled himself out, ran into The Circles and straight downstairs, where he saw Christian and Tommy at the other end of the corridor before they disappeared into the medical centre. As he approached the door he could hear Christian barking out questions inside.

'What in hell is going on?'

'It's Jimi. He's—'

'Another one? This is intolerable!'

Gunzabo was in the doorway now, saw Christian, next to the body, his hand resting on the table. Ken gazed steadfastly at the floor. 'Yes, it is,' he said.

Christian turned away from him, his face warped with fury. Gunzabo moved alongside. 'We cannot lose any more time, Christian. It is certain the murderer has struck again. I must begin my examination immediately, before it is too late.'

Christian laughed ironically. 'It's already too late.'

'I will need full access to the body.'

Christian moved his head slowly to look at Gunzabo, his eyes slits, his voice little more than a hiss. 'You seem to need a lot from me, all of the time. Who is employing who, I wonder to myself?'

Gunzabo looked back at him steadily. 'Let me get on with my job.'

'That won't be necessary,' Christian said dismissively, and then, controlling his anger, he added, 'You can go. The doctor and I can handle this situation.'

Gunzabo stared at him in amazement for a few moments, watched him glaring at the body. 'Why did you bring me here?' he said.

'You were brought here to stop this happening,' Christian answered. 'You failed. You aren't needed here anymore.'

Tommy stepped across the doorway, eyes unblinking as he shuffled forward to force Gunzabo back into the corridor.

'We can speak later,' Gunzabo called out to Ken.

'I doubt it,' Christian said softly.

He made his way back along the corridor, heard the door slam shut as he mounted the stairs.

'That was weird,' said Didi, poking her nose out of his sleeve. 'Do they actually want you to solve this case?'

'No.'

'So what do we do, daddio?'

'We listen.'

Gunzabo hastened back, quietly padding the final few metres to the closed door, where he stood, back to the wall, held his breath and listened.

'You betrayed us for Elysian Fields,' he heard Christian say. 'This has to stop.'

'Yes, I know.'

'Oh you know, do you? There's only one thing that will make me believe that. You know what it is.' Christian's voice carried no emotion. 'Then you can take him away, I don't want him here. Fortunately I have several prospects. We are expecting someone new, not that you would care.'

'I do care, Christian. Of course I do.'

'Don't speak to me. You swore this would not happen again.'

'I had no choice.'

'Shut up.' There was a pause, then Christian said, 'Why did he do it?'

'He was bored.' Ken sounded a little sheepish. 'He didn't take much persuasion.'

'You said John would be the last. I'm a fool for believing that, of course.'

'Listen to me, Christian. I'm sorry, I really am. It's just… everything went wrong. Really wrong. He's dead.'

'I don't care.'

Gunzabo heard movement, the scraping of a chair. 'Did you

hear me?' Ken said. 'I mean John. He's dead.'

'Yes, and now I will never have him. This one I care less about anyhow.'

'I'd better see to him.'

'Do as you will. I don't want to see you again.'

Christian's voice became louder as he approached the door.

'Quick, they'll see us,' whispered Didi. 'Why are you smiling?'

Gunzabo did not answer; neither did he stop smiling. It all made sense. How could he not have seen this earlier? No matter, he decided. The mystery was nearly over, and now, in his mind, the puzzling questions fell neatly into place as he saw in an instant the reasons for every action, every evasive answer of the past four days, and even the time before his arrival.

'Yes, let's go,' he said. 'I've heard enough.'

Elysian Fields. It was the key to everything.

32

'So when are we going back to the medical room?'

'We aren't,' Gunzabo told Didi.

'But you said you wanted to inspect the body.'

'Yes.'

'And now you don't?'

'No.'

Didi sighed. 'You're so annoying.'

He marched past Brian's place, glancing across the newly mowed lawn at the open doors and windows, and at the buckets and cleaning materials gathered neatly on the veranda.

'What were they on about, back there?' said Didi. 'It didn't make sense.'

'It makes perfect sense.'

'Are you joking?'

'I never joke.'

'Go on then, spill the beans.'

'Not yet. Still a few tight ends to loosen.'

He walked past River's house.

'So what about Christian's basement?' asked Didi. 'At least tell me what that means.'

'It means nothing,' Gunzabo said. 'There was nothing worth seeing.'

'Are you serious?'

'How many times have you been in his office? Two, three? That basement is exactly the same thing. If anything more humane. Mere roadkill.'

'But what we saw up at Christian's house,' persisted Didi.

'It's central to the mystery, surely? It must lead to the murderer.'

'What we saw explains the reason for Dead Star Island's existence. But nothing more. It's what we *did not* see that is important. That is what is central to the mystery, Didi. That and what we just heard in the medical room.' He smiled and looked out to sea. 'I can't believe it's taken so long. My brain is rusting. Too much tennis.'

'Too much booze, more like.'

He walked in silence up the beach for a while.

'So where are we going now?' said Didi. 'Are you willing to tell me that?'

'Jimi's place. I want to check a few things. Just to be certain.'

'The tight ends?'

'Precisely.'

He reached the entrance to Jimi's garden and went inside. Bruce, River and Janis were sitting by the pool, silently grieving while staff worked around them, clearing rubbish and sweeping up.

'Hey, Gunzabo,' said Janis. Her face was wet with tears.

'They aren't wasting their time,' said Gunzabo, moving aside as a staff member crawled by, pulling out weeds from between the tiles.

'They wanted to get the place straightened out,' she told him.

'Have they started on the inside?'

'No way, baby,' Bruce said. 'It's not what Jimi would want. They can do what they like out here, but the house is sacrosanct, man.'

'I need to inspect the interior,' said Gunzabo.

Bruce looked at him angrily, but then his face slackened and he said, 'Do what you have to.'

'You are gonna get him, ain't you?' said Janis.

Gunzabo looked at her, astonished at the question. 'Who?'

'Why, the Déjà Vu Killer. I wanna string him up for what he

did to my Jimi.'

'My investigations will be finished today,' he answered dismissively.

'You really think so?' Bruce looked at him, voice filled with bitterness. 'What are you going to do, drink another beer? Work it all out while you're puking in the corner? Man, you make me sick. You all do.' He jumped up. 'I had enough of this talk and pussy footing. It's about time someone did something.'

'So what're you going to do, man?' River said, looking broken and sad as Bruce hopped from foot to foot, saying, 'Fight evil with evil! He should kill me now, before I find him.' Bruce jabbed his fists, speaking in bursts and shadow boxing between each exclamation. 'I'm gonna end this. I can't fight so good now, but I can shoot. I'm gonna hunt that mother down!' Bruce took a few paces towards the house, hands open as if he was already holding the shotgun.

'Oh Bruce!' Janis said. 'You're not well enough. I wish you could. But we can't have you die too.'

'What does it matter?' Bruce darted his fists out again in a series of swift jabs. 'If the man I was ten years ago could see me now, he would be ashamed. It's time I made him proud.'

'She is right,' Gunzabo told him. 'Be patient. The mystery is almost over.'

'Mystery? That's what you're calling it? You kill me, baby, you really do.'

Bruce was wheezing now from the exertion of his shadow boxing and sat down.

'The maid who found Jimi,' Gunzabo asked them. 'Where is she?'

Janis indicated a woman with a long-handled net, scooping cigarette butts out of the swimming pool. He went over and introduced himself. The women looked up quickly, fear in her eyes, then returned to her work.

'You were the one who found Jimi?' he said.

'Yes, sir.' She darted her eyes towards him and blinked rapidly.

'What time was it?'

The woman stopped her work and stared into the pool, determined not to catch his eye. 'Seven o'clock, sir.'

'Exactly seven o'clock?'

'Yes, exactly sir.'

'Tell me what happened.'

'I came to clean the house.'

'I thought Jimi didn't allow this?'

'Every few months we come and clear up some of the mess.' She paused. 'I thought I should check and see who was there. I wanted to make sure Mr Jimi was asleep before I began.' She looked resolutely at the net; the cigarette butts were slowly dispersing back into the pool. 'So I looked in his bedroom. I was about to go. Something was not right. Mr Jimi was so still. And in a strange position.'

'What position?'

'Lying in bed. On his back. But his head was back and to the side. He was so still.'

Gunzabo watched the woman as she stared into the murky pool.

'I went up to the bed. And now I knew things were not right. So I touched him. And at first I thought maybe he is so... wasted, that he is not responding. But then I knew. He is dead.'

'What did you do?'

The woman ventured a quick look at him.

'I was very upset. I didn't know what to do. I used the phone and called for help.'

Gunzabo didn't speak for a while. Eventually he said, 'You're one of Lastri's sisters, aren't you?'

'Yes, sir. She is my older sister.'

'Was it Lastri that you called?'

'Yes.'

'Did you move the body?' he said. 'Did you move anything in the house?'

'Oh no, sir. I just waited.'

'And who was it that arrived?'

'My sister, sir, Lastri. And Ken. He tried to revive Mr Jimi.'

'For how long?'

'I don't know, sir. Ten minutes, maybe?'

'Then what happened?'

'Others came, and—'

'Which others?'

'My other sister, some of my cousins.'

'Female cousins?'

'Yes. We took Mr Jimi to the medical room, then we came back to clear up.'

Gunzabo glanced at the other women working in the garden. 'Have any of you touched anything inside?'

'No, sir. I told you.'

He grunted, left the woman at the pool, walked up to the house and went inside. The place was in an even worse state than before: floor hidden by litter, air filled with the stench of rotting violins, damp clothes, mouldy records and old damp tobacco. He went upstairs to Jimi's bedroom, stepped over the silver spacesuit and a multitude of other outfits which lay crumpled on the floor like an abandoned fancy dress parlour. He knelt down at the mattress.

'Well?' asked Didi.

'Well what?'

'Well, what's going on?'

He did not reply. Scanning the room once more, he went back out, over to the spare bedroom, glanced in, but did not go inside. He moved on to the recording studio. Squeezing between amps, cases and guitars he followed the tangle of leads which led to the mixing desk and piles of lyrics and notes, covered in doodles and crossings out and oversized, uneven handwriting. Buried in the pile he found the front page torn from a magazine.

'Elysian Fields,' he muttered, reading the title. 'This confirms it.'

'Confirms what?' said Didi.

'Both victims had a copy of the same magazine.'

'So did Christian. But what about Brian?'

'Brian is a red herring. We saw him at Christian's underground art gallery.'

He looked around the room again. 'You know, Didi. There's something else not quite right in here.'

'Yeah, you,' said Didi sullenly.

'Can you see it? What has changed?'

He rubbed his forehead, waiting for her to work it out; he was still horrendously hungover. She looked at him blankly.

Finally he said, 'The tape recorder is not here. That is what is different.'

'Have you seen the state of this place? It could be anywhere.'

'It was in here last time,' he told her. 'It is huge, we would have seen it if it was still in the house. Someone has taken it.'

'The killer?'

Gunzabo smiled. 'Not the killer.'

He went back outside, over to where Janis, Bruce and River were still sitting by the pool. The staff were raking the lawn.

'Shall I order some food?' he asked.

Bruce looked at him in disgust. 'My best friend just died.'

'Nothing for me, man,' River said despondently.

A sudden shout came from the entrance to the garden; they all turned: Gusti was bent double, labouring for breath as he held onto the gate.

'Sir, sir,' he said. 'You must come quickly.'

Gunzabo stayed where he was. The others hurried towards

the gate.

'What is it?' Janis asked.

'It is awful.'

'What is, honey?'

'Ken is dead!'

33

He arrived at The Circles with Janis, Bruce and River. Most of the villagers were there, standing inside the restaurant or outside by the glass doors; Jim was on the terrace, running both hands frantically through his beard; Elvis and Diana were sitting at a table, holding hands, dumbstruck.

'Where's Christian?' Gunzabo asked.

Elvis looked up mournfully. 'He's not here.'

'The bodies, are they still in the medical centre?'

'Christian had them taken away.'

'Where?'

'Does it matter?'

'It matters greatly.'

Gunzabo went over to Mrs Bradley, who was quietly standing next to a group of villagers. He put his arm around her.

'Oh Gunzarby,' she said, putting her head against his chest. 'My poor heart can't take much more of this.'

She seemed calmer than earlier, resigned to the shocking events of the day.

'It's nearly over,' he said. 'Where's your husband? Is he with Christian?'

'I expect so,' she said wearily.

'I must find them. Where did they go?'

'I don't know, love. Thomas doesn't tell me anything anymore.'

She disengaged herself, wiped her eyes and stared into space. 'I miss my Kevin so much,' she whispered.

He looked at her, his heart filled with pity, kissed her gently on the forehead, and glanced back across the terrace; the residents from East Beach had arrived, along with Michael, and even Marilyn, in her wheelchair and with all her medical equipment, was being carried across the meadow by a gang of male villagers. Within minutes all of the island's remaining residents were on the terrace, refusing offers of refreshments from the staff, hugging each other sadly and talking in hushed voices.

'Where's Lastri?' Gunzabo asked, approaching one of the waiters.

'With The Director, sir. On the beach.'

He looked across the gardens, over to the beach, and then his eyes followed the path running down towards Palm Grove. He could not see anyone, but he knew they must be there, and stared, deep in thought at the circle of trees, until he sensed movement behind him and turned to see the staff milling around two new arrivals: Rahmad and his wife.

'So, detective,' Rahmad said, as Gunzabo came over. 'You have failed us.' Away from his hut he looked even smaller and rounder, like a pregnant dwarf. Gunzabo did not respond, merely nodded a greeting.

'My eldest daughter told me what has happened,' Rahmad continued. 'It is truly awful. We have only ourselves to blame, you and I.'

Sukma spoke sharply to her husband.

'What?' he said. 'Of course he should! He was brought here to do a job, for which he is being paid handsomely. I take full responsibility for all my mistakes. So should he.'

Sukma spoke again, grinning at Gunzabo and gripping his arm.

'My wife says that you must not blame yourself,' said Rahmad. 'She is of course talking nonsense, but she insists I tell you this.'

Sukma cuffed her husband's ear; he scowled back and continued translating. 'She says it is time for you to leave. And that we will also be leaving soon.' He turned to his wife. 'What do you mean, woman? Nobody is going anywhere.'

Her face creased up in wrinkles and she showed both gums as she laughed at her husband. She began to speak rapidly, while gesturing at the building and the people all around.

'You're insane woman, nothing is over,' said Rahmad. 'It has only just started. You do not believe it was that idiot doctor, do you?'

Sukma stood grinning with her arms folded over her flat chest.

Gunzabo addressed Rahmad: 'Have you spoken to Lastri yet?'

'Ten minutes ago.'

'What did she say about Ken?'

Rahmad shrugged. 'He killed himself. She found him in his surgery with a needle in his arm. There was a note, confessing all, that it was him, he is the Déjà Vu Killer. Such nonsense. It is a cover up, that is clear. Clear to most of us.' He scowled at his wife while she openly laughed back at him.

'Women,' he said. 'Always they are first to see a conspiracy. Never will they believe anything as it is presented to them. But here we are, a killer on the loose, another man dead, and they insist on suicide!'

Sukma moved close to Gunzabo. He felt her bony fingers grip his hand with surprising strength. Looking down at her wrinkled, earnest face, he realised how old and tiny she was, yet so very strong.

'She says you should leave now, while you have the chance. Try the boat, she says. Oh, for goodness sake, woman. Such drama!'

Gunzabo ignored Rahmad now. 'I know everything,' he said, speaking directly to Sukma. 'I will leave or stay as I please. Either way it will be with Christian's consent. I expect the same is true for you.'

Looking back at him with her clear, wrinkled eyes, finally

she nodded and let go of his hand. He was still holding her gaze when he heard angry shouts behind him. Christian had arrived.

'It's over,' he was saying, hands raised in an attempt to make himself heard. But this only allowed the residents to come closer, as they jostled and yelled and demanded explanations. 'Please everybody, try to remain calm.'

'*Remain* calm?' someone shouted.

'It's an outrage!'

'Who's next then? Gonna wait for us all to die, are you, before you actually do something?'

Elvis spoke above the melee. 'Enough! Let him speak.'

Christian glared furtively at Elvis, then smiled his sharp-toothed grin. 'Thank you,' he said, pausing for a moment to gaze around and change his expression to one of sadness. 'My friends, it's finished. Thank goodness, it's finished. The killer is dead. Nobody has anything more to concern themselves about.'

There was a barrage of shouting; Elvis raised his hand; the crowd settled down.

'I have a note here,' Christian said, 'found approximately one hour ago, in the hands of our former doctor, Ken Winter. He confesses fully and unambiguously to the killings of John, Jimi and Brian.'

Christian paused, switching his gaze to Gunzabo, as he continued: 'The matter is resolved. It has been awful, truly awful. On behalf of the staff, I apologise to you all. We let you down. We promised to protect you, to care for you, to make your lives happy and healthy and secure. We messed up. And for that, we are truly sorry.'

Gunzabo stared, watching the performance with amusement, as Christian turned away and now scanned the crowd, wrinkling his eyes in sorrow and affection. 'But on this sad, black day, I make a pledge to each and every one of you: together we will make this wonderful island paradise even more wonderful than before. Today, we mourn our brothers. Tomorrow, we begin again, renewed, reborn. A new beginning for us all. And as part of this, I have some news, quite wonderful news.' He smiled triumphantly. 'For tomorrow, we welcome not one, but two new guests to our shores.'

There were gasps, followed by shouts of 'Who is it?' and 'Tell us!' and 'Right on!'

Christian raised his hands, smiling happily. 'I cannot tell you today. You know I like to surprise you.' He looked around, soberness returning to his face. 'And it would not be fitting on this day, this day of goodbyes.'

There were murmurs of agreement from the crowd.

'Please everyone,' he said. 'Let us go down to the Grove, put Jimi to rest.'

Christian smiled, turned and stepped onto the path towards Palm Grove, followed by the Bradleys, Lastri and her parents. Gunzabo waited at the edge of the terrace, while the residents and staff looked uncertainly at Elvis.

'Come,' he said. 'Let's go bury our friend.'

34

Gunzabo made his way down to Palm Grove, walking solemnly behind the line of islanders which stretched down to the beach.

As he came to the outer circle of trees he saw, beyond the people filing inside, men already in the grove preparing the ground for burial. He stopped and watched them finish their work, put their shovels aside, then pick up two ladders which they carried away.

'Strange equipment for a burial,' he said to Lastri, who was standing next to him.

'For checking coconuts,' she said, refusing to look at him. 'We have had enough deaths for one day.'

He glanced up at the treetops, remembered his first visit, on the night of the storm. Giving her one last bemused look, he went inside.

Seventy mourners stood on the shaded sand, a silent, unbroken line encircling the graves of the dead. He watched them shift their feet and look across the grove with sad, expectant eyes, or stare at the ground while others offered silent comfort. Christian was giving instructions to a group of male villagers, who then hurried outside, past where Gunzabo stood on the fringes. The mourners waited and the black trees swayed overhead and threw shadowed stripes across their faces. The sea hissed into the sand. Janis wept uncontrollably at the open grave. Then everyone turned and the circle parted to allow the funeral procession to enter: four men grimly carrying a white coffin on their shoulders. There was no music; there was just the crunch of sand as they walked slowly to the grave. They stopped.

Christian spoke. 'This has been a terrible week in the history of Dead Star Island. We have lost friends and family over the years. But nothing can compare to this past week. Words cannot express my sorrow at the passing of our dear friends. Today we mourn Jimi.'

The gathering stood in silence. The men shifted under the weight of the coffin. Gunzabo rubbed his chin, amused at the almost saintly expression on Christian's face.

'Would anybody like to say a few words?' Christian said.

Everyone looked around the circle, their eyes drawn to Janis.

'I guess so,' Janis murmured, conscious of the expectant crowd. She raised her voice, 'I'd just like to say, Jimi, you never knew how special you were. Not really. There will never be another like you on this Earth. You were so... so bright. I always loved you. I always will.'

She gazed up at the sky, then looked down, put her hand over her face. Bruce took her away from the grave. Christian nodded to the men, who brought the coffin down off their shoulders, and lowered it into the ground, working quickly to fill the hole. Finally they stepped back. Silence returned; the breeze dropped; the trees stilled their leaves and squeezed the faint patches of light into static shards. It felt almost cold.

Gunzabo cleared his throat. 'I would like to say something,' he said.

He moved forward, alongside the graves.

'He didn't mean you,' Bruce said, his face taut with anger.

Janis pulled him back. 'No,' she said. 'Let him speak.'

Gunzabo ignored them both. 'I want to speak about the events Christian referred to in his brief eulogy.'

He paused and straightened his back. He looked around the gathering and at the trees with their canopies bowed down to Earth, as if they too were watching the drama unfold.

'Can we discuss this later, Maz?' said Elvis. 'We've just come here to pay our respects.'

'No,' Gunzabo said. 'This cannot wait.'

He did not look at Elvis, but addressed the entire gathering, feeling every eye now focussed on him. 'You must all listen now. Just as I have listened to you, these last few days.'

They remained silent. Then he began.

'You all know why I was brought to this island,' he said. 'To answer an important question: who killed John? And a second question: who killed Brian? Two men die within a month, one violently, the other in suspicious circumstances.' He paced up and down in front of Jimi's grave as he spoke. 'And what of the others? This murderer, this Déjà Vu Killer; how far back does his killing spree go? How many has he killed? But we'll come to Brian and the others later. First, I want to speak of John.'

Gunzabo smiled briefly at Christian, did not wait to see his reaction before continuing. 'John had enemies. You all told me so, one way or another. He was a fighter, he did not hesitate to say what he thought, regardless of the effect his words might have. But he was a lover too. And he was loved. You all, it seems to me, loved him, in one way or another.

'In the course of my investigations I discovered this, and many other things. John had a lover: the mysterious Iris. Not such a mystery, of course. Iris was Diana, his beloved for some years. Many of you know this, I think, including those who are supposed not to know. It was a turbulent affair, by all accounts, and it ended painfully. Particularly for John.'

'Hey now,' said Kurt. 'I'm with Elvis, man. I'm not sure we want to hear this. I mean, it's pretty rotten, talking about a dead man like this. We are at a funeral in case you forgot.'

Gunzabo looked back at him. 'No, I have not forgotten. And yes it is a rotten thing. All of it is rotten, to the very core. That is exactly why we must talk about it. It is time to end the charade.'

Mrs Bradley spoke out: 'Look love,' she said, 'I know this is your moment, but we all know Ken did it. I read the note with my own eyes. It was his writing, he owned up to everything.'

The residents began murmuring.

'You are joking?' Bruce said scornfully. 'That's just too tidy. And besides: Ken, he ain't got the balls, man. I say Christian did it.'

'Christian? He wouldn't hurt a fly, love,' Mrs Bradley said. 'If you want the truth, I always thought it was Jimi.'

'I thought you said it was Ken?' observed River.

'Well, yes, but—'

'Here we have the problem, in a seashell,' said Gunzabo. He gazed across the entire circle, hand raised to quieten them down. 'So many possibilities, so many opinions. I will come to all of these suspects – and others – shortly. But for now, I will talk about the victim.' He resumed his pacing. 'So: John and Diana. After several years, their relationship ended. He was heartbroken. I have seen the letters. Did he want to continue the affair? Yes. But it did not continue, because she did not want this. That much Diana told me, and I believe her. And so should you.' He looked meaningfully at Elvis, before continuing. 'He began another affair. He found another Iris: the lovely Lastri. I discovered these liaisons early in my investigations, but I wondered how I could use this to penetrate the mystery of his death. However, I must digress now, and talk not about John, but about you all.'

He looked around the watching audience, satisfied that now, they waited on his every word.

'When I discovered the extraordinary nature of this island and its residents, and when I met you, the first question that struck me was this: why did you come here? Why did you give up so much? Some of you provided explanations, some I deduced, but as my investigation progressed, as I got to know you, I realised this question had very little significance. None in fact. What really intrigued me, even baffled me, was a similar but quite different

266

question.' He paused dramatically. 'Why are you still here? What is it that keeps you here? Is it the sun, the sea? Luxury? Being treated like gods, like immortalised heroes? Surely it is not those things. Those things you can have anywhere. Most of you did have them, did you not? No.' He paused, gazing at all the faces directed at him. 'Some of you I think, truly love it here. You are born again, your life refreshed. Your old life was a misery, and your new existence is a revelation. Others? It's where you are. Habit. It's very easy, everything is provided. It spares a lot of pain. Change is painful, we all know this. You took a dramatic step in coming here, many of you quite literally, and there is no going back.

'For others, I think perhaps you take the view that it does not matter where you are; you transcend time and place, or at least you attempt this. Life here, this island, is merely a test, a challenge to overcome. And maybe you realise also that the reasons you came here, the things you ran from, they followed you. You fled your demons and they met you on arrival, here on the beach. So why leave, if you cannot leave your troubles behind?

'And John? Why was John here? He came to Dead Star Island in fear of his life, and his presence was tolerated from afar. Apparently. I cannot confirm this, but it does not surprise me. He was unwilling to forfeit his life. If life is what you call living here.

'All these things and more, these are what I considered to be among the reasons for your remaining here. Or at least, these are what I consider *you* believe are the reasons. For they are not true. Like your lives themselves, like your very existence, these are an illusion. Yes! There is only one reason why you are all still here. It is the same single reason why *everyone* is here, staff included.'

He paused, enjoying the dazed silence of the onlooking residents and staff, as they waited for him to continue.

'It is because you cannot leave. It is not permitted. None of you try, because you have cloaked yourselves in the reassurance of your daily concerns. But in fact, you are imprisoned here.'

35

The residents began shouting angrily.

'Like it or not, it is true,' he told them, when they had begun to settle down. 'But let us move on to one more question. It is in the same artery. This question I shall answer for you immediately. Why is Christian here?' He turned to Christian, smiled pleasantly at him. 'Will you tell them? Come, don't be shy.'

Christian watched silently, his small eyes glittering. Gunzabo shrugged. 'It seems I will have to tell the story.

'Christian has always been fascinated by death. As some of you know, we grew up together. We were companions, brothers even. But you could not imagine two boys more distant. I remember how Christian would gather the bluebottles that lay still and brittle on the windowsill. He collected insects and small creatures of every variety. If he found a bird or a rabbit dead in a field it was like a holy relic. When our cat died we did not know where the body went until the stench from his room filled the house.'

'I merely seek to preserve life,' Christian said, giving Gunzabo a look of alienated hurt. 'Is that so terrible?'

Gunzabo smiled, and continued addressing the crowd. 'What Christian is doing is to preserve *death*, to take the shell of a being and to maintain it, frozen at the very instant of death. Trap it in his underworld, preside over his subjects. It is rather sick, really. Oh, it is Christian! Look at everyone's faces.'

'I do not hide it,' Christian said. 'Everybody has been to my office.'

'Yes. But I have been to your *house*, Christian. I went there this morning. I went *under* your house. Into the basement.'

Christian went pale.

'Yes, I'm afraid so,' Gunzabo said. 'It is quite brilliant, in many ways. One has to admire the compulsion, the dedication, the patience. Perhaps I should demonstrate.'

He took a shovel from one of the gravedigger's hands, using it like an oversized trowel as he began digging at Steve's grave with his one arm.

'What on earth,' began Diana.

Her words dissipated into the silence as everyone watched Gunzabo dig into the sand. He asked one of the gravediggers to help him. The sand moved easily; a few feet down it became sodden and they hit solid wood. He grunted now as he stooped and cleared the remaining sand from the top of the coffin. The crowd pressed inwards, morbidly fascinated. Gunzabo threw open the lid.

There were gasps. It was empty.

He moved on to Brian's grave. Everyone was silent and there was just the sound of the shovels and the waves on the beach and heavy breathing as they cleared the grave. Gunzabo opened up the empty coffin.

'I could continue of course. But I think you have the idea. Can you guess where the bodies are?'

'Christian...' growled Elvis.

'Yes, that's right,' Gunzabo said. 'Oh you should see it! Perhaps you will. It truly is a sight to behold. Such a shame, Christian, for you not to share it with everyone. How shall I describe it? He has created for himself... a surprise party, you might call it. A room where he is the star, where the others wait for him, their whole lives. Or deaths, I should say. Try to imagine this place: he enters, underground, after a long day at the office, and they are there, waiting for him. They listen, he talks, they smile, he jokes; they sigh at his wonderful stories; his wit, his insight, his intellect dazzles them. This is his private fantasy, compelling him in all he does. And he has made it come true.

'I suspected this for some time. You only have to sit in his office for one minute to see how his childhood fascination has become an obsession. But how much of an obsession? Enough to kill? Well, we shall see.

'It was enough, certainly, to create this place. Quite an achievement in itself. You were all successful people, you residents. What drove your desire for success? Think of Christian, think of the burning ambition, raging inside, that drove him to seduce every one of you. This island, Dead Star Island, it is his *raison d'être*. He craves your company, desires your celebrity. And celebrity is four dimensional taxidermy. Everything he has ever done, everything he has ever said, promised, asked, all solely to realise this dream, to build this underground cavern. And in the meantime, before he takes you there? Well, you are here, shades, moving exhibits, in some outer circle of Hades' waiting room.

'But how does he get each of you from the waiting room, into the cavern? How will you become the next guest of that underground party? You won't answer me, Christian? You brought me here as a charade, I know. But I always intended to earn my money. I was the premier detective in the whole of Greece! Do not underestimate me, ever.

'To answer this question, this possibility of Christian being the Déjà Vu Killer, firstly consider the man: he deals with death; he wishes for your deaths; he poisons his staff in order to suppress their numbers and control their society. But he does not kill. He anticipates. He waits. Even the animals in his office, he finds them, already dead, or waits for them eventually to die. And consider the evidence: Christian was not on the island when John was shot. At the very least he did not pull the trigger.

'No. Christian was as shocked as everyone else. And then he received another, even greater shock. Imagine his excitement at the thought of digging up John's body, taking it to his workshop? Another guest at the party, only weeks after the last one. Brian, he already had – I saw him there, in the basement. But John?

'Christian had to wait an extra night after the funeral, due to the power of the storm which struck the island. And there was a second storm, the following night. But this passed and he was able to act. Finally he got to the grave. I interrupted his work, but he came again, later, and he was now alone, ready to exhume his newest guest. Think of him, here, in the first hours of morning, digging the wet sand, reaching the lid of the coffin as I did just now for Steve and Brian. Think of his anticipation, his arousal. And imagine his dismay when he lifted the lid, and... it was empty! As empty as all the others! I heard his dismay with my own ears, though I did not realise at the time, and thought it but a dream. I heard his screams in my sleep. It was robbery! How ironic. The man who has plundered each and every other grave, digs up John and finds? Nothing!'

He paused, looked in satisfaction at the shocked faces surrounding him.

'All very dramatic, baby,' said Bruce. 'Are you actually going to tell us who did it? Get on with it, man.'

Gunzabo smiled. 'Very well. I shall talk less of psychology, and more of facts. Let us return to the moment of the shooting.

'At first I despaired. I was getting nowhere. Half of you had stainless steel alibis: you were not even on the island. But the other half, there were so many of you with corroborating stories, but from too few of your friends and colleagues. Who could I trust? There was much talk, but little hard evidence. Finally I got my break: Jim had made a film. I could have danced when I discovered there was footage of the incident. How wonderful! A chance to be transported to the day of the shooting, even to witness the succession of events in the days leading up to it. It did not let me down. It provided the most interesting oddity. Did anyone else notice? No? You all saw the film, did you not? Jim? You spent hours, if not days, editing that footage. You neither? Well, at least you provided yourself with a perfectly documented alibi.

'It was a game of spot the difference. Jim's film examined the monotony of life on the island. He examined it thoroughly. Day after day the men run past, the staff make their way to work. Hardly anyone else features. There is the sea, the beach, the jungle. You've seen the film!

'So what was different on the day of the shooting? At first, all I had was a sense that something was not right. But then I saw. It was this: why was it, whilst on an arduous run, on the hottest day of the year – and unlike every day preceding it – that John was wearing a long-sleeved top?'

He looked around, waiting for an answer. The crowd watched expectantly.

'I shall return to this point presently. I was talking about suspects, so I shall talk some more about this part of the investigation. It proved a difficult area, for reasons already stated. Not enough hard facts, too much hearsay. Yes, there were motives, possibilities: jealousy, anger, cowardice, retribution. Or perhaps just a terrible accident. Unfriendly fire. What do you say, Bruce? Was it like that? You aren't talking either, never mind, you did not do it, be as sullen as you like. Neither did Jimi. Besides, he's dead. He cannot be the serial killer, can he? And others of course: you Michael, Diana maybe, or perhaps Marilyn is faking her incapacity and has some nameless grudge. One should always look for those least likely in these murder mysteries.

'But I shall not bore you, or insult you all by reviewing the credits and debits against each of you. For we have a prime suspect, as Mrs Bradley herself pointed out: Ken. I wonder where he is?'

'His body's in the medical room, love,' said Mrs Bradley.

'We didn't think it was right to bury him with Jimi.'

'Quite right. As it should be. But I thought we might ask him ourselves...' Gunzabo craned his neck to look up at the treetops. 'Ken!' he called out. He banged on the tree trunks. 'Come on, we know you're up there.'

Some of the crowd started tittering, but were immediately hushed by the others. They waited while he moved from tree to tree, looking up into the foliage.

'Come on, Ken. The game is up now. You can bring Jimi down too.'

'We're not here,' said a voice from one of the shorter palm trees. There was a guffaw. The crowd gasped and now everyone was peering up and trying to identify where the voice and laughter were coming from.

'Is someone going to bring a ladder, then?' said the voice. 'I'm not as nimble as I used to be.'

Staff brought ladders to the tree. Two men appeared in the branches above, climbed down and stepped onto the sand.

'Alright, alright,' said Ken. 'It's a fair cop. You got us good and proper.'

'Yeah, uh, it's kinda awkward I guess,' mumbled Jimi. 'I didn't exactly mean it to go like this.'

Janis moved over to them. Her tears were gone, and she was smiling broadly. She and Jimi embraced. 'Looks like we're leaving together, honey,' she said. 'Did I do good?'

He grinned at her, full of love. 'I always said you should be an actor, baby.'

Ken was grinning too. 'Anyone else fancy coming?' he said.

Christian stepped towards them, white-faced with fury. 'That is not what we agreed,' he said, with dangerous softness.

'What?' said Bruce. 'Where are you going? What the hell is happening, man?'

'They are talking of their destination,' said Gunzabo. 'They are talking of Elysian Fields.'

'Elysian what?'

Diana laughed. 'Is that what this is all about? Oh, now I see. You're doing a bit of island hopping, are you? Faking your deaths, yet again, moving on, starting all over.'

'Yes,' Gunzabo said. 'Elysian Fields, the new kid on the street, bitter rival to Dead Star Island.'

'Hardly a rival,' sneered Christian. 'Who have they got? Bob? A few other singers no one's ever heard of. They've got *nobody*.' He spat this final word contemptuously.

'Had nobody,' corrected Gunzabo. He stepped back into the centre of the crowd. 'You see, Dead Star Island is not the only option these days, in the, what do you call your industry, Christian?'

'The superstar resettlement sector.' Christian could barely bring himself to move his lips.

'Yes, the superstar resettlement sector,' said Gunzabo. 'Strolls off the tongue, doesn't it?

'I should have deduced this days ago. I saw the brochure for the resort on Christian's desk, glossy and new. But I assumed it was promotional material for Dead Star Island itself. I saw it also in John's house, and this morning in Jimi's house, and by then its significance was very clear. It is capitalism in action. It is the end of the monopoly. An alternative reality for death. And it has made Christian even more impotent than he already is.'

He smiled at the dumb, dazed faces around him.

'I cannot tell you all for certain what happened, but it seems Christian and Ken came to an arrangement, once Christian realised that John was not dead. He would instantly have known that only Ken could have done this. But he had only one choice: accept the loss and move on, find a way to tie up the knots and then expel the treacherous doctor. Except it wasn't that easy: nobody leaves the island. He could not just let Ken hand in his notice and go. The rest of you might start getting ideas. So he had to wait until an opportunity presented itself, to kill off Ken, or make it appear so.

'And there was another problem: by now, everyone was terrified of the Déjà Vu Killer. This invention of Ken's proved very useful. Faking his death would cause even more panic. Also, there was me, brought here by unpopular demand, wandering about causing mischief. And there was Ken himself: he did not want to leave quite yet. Did you Ken?'

All this time, Ken had been darting his eyes around, looking to gauge the attitude of the crowd and he smiled now, confident they had turned fully against Christian.

'You stop laughing, boy,' Elvis told him.

'We've been living in fear of our lives, man,' said Marc.

'And what about the rest of us?' Keith said. 'You were just gonna leave us here, weren't you?'

Elvis gestured for everyone to quieten down, to allow Ken to speak.

'Look, it all just went tits up, alright?' said Ken. He spoke in a quiet, serious voice, looking down at the sand. 'I tried my best. Sometimes events conspire against you.'

'Something happened, didn't it?' Gunzabo said.

Ken looked at him resentfully. 'So why don't you tell them? You seem to know everything.'

'Not everything.'

Ken bowed his head, shuffled his feet on the sand. 'It's complicated,' he said.

'You have a good life here,' Gunzabo continued. 'You escaped your wives and debts. Why risk it all? Or was it the risk itself that impelled you to do this?'

Ken looked up. 'I dunno,' he said. 'I just sort of did it. They approached me – I've still got a few contacts I keep in touch with – and well, no offence, but it is pretty boring here. Everyone's a religious nut these days, or they're in therapy, or playing video games all day and night. I just want a bit of fun really. Life's too short. Besides, I've had enough of arranging parties. It's about time someone else did. That's what I thought. They told me I could be one of the residents. You know, a famous doctor. Well I am. But everyone treats me like a skivvy round here.'

'But what they really wanted,' Gunzabo said, 'what they needed, was someone big. A trophy, a figurehead, to market their new island to all the wealthy, disaffected stars out there. Money was no object. And Ken could not resist.'

Gunzabo looked exultantly around him. 'So, here we are,' he said. 'At a funeral where no one died. At a graveyard where no one is buried. But something went wrong. This is what I want to find out. What happened?'

Ken looked down at the sand again. He rubbed his neck as he spoke.

'It was only ever supposed to be one. Get us John or Jimi. That's what they said. And John, well, he wanted to go. He wanted out. He hated Christian. He'd had enough of it here, all the lies and the politics. He was through with this place, that's what he told me. I remember one day, he said, "Ken, I've tried my best to change this island. And I can't. I can only change myself." So I made the arrangements. I already had the blood, it was his. Nice touch, I thought. I had a boat ready, they'd finally managed to pinpoint the island. That was supposed to be it. Job done.'

'The storm prevented you from leaving the first night, I suppose?'

'Yeah, blinking weather. We rearranged it for the next night. Christian still didn't know what had happened, but he was really suspicious. He had me watched day and night, so John went on his own. I thought I'd wait here on the island, let the heat die down, go later. Except it all went wrong.'

'What went wrong?'

Ken looked at Gunzabo, then at the crowd. His lips trembled, as he spoke in a near whisper: 'He died.'

He winced, shaking his head sadly. 'He fell overboard. It was only a small boat. That's what they told me. The sea got really rough, the storm came back. And he was gone. They spent hours looking. They never found the body. That's when they said they needed Jimi.'

'You never told me that,' said Jimi. 'You cold cat, man, you kept that to yourself. You said he was safe on the island, waiting for us.'

'I couldn't tell you, Jim, could I?' Ken said. 'You never would have come.'

'You bet I wouldn't.'

'Well, you're not staying here,' said Christian. He spoke softly, eyes gleaming with hatred. 'We don't want you. This island doesn't *need* you. Either of you. Not after your behaviour, and your attitude.'

Elvis spoke now, taking a step towards Christian. 'You no longer have any right to tell us what we can or cannot do. It's time for the people of this island to have their say.'

Christian turned to him in fury. 'Oh, I'm sorry,' he said viciously. 'Who made you their leader? What is it you do again? Nothing.' His teeth were fully bared, and pieces of saliva appeared on his lips as he pronounced each syllable. 'You do nothing for our community,' he said, 'and you stand there and moralise? Everything here, everything you see, all of it, was built by me! It was my vision. You would be nothing without me.' He looked around now, shaking with emotion. 'None of you. Nothing.'

The residents began to move away and out of the grove.

'Come back!' he spat at them. 'You're not going anywhere!'

The staff were now leaving, and even the Bradleys walked away, holding hands tightly. Gunzabo stood, watching impassively as Christian fell to the sand, started pushing the lids back on the coffins. His glasses had fallen off, and it was strange how very different he now looked: face old and bare and vulnerable as he clawed weakly at the legs of those passing by; then he returned to the coffins, scrambling blindly on his hands and knees, dragging each lid into place, oblivious to the sand which now covered his body.

'Is that it, then?' asked River, still lingering in the grove.

'That's it,' said Gunzabo. 'I have nothing more to add. You all know the truth. The rest you must work out for yourselves.'

He waited as the remaining staff made their way out. Christian was still on the ground, sobbing now, obsessively collecting the loose sand and pushing it into the open graves. Gunzabo knelt down beside him, put his hand gently on his shoulder. Christian angrily pushed him away.

'I need a drink,' Gunzabo muttered.

He stood up and followed the others back up towards The Circles, stroking Didi fondly under his shirt.

36

'So what will you do, Gunzabo?'

He sipped his beer on the restaurant terrace.

'Go home to my ladies who lunch. They don't learn tennis by themselves, you know.'

Lastri smiled. 'What about the ones here? We won't know what to do with ourselves.'

'We both know that's not true.' He called for another drink. 'You were having me followed the whole time, weren't you?'

Lastri tilted her head slightly. 'We wanted to keep an eye on you. Make sure you didn't get into any trouble.'

'You ladies.'

'Us ladies.'

Another beer arrived. He took a sip, sweeping his gaze along the beach and over to the north, across the dark forest canopy. The buzz of insects and mating calls of birds were in his ears: the exuberant, throbbing pulse of the jungle. There was so much life in there, hidden under the forest roof: creatures living and dying and being born; plants and trees competing for light and space on the forest floor; all exulting in the world, living without fear of their ultimate fate: to no longer be themselves, to be incorporated back into the jungle. He nodded with approval.

Sing on! he told them. *Live! Raise hell!*

There was so little time in which to be heard. And he had wasted so many years. But it did not matter. All that mattered was that now there could be life after death. He sensed Lastri looking at him, came out of his reverie, remembered their conversation.

'Christian suspects, of course?' he asked her.

'Of course,' answered Lastri. 'But what can he do? He needs us.'

He smiled at her. 'It took you a long time to realise that.'

She smiled back. 'Far too long. But things have changed now.'

'Will you stay?'

'For now. This is our home. Most of us know nothing else.'

Gunzabo scratched his arm; not because it was irritating him, rather from force of habit. 'Was it you I saw in the jungle the other night? Going to the hut.'

Lastri inclined her head. 'You and Thomas gave me quite a shock.'

He nodded thoughtfully. 'For days I thought I had found the killer's lair. But it was just a waiting room, wasn't it? A crude departure lounge, well stocked with beer.' He grinned briefly, imitating Christian. 'Apart from when I stayed there.'

He looked into her dark, smiling eyes. Although she was still beautiful, he did not find it painful to be with her anymore. 'John needed food and shelter,' he said, 'he needed help to get off the island, all easy enough to provide. But the shooting. Who was it? Who waved the gun?'

Lastri smoothed out her sari. 'Tell me your suspects, detective.'

'Everyone is accounted for. Except three: your son and your parents. Your son is too young. Your father was probably asleep, as he said.' As he looked at her, for a moment, he felt he knew everything in her mind, as decades-long lovers do. A brief flash of desire flared in him, but then he blinked and it was gone and he saw she knew nothing of what was going on inside him.

'She is an amazing woman,' she said.

'I hope I am as agile at that age.'

'We all wanted to do it,' Lastri said. 'But mother was the best option, by far.'

'All of you?'

'All of us.'

'The men are blissfully ignorant?'

'Always.'

'That includes Ken, I assume?' said Gunzabo.

She smiled delicately, the faintest of dimples marking her flawless cheeks, and then her eyes were full of joy as her son trotted up to them. She kissed his forehead, brought him close.

'Did you know that three of my cousins are now pregnant?' she said. 'I was telling my father for months about the water. He refused to listen, just as he has refused to do anything for years. I would call it collusion, if he wasn't my father.'

'So you took John's advice.'

'Yes.'

She looked sad for an instant, then gazed at her son and smiled joyously.

'It must have been difficult, letting him go,' Gunzabo said.

'Yes. But I understood. It is what you do when you love someone.'

'It won't be easy for him, in the outside world.'

'I suppose not.' She kissed her son on the top of his head. 'It is his choice, and it is for him to explain. I respect that. I knew him very well, Gunzabo. We spoke a lot about this.' She laughed gently. 'But he missed all the action. He would have loved it.'

'There's plenty more to come.'

'I hope so. It would be boring otherwise.' Lastri stood up. 'Come on little one,' she said to her son. 'Say goodbye to Uncle Gunzabo.'

The boy looked at him with his dark, bright eyes, and turned and walked off holding his mother's hand. Gunzabo smiled as he sipped his beer.

'What's going on?' asked Didi.

'Not a lot.'

'How long was I asleep for? I slept like the dead, did I miss anything?'

'You missed everything,' he told her.

'You're joking? So are you going to tell me?'

'I'll tell you on the boat back.'

He finished his beer. Christian's dog came scampering up. He reached down to stroke him; Cerberus snarled and nipped his finger.

'I wonder if your owner will miss you?' Gunzabo said, picking up Cerberus and setting him down in his lap, where he wriggled around like an angry toddler. 'Do you want to come with us? You know what awaits you otherwise.'

'Let's take him,' Didi said, 'He's cute. I like his attitude, he's sort of like a cousin in a way, isn't he?'

She jumped onto the table and perched next to Gunzabo's empty glass. 'So you solved the mystery, did you?'

'I solved the mystery.'

'Well I never. You're back in business, what you always wanted. You know, I'm actually a little bit proud of you.'

He grunted. 'You made my day.'

She was sitting on her hind legs, looking at him with her head tilted to one side. 'And am I the daughter you always wanted?'

'No.'

'I knew you'd say that.'

Didi smiled sweetly, then dashed up Gunzabo's empty sleeve.

Epilogue

The room was packed. All the seats were taken two hours before. A hundred people jostled for standing room; a hundred more stood outside.

A man stepped onto the stage. The buzz of the crowd grew intense and expectant. He switched on the microphones, moved the two chairs back to allow easy access to the table. He spoke into a walkie-talkie, then left the stage, pushing his way to the back of the room.

Fifteen minutes passed. Still no one appeared. The audience were used to waiting. They checked their own microphones and recording devices. They talked urgently to each other, as excited as they were puzzled. Something big was about to happen.

Behind the curtain the old man closed his eyes for another minute.

'Are you sure you want to do this?' asked the woman beside him.

The man did not answer. He opened his eyes and smiled at her. He returned to his breathing.

'It's all happening so quickly. And we've missed so much together. A whole lifetime.'

She watched him meditate. She scanned every centimetre of his features. His hair was white now, but it was still thick and full. His nose was larger, and his ears; and his brow was tanned and corrugated. There was a deep vertical line in each cheek that she'd seen a hint of years before.

'Are you sure about this?' she said, still studying him. 'They'll tear us apart.'

'They always did.'

'Why don't we leave here? Go somewhere quiet for a while.'

The man laughed. 'I know somewhere nice, if you fancy a long break.'

The woman looked hurt. He opened his eyes, saw her expression and smiled gently.

She did not smile back. It had taken months for her even to speak to him. He was supposed to have been gone for two or three years, five maximum.

'What about the idea I had?' said the woman. 'The second coming. You know they're going to demand explanations.'

'No. This is real.'

He grabbed her hand. 'Come on,' he said.

He pulled apart the curtains and strode onto the stage.

END

Acknowledgements

Thanks so much to everyone who helped me with this novel.
Firstly my early readers: Leo, the Shants, Martin, Eoin, Mac,
and especially Frank for some very tough but fair feedback
on the early drafts. Thanks also to Jess, Joel and Mark for
the artwork you see in this book and on my website.

A big thank you to everyone at APP, for believing in the book
and all the time and effort you have put into it.

Finally, the biggest thank you of all to Gaynor – my muse,
sounding board and partner in this and in everything else.

Lightning Source UK Ltd.
Milton Keynes UK
UKOW06f1834100715

254983UK00012B/241/P